CALLED TO THE WILD

She didn't seem to have heard Joshua yet, either, or
perhaps she was simply too engrossed in what she was
[...]ing, kneeling on the bed, her bottom raised to him, her
[...]blue pleated skirt rucked up over the taut white
[...] of her buttocks, a dark, hairy hand busy between
[...]. Her shirt was open, and her white bra had been
[...]own, her pale breasts exposed, long pink nipples
[...]own. Joshua wanted to turn away, not to see her
[...]s, but he was frozen, unable to stop looking. Beth's
[...]ere rotating from side to side as she buried her face
[...]n the intruder's legs, her eyes closed, cradling his
[...]ith one hand, bobbing her head up and down on his
[...] thick it was straining her lips.

CALLED TO THE WILD

Angel Blake

This book is a work of fiction.
In real life, make sure you practise safe, sane and consensual sex.

First published in 2006 by
Nexus
Thames Wharf Studios
Rainville Rd
London W6 9HA

www.nexus-books.co.uk

Typeset by TW Typesetting, Plymouth, Devon
Printed and bound by Clays Ltd, St Ives PLC

ISBN 0 352 34067 3
ISBN 9 780352 340672

One

She was late. Steve checked his watch again and looked anxiously around. Maybe it wasn't such a good idea after all. The museum was closed now; he'd been ushering crowds of tourists towards the main doors for the last twenty minutes. God only knew where she'd managed to hide herself. She'd probably been found, led to the doors like the rest of them, and for a second he found himself hoping that it was true.

But then he remembered. The way she'd come up to him, so sweetly, asking the way to the Ancient Britain room. He'd got used to seeing beautiful women here: foreign students, dusky exotics, even the prim bespectacled teachers had haunted his fantasies ever since he'd taken the security job. But this girl was different. He'd felt his cock twitch when he first saw her, and she'd locked eyes with him like she knew exactly what he was thinking and didn't mind, even encouraged it.

Her face was unusual: elfin features framed by long straight black hair, the dark colouring giving her strong eyebrows above the greenest eyes he'd ever seen. Steve had felt himself falling into those eyes, and it had taken him a second to register that she was talking to him.

And although she'd asked him to take her to the

1

Ancient Britain room – to look at some kind of wolf amulet or something – she'd walked in front of him at first like she knew which way it was, giving him time to admire her from behind, the contours of her bottom clearly visible under the thin jogging pants she wore. He hadn't been able to see any VPL tell-tales under the joggers so she was either wearing a thong, or – and the thought brought a lump to his throat – nothing at all. When she turned her head to wink coquettishly at him, catching him staring at her and surreptitiously rearranging his crotch, she'd stared at him in turn, her eyes widening when she took in the bulge between his legs, and she dropped back to talk to him, suggesting a private tour and brushing the back of her hand against his cock, thick now and bulging against his trousers.

He'd been too excited to do anything but agree breathlessly. The idea of turning this opportunity down to go home and eat a microwave meal in front of the TV had seemed unthinkable at the time, although now part of him was wishing that he hadn't appeared so keen. He knew he'd be sacked instantly if he was caught with a visitor after hours; knew that it went against all the security regulations, everything he'd been taught. Knew also that he'd do anything to relieve the sweet pain in his crotch, to see those green eyes widen in excitement again.

Steve was staring at the wolf amulet, an ugly, shrivelled paw dangling from a dully glinting chain, and was thinking of how long and strong the claws looked, even now, when he heard her whispered 'Hey'.

He spun round to find her behind him, a lopsided grin on her face.

'I'm glad you waited. Did you miss me?' she asked, her voice low and even.

He managed to muster a passable 'Yes,' unsure of what would happen next, when she moved closer to him.

'Are we alone here?' she purred.

'The – the museum's closed now. I really shouldn't be doing this, you know,' he stammered.

The girl pouted and looked crestfallen for a second, then smiled again and looked pointedly down at his crotch. Steve felt himself flush, and instinctively drew a hand towards the swelling to cover it from view. But she beat him to it, brushing her hand a second time over his bulge. He drew back with a gasp.

'I love your uniform,' she said breathlessly, then looked around. 'But we won't get caught, will we? Are there any other guards?'

He knew that his 'No' sounded strangled but there was no mistaking what she was doing now, rubbing him through his pants. He was stiff and astonished: still conscious of the dangers of the situation, but every stroke of her small hand drove them from his mind. 'This way,' he said thickly, taking her by the arm then pulling her back with him until he reached the wall. She made no move to resist and watched him expectantly. 'There's a camera up there.' He nodded towards the unblinking electronic eye embedded in the corner of the ceiling. She glanced at it, then looked back at him and grinned.

As the girl dropped down to squat in front of Steve, reaching up to pull his zip down, he made a last half-hearted attempt to stop her, a final glimmer of dutiful panic before he succumbed for good. 'Are you sure you –' But his sentence was broken off when her full lips closed over the angry-looking red head of his cock, which seemed bigger than ever against her small face. She looked up at him, the shaft stuffed into her mouth, and the wide-eyed thrill in her stare melted the last of his reserve as he slid his cock in as far as it would go.

She closed a hand around the shaft and began to pump it slowly, her tongue coiling lovingly over the tip, her cheeks hollowing as she sucked hard. With her other hand she pulled up her top, exposing the creamy whiteness of two small, firm breasts topped with the pinkest nipples Steve had ever seen, stiff enough to stop her top from rolling back down. He reached down to tug on one and was rewarded with a groan from her and a sequence of vigorous head bobs.

Her eyes were closed now and she seemed oblivious of the long streamer of saliva that dangled from her lips as she slavered over his cock. Her other hand had worked its way down under her joggers and he could see it wriggling around in her crotch, her fingers burrowing frantically.

A shadow flickered past at the edge of his field of vision and Steve pulled away from her momentarily. 'What was that?' he muttered, trying to ignore her moan of disappointment as his stare darted around the room. There was another movement and he turned quickly. There was nothing. Maybe his eyes were playing tricks on him.

'Don't you want me?' the girl pleaded, tugging on the back of his trousers. When he looked back at her, desperately excited but also a little scared now, warning bells ringing faintly in his head, she leaned back and pulled her joggers down to pool around her ankles. Then she spread her legs to expose herself to him and all thoughts of fear or doubt evaporated.

She hadn't been wearing any underwear. Her slit glistened wetly in the dim light, the sides shaved and a tuft of thick black hair remaining above. She peeled her lower lips open with one hand, showing him the pink oiliness in the crease. The clit was clearly visible, a pearly ball that she now strummed with one hand, her legs trembling as she touched it.

'You want to fuck me?' she asked, biting her lip. Steve knew as he looked into her wide eyes that he didn't even have to answer, just to watch, his balls already tight and full. Still holding his gaze, she unexpectedly cocked her hips to the side, close up against the wall now. Then, before he could stop her, she sprayed a long jet of urine out onto the wall, the hot yellow liquid leaving a dark trail then spreading out in an ever-widening puddle on the floor.

'What the fuck?' he managed, his mind reeling as he pictured the cleaners finding the mess, reporting it to the duty chief, who would be sure to check the cameras for the sector and find not only him there but the woman too.

But even as Steve stared at the girl, incredulous, she was stroking herself. Although every nerve screamed at him to get away, alerting him that there was something wrong here, his cock remained hard and he unconsciously moved a hand down to it, his stare still riveted by the inviting wetness between the girl's legs. He stepped towards her, his heart beating violently with the thought of what he was about to do, when a sharp, entirely unexpected pain caught him above the right ear and everything went black.

'Get inside, woman, quick!' Joshua leaned out of the kitchen door and called to his wife.

Mary turned from the end of the garden where she was hurriedly taking the washing off the line and gestured with her head to the sky, where bruised clouds massed, the lowest tinged with pink from the dying sun. The air was still and heavy. 'I've got to take in the washing, Joshua; a storm's coming in!'

The hairs on the back of Joshua's neck bristled and he pulled impatiently on his beard. Then he ran out to help her, muttering to himself as he moved out of the house. He'd only pulled down two shirts, pocketing the wooden pegs in his trousers, before the first fat drops of rain fell, spattering onto his top. 'Faster, woman!'

'I'm doing my best!' Mary wailed, her worn face agitated, as she struggled with the sheets that flapped in the wind that had picked up. Their fabric was growing wet and heavy in the rain.

'For God's sake,' muttered Joshua as he pulled the last sheet off, bundled the wet mess against his chest and then reached out with his spare hand to grab his wife. 'Get inside – *now*.'

As Mary began to run towards the house, slipping once on the wet grass, Joshua heard the howl again, a long, mournful cry that seemed to linger in the air. A chill coiled through his intestines. It was closer now. Much closer.

As soon as they were both inside he closed and bolted the door, then called for his son. 'Jimmy!'

The boy ran down the stairs, still gangly at fifteen, his clothes hanging loosely off his skinny arms and legs. 'What is it, Dad?' He looked pale and Joshua knew that he'd heard it too.

'Get a couple of hammers and some nails from the cellar. There are some short pieces of wood down there as well. Bring them up – we'll need them.'

Jimmy nodded, looking as though he was about to ask something else, then ran down the stairs to the cellar as instructed. Joshua spun round to his wife.

'Where's Beth?' he demanded.

'She's in her room, sleeping,' replied Mary, wringing her hands anxiously. 'She's been working so hard for her exams – best not to disturb her, eh?' She looked pleadingly at her husband who paused, uncertain. There was no door to the outside from Beth's room, at least, and her first exams began next week. Perhaps it would be best to leave her alone. He nodded to his wife who smiled tentatively at him and reached out her arms, beckoning him to her.

Joshua stepped forward and moved as though to hold her. But the howl sounded again. He could have sworn it was right by the house now. Mary shrieked and lunged towards him to bury her face in his chest, sobbing, but he pushed her away, his lips set in a grim line. 'There's no time for that, woman. Get back further into the house – go on. Stand guard by Beth's door – that's where he'll be wanting to go.'

His wife stared at him, uncomprehending until the realisation of what he meant dawned and a spasm of pain crossed her face. Choking back a sob, she turned and moved quickly down the hall towards Beth's room.

The cellar door swung open behind Joshua and he turned to see his son waiting expectantly, one hand holding two hammers and a bag of nails, the other clasping an armful of short planks to his side.

'Good lad,' said Joshua encouragingly, nodding at his son. 'I've locked the doors already, but we're going to board up the windows to be safe. I've heard tell that they sometimes come in through the windows.'

His son mutely held out a hammer and the bag of nails. Joshua dug inside to pull out a fistful, then took the proffered wood from his son's other arm. 'Do we do the windows upstairs too, Dad?' asked Jimmy, finally finding his voice, the fear he felt and was obviously trying to hide betrayed by a quavering tone.

Joshua shook his head and tried to sound reassuring. 'No, lad, just down here. They've not got wings

– not so far as I know, anyway.' He tried to smile at his son but he could tell from the expression on Jimmy's face that it had not worked, had emerged as some grotesque grimace.

'I'll take the front room, then, and the toilet, if you do the kitchen and the hall.' Jimmy nodded and ran off, and Joshua went into the front room and switched on the light. He paused on the threshold of the room, suddenly struck by the homeliness of the scene: the old sofa, its cushions sagging towards the middle, covered in a rug that he and Mary had received as a wedding gift, threadbare now but still loved, part of the family; the books, some he'd had since childhood, prizes for hockey, natural history, lining the wall; the framed paintings hanging above the sofa, one of which he'd inherited from his parents, a view of the coastal holiday cottage from which he'd taken some of his happiest childhood memories. He felt his eyes moisten, his throat tighten, at the contrast between the comfort he felt here, the sense of being at home, in his proper place, and what he was now being forced to do.

With a heavy heart, he stepped across the rug and, sitting on an arm of the sofa, placed one of the planks across the recessed window. At least the wood fitted. They'd be able to take it away, when it was all over. He heard the sounds of hammering coming from the next room. Jimmy was a good boy, he did what he was told. As tears began to blur his vision, Joshua struck the first nail hard, then put all his rage and grief into the blows, sinking it deep into the wall with two sharp raps. Then he added another nail, which he hit so furiously that it was driven home on the first tap.

Something brushed against his leg and his stomach leapt. He turned, hammer raised, to see his dog Basil, a Yorkshire terrier he'd had for ten years now, cowering away from him, eyes wide and staring at him, ears pinned back, hindquarters quivering on the sofa.

Letting out a groan and wiping the moisture from his eyes with the back of his hand, Joshua put the hammer down and scratched his dog behind the ears. Basil let out a tiny questioning whine and Joshua picked him up and hugged him. The dog was scared too, of course he was, he'd heard it outside like the rest of them, and Joshua felt a sudden access of emotion, a rush of love – for his children, his wife, his dog – mixed with an urge to protect them all that almost overwhelmed him.

But now was not the time for emotion, he told himself. He put the dog down, its tail wagging slightly now, the animal happy to have been given some attention. Then Joshua turned back to the window to fix the other end of the plank in place.

When he'd finished with the window he walked out through the hall to the toilet, Basil following faithfully at his heels. The window in there was small, but just about big enough to let a man – or something shaped like a man – through. Joshua hadn't heard the howl for a while, though, and he let himself hope that it had gone, that they were safe. Still, they'd started, and Jimmy's hammering had been so forceful and consistent that he must have almost finished the rooms that Joshua had charged him with.

Joshua smiled despite himself at the thought that Jimmy might catch his father with his own task unfinished, having grown sentimental. That would never do. And with that thought, he placed one end of a plank over the toilet window and began to hammer in a nail. It was curious that Basil wasn't barking; hadn't barked once. He would have expected that, at least, of the dog, but Basil still seemed cowed.

Joshua turned away from the window, cramped in the close confines of the small room, satisfied with a job well done, only to see his wife standing in the hall. Even through the gloom he could see that she looked agitated.

'What is it?' He moved forward and took her by the arms, letting the hammer and nails drop to the floor. 'Mary? What is it?' he asked more forcefully.

She stared back at him, biting her lip, her eyes welling with tears. 'It's the sounds. There's sounds coming from Beth's room.'

'What do you mean?' Joshua shook her. 'What sounds?' But she just stared back at him and started to sob, gently at first. Then her whole body grew racked with spasms and he pushed her aside, panic rising in his mind now, taking long strides, then running, across the hall, turning at the passage at the end, brushing against the light hanging from the ceiling, leaving crazy shadows swinging in his wake until he stood in front of his daughter's door.

Go in! he told himself. But his hand paused before it reached the handle and he listened, his ears pricked for the faintest sound. The blood drained from his face and his stomach seemed to twist inside him as he heard it: soft, girlish moans and giggles and some kind of slurping sound, answered by a low masculine growl.

Giddy, horror-struck, Joshua pushed the door open. The choked 'Beth' died on his lips as his eyes took in the scene. His daughter's A-level revision books were strewn all over the floor, one marked with a muddy footprint from where it had been dislodged from the windowsill. The window was wide open and he realised sickly that his daughter must have let *him* in.

Beth was still dressed in her school uniform, too; she must have lied to her mother, she hadn't been in bed at all, hadn't been asleep, but had been waiting,

waiting for this to happen, welcoming the violator into her room. She didn't seem to have heard Joshua yet, either, or perhaps she was simply too engrossed in what she was doing, kneeling on the bed, her bottom raised to him, her navy-blue pleated skirt rucked up over the taut white globes of her buttocks, a dark, hairy hand busy in the oily slit between her legs. Her shirt was open and her white bra had been pushed down, her pale breasts exposed, long pink nipples hanging down. Joshua wanted to turn away, not to see her like this, but he was frozen, unable to stop looking. Beth's hips were rotating from side to side as she buried her face between the intruder's legs, her eyes closed, cradling his balls with one hand, bobbing her head up and down on his cock, so thick it was straining her lips.

And all the while the man – naked, lying on Joshua's daughter's bed, hairy but human, not the beast he'd half-expected to find here – stared back at Joshua, stroking his daughter's quim, sinking his cock into her throat, with a gently mocking expression in his bright green eyes.

'Tales of humans transforming, shape-shifting into animals, are common throughout the world – and not only in primitive mythology.' Dr Cavendish's deep voice filled the auditorium as he looked up from his notes. The hall was almost full: the doctor's lectures were popular. Emma looked over to where Miriam was sitting and saw that she was watching him with rapt attention. At the sight a pang of jealousy coursed through her, one she suppressed as fiercely as it had struck her. Her bottom lip quivering, she listened again to the lecturer.

'The account I'm going to read out to you was given by a respected British surgeon in Zimbabwe

11

some eighty years ago. You'll need to excuse some of the more, ah, colourful descriptions of Africa in the account, I'm afraid. But I still think it valuable.' He cleared his throat, rustled his notes and began, deepening his voice.

' "One of the most secret rites in Africa today is the ritual of the animal dance. I am one of the dozen or so Europeans who have ever seen one of these. And one moonlit night in a clearing of what at home people call 'the jungle', I saw the 'Nyan na lo Laklass' – the dance of the jackal. I saw men and women stealthily collecting, forming a circle, drinking furiously – drinking, drinking, drinking. The tom-toms are beating that maddening rhythm so impossible to reproduce, so ventriloquial that it seems to come from inside one's head. The beaters glisten with sweat as their bare hands strike with incredible rapidity upon the stretched skin.

' "In the circle drunken men and women are dancing, each in their place faster and faster as the drums' fierce rhythm seeps into their blood and the beer inflames them. Then there is a hush as the witch doctor, in his beads and teeth and jackal tails, begins his amazing dance." ' Cavendish's voice dropped and he looked up. 'The surgeon's a little vague as to the details of what happens to the witch doctor, apart from saying that he goes into a trance, but what follows is very interesting.

' "The scream of a hunted jackal echoes through the trees. The drums cease. A shiver runs through the squatting bodies, a little movement as of wind in standing corn. A woman whimpers – like a jackal bitch. A man growls – like a jackal dog. And then it begins. The details are horrible." Damn these censorious colonials,' Cavendish muttered as an aside in his normal voice, before resuming. ' "I can only say that these men and women imitate the actions of jackals with such uncanny accuracy that one is compelled to believe that they take on the nature, if not the form, of the beast.

' "Now the climax. Exhausted, the jackal men and women crawl back to their circle to growl and lick their wounds. The witch doctor comes out of his trance and dances again, and again falls, this time apparently into the deepest coma. And now a boy and girl leap into the circle to dance. If the imitations of the crowd are uncanny, those of this pair are miraculous. More and more nearly do they resemble the animals they portray until suddenly, before my eyes, two jackals are standing in that ring. One noses the entranced witch doctor with canine curiosity. Then they leap off and away while I blame my fatigue for a trick of the sight. But was it? I do not know. Perhaps it was a coincidence that I treated a native girl in the district for severe jackal scratches (an unheard-of thing). Perhaps! I am not sure." '

Dr Cavendish looked up. A hush fell over the auditorium, the students waiting to see if he'd finished. Then one put his head back and howled, a thin sound after the bass rumble of Cavendish's story, and a couple of students laughed. Cavendish, who Emma thought might have been annoyed, smiled and nodded. 'See you on Thursday,' he boomed and gathered his papers from the desk.

Students were already starting to mill around him. Miriam would never dare approach him, though, and Emma took some consolation in the thought. Her friend was shy in some matters, if almost too bold in others – she thought nothing of the dancing work they did, even if neither she nor Emma would ever tell any of the other students about it and lived in a perpetual fear that one of them might come to the

13

pub to watch – and approaching men wasn't her style. Especially men she had a crush on, and even more so men she was in awe of.

Emma had found out how Miriam felt during a row they'd had a couple of weeks ago. She'd known already that Miriam liked men, more than she did herself: her friend had taken a couple of boyfriends in the first year, by all accounts mutually enjoyable experiences, while Emma, trying hard to keep her own sexual leanings under wraps, had only managed to convince a few of the more forward male students that she was 'frigid'. She probably wouldn't have made a pass at Miriam at all if her friend hadn't drunkenly confessed that she fancied her one night. The dancing must have had something to do with it: Emma had always enjoyed watching Miriam strip and flaunt herself in front of hard-eyed strangers, but it had been a shock to discover that Miriam enjoyed watching her just as much.

The row had started when Emma suggested they could make a lot more money by putting on the occasional private show in the pub, not doing any-thing they didn't do together at home but not leaving much of it out, either. She'd thought Miriam would be game, considering how easily she'd taken to the stage, but instead her friend seemed to use it as an excuse to vent all the petty irritations she'd been building up over their relationship. Then she'd finally burst into tears when she'd admitted that she fanta-sised about Dr Cavendish.

They weren't even normal fantasies, either. Emma could have coped with that: she didn't expect Miriam's erotic imagination to dry up just because she was with her. But they were sordid dreams, tainted by whips, rubber masks and degrading acts. Miriam admitted that she'd often made herself come by thinking about Dr Cavendish forcing his cock down her throat and making her gag, or caning and buggering her, hard, taking his pleasure, using her and leaving her.

Maybe Miriam had thought that if she told Emma about the fantasies it would clear the air between them. Whatever the case, it had done exactly the opposite. Their time together seemed a little forced these days: they still cooked for each other, slept together, alternating visits between each other's flats, but now there was an unspoken barrier between them.

Emma caught up with Miriam as they filed out of the auditorium.

'Fancy some lunch?' she asked casually, trying to keep her voice light.

Miriam looked up, caught Emma's gaze and flushed, then looked away and nodded.

The refectory was filling up fast, huddles of students talking animatedly among the tables. Emma and Miriam took trays and piled salads high on their plates, then scoured the room until they found an empty table.

They ate in silence, Miriam picking at her food, until Emma saw what she'd hoped to find and only paused for a second before deciding to go through with it. Dr Cavendish was holding a mug of coffee and walking uncertainly across the floor, blinking owlishly behind his glasses.

'Dr Cavendish!' Emma half stood, and beckoned to him. A few students turned to look at her, and Cavendish beamed and moved towards their table, then faltered as he took a closer look. It was no surprise if he didn't recognise them, Emma reflected; but he had a reputation for being friendly with the students, and after his initial hesitation he came over with a determined stride.

'Hello,' he said, beaming. 'I don't know I've had the pleasure, Miss . . .'

'Oh, it's Emma Wall.' Emma smiled back. 'And this is Miriam – Miriam Price. We're in the third year, Anthropology students. I just wanted to say how much I've been enjoying your lectures. Won't you sit down?' Emma swung out of her seat to join Miriam on her side.

The older man, clearly flattered by the attention, sat in Emma's vacated seat. 'Of course, it's a fascinating subject,' he began. 'There are still reports of werewolves in the Caucasus and Ural mountains, to say nothing of Finland and Lapland, although they've generally died out in the British Isles. Ireland saw the most recent stories, accounts being given well into the middle of the nineteenth century, probably because wolves survived there longer than they did anywhere else in Britain.

'Interestingly, there was a recent robbery at the British Museum that ties in with this. You might have heard of it – no? I can't think why thieves would want to steal it, especially with the other valuable antiquities on display, but an Ancient British wolf amulet was taken and a guard knocked out. It's a tragedy for scholarship in the area, of course: opinions varied as to the use of the amulet, but my money's on it being one of the few remaining artefacts of a wolf-worshipping cult that, it has been argued, flourished in the British islands in pre-Roman times. But I'm boring you.' Dr Cavendish smiled. 'May I ask what your particular interest in the topic is?'

'Actually,' Emma replied, 'I called you over because I think Miriam has something she wants to tell you.'

'Oh?' Cavendish sat up straighter in his chair and stared at Miriam, whose gaze had dropped to the floor. He leaned forwards. 'What is it, my dear girl?'

Miriam made a squeak of protest and bit her lower lip, her hands fidgeting in her lap.

'Come on, Miriam! Why don't you tell the doctor what you told me the other day?' Emma cajoled. Still Miriam made no move, but a pink flush had started on her neck and was slowly suffusing her cheeks. The doctor sat patiently, watching the two of them, but there was a more acute interest in his eyes now, something sharper than the fuzzy warmth and good humour he normally gave off.

'Well, if she won't tell you, I suppose *I*'ll have to,' said Emma, turning from her friend back to the doctor. Miriam whispered a muffled 'No' and tugged at Emma's sleeve.

'Maybe I'd better, ah –' the doctor made as though to leave.

'Don't!' Emma said sharply. 'You'll want to hear this.'

The doctor sat down again.

'Miriam tells me she thinks about you, often, when you're not around.'

'Well, that's very pleasant, but I don't see why it –' the doctor blustered.

'She has fantasies – how often, Miriam? Nightly?' Emma prodded Miriam, whose whole body was shaking now in an effort to suppress her tears. 'Let's say a few times a week, for the sake of argument. She likes to imagine that you're her tutor, and that she has to take an essay to hand in to you in your office. She knows it's not good, she knows she's copied great chunks of it directly from another book, but she hopes you won't notice.' The doctor's gaze flicked back and forth between the two girls.

'You do, of course, but you don't shout at her, or fail her essay, or anything like that. It's much worse. You just stand up, and in a quiet but firm voice tell her to bend over the back of the chair and hold the seat, standing on tiptoe. She likes to imagine that you have a row of canes, a selection – ferrules, malaccas, bamboo rods – hanging on a rail on your wall. I'm sure you don't –' the doctor blinked '– but that's her fantasy. She's been in your office before, of course, and seen them, but thought they were just for decoration. But now she suspects that they're used on bad students, particularly on girls who waste your time. And now that she thinks about it, she can see that they're worn with use, that they're clearly taken down – and regularly, too.

'You select one and test its springiness between your hands, flexing it and then letting the tip swing free. Miriam's watching it, listening to it, and her legs are starting to shake with the effort of staying on her toes. You move behind her, and she knows what's going to happen, but daren't move out of the way. You lift her skirt up, some flouncy little number that you probably think is entirely unsuitable wear for a scholar, the kind of thing a tart would wear to show off to some brute of a boyfriend. You take her knickers – something fancy, silky with lace frills – and pull them down to inspect them.'

Emma paused. Cavendish was leaning back in his chair now, his face pale as he watched Miriam. She turned to her friend. A single tear rolled down Miriam's cheek.

'There are two things you find on her knickers. The first, which is bad enough, is that she's been scratching her dirty arse during the morning, and there's a skid mark there, a brown streak across the seat of her pants. You point this out to her, and tell her that you don't think it's appropriate behaviour to come and see your tutor with a dirty arse. But what's worse than this, what she's even more ashamed of, is the fact that she's juiced all over her knickers, that they're soaking with her excitement, damp all the way through. And when you find this you're shocked. How can she respond like this? Doesn't she know that she's going to be punished?

'And with that you take a few paces back and ask her how many strokes she thinks she deserves. She'll suggest some paltry number, three or something, and you'll point out that you aren't only punishing her for the essay, which is an insult to your intelligence at the very least, but for having the gall to approach you with dirty pants, and for behaving like a slut in your office. She may suggest six then, but you'll laugh and double it to twelve. She'll probably start whimpering or even crying then, like she is now.' The tears were rolling down Miriam's hotly flushed cheeks, and she was biting her lower lip, her shoulders shaking.

'Steady on,' the doctor said in an uncertain voice.

'You'll tell her to count the strokes, then give her the first without any warning. She'll jump up, try not to scream, and reach back with her hands to soothe the poor bruised flesh of her buttocks. You won't let her count that one off because she didn't stay in position. Then you'll lay the second stroke right on top of the first and stand back to watch it go red, then raise up, a bright red weal against the white flesh. But she'll have learned her lesson now – she doesn't want to take any more than she has to – and she'll stay in position, no matter how much it hurts.

'By the fourth blow she'll be blubbing properly, and you'll enjoy hearing the tears in her voice as she counts down the strokes. You'll take your time over it, laying each one in a criss-cross pattern, a methodical and skilled job, across both cheeks, until they're scarlet and hugely swollen, starting to go purple with the bruises. You'll use the tip of the cane to open her cunt, which will be dripping wet by now, and rub it along the crease, and you'll make sure that with the last few blows the tip cracks across the lips – enjoying her squeals when they land – or just under the tuck of her cheeks, across the tops of her thighs, where you know it'll hurt her even more.

'She'll scream at this, of course, but she'll know enough not to move until she's told to. But you have no intention of making her move. You want her to stay exactly where she is, her arse a mess of purple blotches. You move behind her and press your thumb into her cunt, telling her she's a filthy whore to be excited by a caning. You'll smear her juices all over her cunt, but you won't touch her clit, which will be standing up hard, even though she tries to push back onto you, to get some friction on it. Then you'll push your thumb against her tight arsehole and she'll complain, try to stop you, but you'll ignore her and she'll give up and let it in.

'You'll stretch her like that for a while, then you'll get your cock out and oil it up with her grease, although you won't fuck her where she wants it, even though she'll start begging you, wanting you to fill her up, pleading with you not to fuck her poor tender arse but to fill her juicy cunt. But you'll ignore her, and you'll press the end of your stiff cock against her dirty hole and push it in, slowly stretching her arse until it's all the way in. She'll be squealing again now, telling you to stop, it's too big, but it's going in, you're not about to stop now, and then you'll start to fuck it, long, slow strokes at first, gripping the sides of her welted arse, ignoring her cries of pain, then fucking it harder, feeling your balls slapping against her juicy slit, getting greasy now from the juice dripping down.

'After a while her grunts will turn into moans, and you'll pull away to let the ring close slowly on air. Then you'll stretch it again, just with the tip of your cock, and pull it out again, holding her cheeks wide apart with your hands. Soon it'll be enough for you, your balls will be tight and you'll want to spurt it out, but you'll bring yourself off with your hand, shooting it all onto her slowly closing hole, so that some of it goes right in and the rest oozes out as her dirty arse closes on it.

'You'll make her stand up again then, and pull the knickers back on to catch all the come, and make her wear them with it soaking through them, make her walk out of the office and back to her flat with your come still being squeezed out of her arsehole.'

Emma paused. Both Cavendish and Miriam were flushed now, and Miriam had stopped crying. Her eyes glittered as she looked furtively at the doctor. He pushed his chair back, clumsily spilling his coffee as he did so.

'I'd better go.' He tried to stand, but he was hard, Emma could tell, as he hunched over.

'Wait!' Emma instructed, and Cavendish paused, a professional smile frozen on his lips.

She turned to her friend. 'Miriam, give them to him.'

Miriam shook her head. Emma sighed and reached under Miriam's skirt, bunching it up around her waist, ignoring the attention they were drawing now from the students at the other tables. With a hard wrench and a tearing sound they were free, and Emma pulled Miriam's knickers away from her crotch. They were soaked, just as she'd known they would be. She offered them to the doctor, who held them delicately, staring at them as though he'd never seen female underwear before.

'Just to show you I wasn't making any of it up,' Emma said, smiling sweetly.

Dr Cavendish gave each of them a hurried glance, put the damp knickers in his pocket absent-mindedly, turned and walked uncomfortably away.

Two

He hadn't been keen on the idea from the start. It wasn't a question of money, after all, but he'd been foolish enough to ask Barbara where she'd like to go on a long weekend away. Paris? Rome? And the silly girl had picked this godforsaken Scottish village in the middle of nowhere, with only a couple of other godforsaken Scottish villages to break up the vast expanse of nothingness. Paul had heard of the Cuillins and places like Rannoch Moor, of course, but this wasn't even near the national parks; on the map it looked like it was in the middle of precisely nothing, which was exactly how it felt now on the moors. In summer it might have been all right, but early April didn't even count as spring to Paul. He took out the Ordnance Survey map and tried to open it, fighting against its flapping in the wind. It was no use.

'Barbara, I think we're lost.'

'I'm sure it's this way, Paul. Don't be a spoilsport – come on.' And she was bounding off again through the mist, unexpectedly nimble over the treacherous ground. Paul trudged after her resignedly. All this empty land seemed such a waste. Barbara always asked him to leave his work at the office, but he couldn't help thinking about development, how the boggy patches up here could be drained, new roads put in, grids of four- or five-bedroom houses, perhaps a landscaped golf course. At the moment it was just a barren wasteland.

Of course, Barbara didn't think so, skipping merrily ahead and pointing out lichens, mosses and birds to Paul. She seemed oblivious to the fact that they couldn't see the hill they'd been heading for earlier at all now; the mist had come down suddenly and now enveloped them so that they could only see clearly a few metres in any direction.

Paul checked his watch. It was five now, and it would start to get dark soon. He ran on, trying to catch up with Barbara, panting with the exertion. 'Barbara! I think we should stop now. Let's try and get back.'

She turned to face him and smiled, gently mocking. 'And if we're so lost, Paul, how do you hope to get us back again?'

'I think it's more or less this way.' He turned, although he wasn't at all sure. It looked the same in every direction: clumps of grass and pools of water, broken up only by the occasional fence or stone wall. 'If we find a stream, that'll get us off the moor; we just need to follow it down.'

Barbara came to him and rubbed his shoulder affectionately. 'Tired, are we?' Paul was about to protest, riled suddenly, but she went on. 'I must admit, this ground's a bit taxing.' She jumped experimentally from one clump of grass to the next, then looked up, beaming. 'OK, then. You're the leader. Show us the way.'

It took them half an hour to find a proper stream – most of the other rivulets ended in pools. There was noticeably less light than before and it was even darker in the stream gully; Paul almost slipped on the stones crossing the watercourse, trying to pick a trail down the side. Barbara had not been quite able to stifle a giggle.

Soon they came to a small clearing, with soot-blackened stones around the remains of a fire. There was a long stick upright in the ground, and Paul found a bleached sheep's skull by the fire. He picked it up and hung it on the top of the stick, then turned to Barbara, leering horribly.

'Here be witches.'

Barbara smiled absently and walked on. Slightly embarrassed, Paul began to follow, then looked back at the tableau. Suddenly frightened by the way the skull lolled, he kicked the stick, then crushed the fallen skull with his boot and hurried after Barbara.

Here they weren't far from the road and in the last of the light they worked out which way to go to return to the pub. There were no pavements, of course – another disadvantage to rural Britain, Paul thought bitterly – and the condition of the road was so bad, marred by great cracks and with tall weeds sprouting from the uneven tarmac, that walking on it was hard enough.

At least there were no cars. Although that had struck him as one of the strangest things of all about this place. When he'd called to book a room he'd asked about parking and had been told that he'd better leave his car outside the village and walk to the inn. He hadn't been quite able to believe what he'd heard but when he'd pressed the landlord for information all he could discover was that the roads were in very poor repair and that a Lord Garner, who owned most of the land thereabouts and lived in the castle next to the village, disapproved of cars. It sounded like the Middle Ages to Paul, who never walked anywhere if he could help it. But when he'd told Barbara about it she'd clapped her hands together with glee and had started to tell him about childhood holidays in Sark, which had also banned the use of cars, and how much she'd loved the place. In fairness, though, she hadn't expected him to carry the luggage all the way from the car by himself, volunteering gamely to carry her own bag, which was smaller than Paul's – a first in his experience.

It had gone seven by the time they saw the lights of the village; Paul had never expected to feel so happy to find the pub again. The bar was only half full, despite it being a Friday, and the landlord caught Paul's eye as they came in and nodded to him. 'Good walking, then?'

Paul raised an eyebrow. 'We were heading for that big hill, but we got lost in the fog.'

The landlord nodded. 'You'll be wanting dinner soon?'

Paul's stomach had been rumbling for some time now. 'Yes – we'll be down in a bit. Just need to wash up, you know.'

The landlord looked from him to Barbara, smirked, then nodded again. He'd been like this ever since they'd arrived, first asking incredulously if they were sure they wanted a double bed, then making subtle references to their age difference. At least, that was how it had seemed to Paul, although he'd wondered if he wasn't being a little paranoid – nobody batted an eyelid at the two of them together in London, but he hadn't been anywhere like this with her before. It was envy, Paul supposed; the landlady was matronly and grey, and Barbara was beautiful by anyone's standards.

In the room, he threw himself on the bed. He hadn't realised how tired he was.

'I'm going to have a shower,' Barbara announced. But instead of going straight to the bathroom she stood at the foot of the bed, watching Paul as she started to undress. She'd done this for him before, stripping slowly for him, and it had always turned him on. Yet this time, even though he could appreciate it and tried to make the correct sounds of approval as she pulled the bra cups from her breasts, or bent over to stick her bum out then work the knickers down over her thighs, inch by inch, it just wasn't doing it for him.

He couldn't disguise it, either. She came up to him and brushed her hand against his trousers, clearly disappointed by his lack of reaction. She brushed harder, then cupped his balls and reached for the zip. He pushed her hand away.

'Barbara, I'm tired.'

She sighed, and walked to the bathroom. As she showered, Paul looked through the window. There wasn't much of a view, just the narrow street and the unlit house opposite. In the distance he thought he could hear a drum.

The sound was more noticeable while they were eating: a steady thump coming from somewhere in the village. Partly because he was genuinely curious, partly in a bid to lighten the atmosphere – Barbara was sulking, and had hardly touched her food – Paul asked the landlady what it was.

At first he thought she hadn't heard him, as her only response was to ask Barbara if there was a problem with her food. Barbara shook her head, smiled wanly and started to eat again, encouraged by the landlady's prompting. So he asked again.

'That sound, like drums. Is there a festival in the village tonight, or something?'

The landlady tried to laugh. 'It's not a festival, no. There are some dances, not the kind of thing we approve of.'

'Oh? And why not?'

27

'I'd rather not say, sir, just that it's not godly. Going about as animals and that.'

That got his attention, Barbara's too, but the landlady was fidgeting, clearly keen to get away. Anticipating his next question, she went on, 'I wouldn't go out tonight. The locals here aren't too welcoming this time of year.'

'You're not local yourselves, then?'

'Oh, no, we've only been here twenty years.'

'Paul, I have a headache. I think I'll go upstairs.' Barbara pushed her plate away, the food only half finished, then stood up. Paul rose too, to join her, but she stopped him. 'You stay, if you like. Have a few more drinks.'

Perhaps he would. His reluctance earlier had clearly hurt Barbara's feelings, and there probably wasn't any point in trying to smooth them over now. He'd let her sleep on it, and everything would be all right in the morning. Paul nodded to the landlady, who was waiting impassively, to show that he'd finished, and walked to the bar.

There were a few people sitting huddled over their drinks at the tables, and a man of Paul's age was sitting on a bar stool. Paul ordered a pint of lager, then sat down next to the man. He could still hear the sound of the drum.

'Do you know anything about these dances, then?' he asked the man, who turned to stare at Paul before returning to his drink.

'It's nothing, just some locals getting drunk.'

'But she –' Paul nodded towards the landlady '– said something about them dressing up as animals, or something.'

The man sighed. 'I wouldn't know about that. And I wouldn't much care, either. So long as they don't go on my property, they can do what they like.'

The mention of property returned Paul to familiar territory, and soon they were talking about planning permission, ways to put pressure on reluctant councillors, and the financial potential of undeveloped land. One pint led to another, and soon Paul had had four and was feeling a little wobbly. The man had quite similar interests to him, it turned out, and they'd talked about golf and cars, making half-hearted promises to play a round together. But his new friend's easy affability had soured when Paul had tipsily revealed to him that he'd paid two men fifty quid to chainsaw a couple of old oaks that had been preventing him from developing an old vicarage and its garden into a block of new flats. He couldn't understand the man's rancour – he was bringing work to people, and providing essential new housing, and although he'd never have told Barbara some of what his job involved the man had seemed to have a sympathetic ear.

Paul walked unsteadily up the stairs, overtired now and ready for bed. The light was off, and he whispered as he entered the room: 'Barbara?' There was no reply, and he tried to walk to the bathroom without disturbing her, but only succeeded in shinning himself on the bed frame. There was no response to his yelp, either, and when he put the bathroom light on and looked back he saw that the bed was empty. It didn't, in fact, look like it had been used at all, apart from the dent where he'd lain down earlier. And Barbara wasn't in the bathroom, either.

The sound of the drum was louder now, and it was moving. Paul stepped over to the window and peered out. The moon was fat and bright, and he saw a figure turn the corner then pass out of sight, vanishing as the drum grew quiet. The silvery light of the moon cast curious shadows and for a second he thought he'd seen antlers on the figure's head.

He walked back downstairs and returned to the bar. Unsure how to broach the subject, he decided on a direct approach and asked the landlord, 'You haven't seen Barbara, have you?'

A couple of the heads at the tables looked up, and the man he'd been talking to before turned as well. He must have spoken more loudly than he thought. The landlord shook his head.

'She's not upstairs. She said, you know, she was going upstairs, she had a headache, but she's not there now.' Paul paused, then looked at the door. 'You would have seen if she went out, though?'

'If she'd used that door, yes. But there's a back entrance as well. I'm sure she's OK, probably just popped out for a bit of fresh air. Why don't you sit down and have another pint; she'll be back in no time.'

Paul grimaced, then walked towards the back door that the landlord had indicated, aware that most of the other drinkers had stopped talking and were watching him. He wasn't going to wait for her, let her show him up like this. Suddenly he was angry at her for putting him in this situation, having brought him to this place, and he wanted to let her know.

But there was no sign of Barbara outside the back door. The night air was cold and sobered him up. She might have gone for a walk. She might even have gone to see what the dancers were doing, in which case he should follow the sound of the drums.

The roofs of the buildings shone in the moonlight, but the shadows it cast were dark and Paul couldn't remember the layout of the village. It wasn't very big, though, and once he'd found the church he'd be able to orientate himself; if not that, there were always the lights in the castle on the hill. He called out once, 'Barbara?', but there was no reply, only the drumming, fainter now, and he set off.

Paul and Barbara had walked around the streets before, but they seemed more narrow now, more tightly winding. There was no one out, and hardly any lights on in any of the houses. He tried to follow the sound of the drumming, but some of the streets it took him down were dead ends and others forced him into a maze of tortuous back streets, so that before Paul knew it he was lost, and cold.

Still, he wasn't about to give up. He was noticing things about the houses that he hadn't seen before, the moonlight picking out fresh details – the carved faces over the lintels of some of the older houses, and the figures lined up in a few of the windows. Paul had seen them before, in a book he'd read as a child, and tried to dredge up their name – corn dollies, some kind of fertility figure, which must have been made from the previous year's harvest. He'd seen photos of them in other books too, although not since his childhood, but while those had seemed benign these looked more sinister, their wizened sheaves mocking his tired body. He hadn't realised these people were so backward, and the thought frightened him.

Wandering aimlessly now, trying to find a landmark he recognised – the church steeple remained invisible – Paul came across a small green. A low, flat building squatted on the other side, its doors open, and light and music spilled out. The drumming was stronger again now, and seemed to be coming from inside. Suddenly hopeful, Paul crossed the green and pulled the door wide open, then stepped back.

There was a large room, dimly lit, with a crowd gathered around a door at the far end. Other people, mostly men, were sitting or lying around the sides of the room, holding bottles or passed out. Some were dressed in the normal farm-wear he'd seen most of the people here wearing, but a few looked different: one had horns that had fallen slightly askew as he slept, another was covered in green leaves, a halo of the largest ones arranged around his face, which was also painted green, and a few were wearing tunics and short trousers, looking like a uniform of some kind or an outfit for a medieval re-enactment.

Paul stepped in. There were other sounds as well as the drumming here too, all coming from the door at the far end. The fast music, a manic fiddle punctuated by drumbeats, mixed with laughter, the chinking of glasses and shouts of approval. But over these there was something else, something that made Paul feel queasy – a series of high-pitched moans and squeals, sounds he recognised clearly enough. They were the unmistakable sounds of a woman in a state of high sexual excitement.

Blanching now, Paul moved towards the crowd. Everyone was jockeying for a better look, leaping up on their companions' backs. Nobody noticed him joining them, or if they did they didn't show it, intent as they were on the activity in the far room. The light in there was even dimmer, and it took his eyes a few seconds to adjust to the gloom. Almost all the men there were in costumes, huge antlers or long goat horns strapped to their heads, or wearing full animal masks. In the centre was a man in a wolf mask, his trousers pushed down and his hindquarters pumping as he drove his cock into some local tart, some slut who . . .

Paul almost didn't recognise her at first. The front of her hair was thick and ropy with something sticky, and her face glistened, white drops running down her chin and over her cheeks. Her eyes were closed, but

Paul could see with a sickening lurch that she was in ecstasy, more than she'd ever been with him. There were men standing around her, their cocks out and level with her face, and she'd turn her head this way and that, giving one a lick while pumping another with her hand, then bobbing her head furiously up and down, or putting her head back and gasping as the man inside her pumped harder.

'Barbara!' he couldn't help calling out in a strangled voice. Almost immediately the crowd began to part, some of the men pushing him forward, others just slapping him on the back or pulling at his clothes.

Paul could dimly hear the calls around him. 'It's the husband!' 'The boyfriend!' 'This one knows her, he does!' All the cries were met with riotous laughter and cheers, until he was at the front of the crowd, sobbing as he watched. Barbara's eyes opened, glittering, and he stared at her. She didn't seem to recognise him.

A few of the women from the crowd surrounded him now and were tugging at his clothes. 'Get these off him!' they encouraged each other, and although he tried to stop them, crying out 'No! No!', batting at their hands and wrapping his arms around his chest, he was soon on the ground as the women struggled to pull off first his coat and jumper, then his shoes, socks and trousers. Finally he was just in his pants, but the women's hands were still rubbing all over him, accompanied by the sounds of laughter from the men, and they were squabbling over the prize, each pushing the others' hands away until one took a firm grip and ripped the pants down off his crotch.

Paul's instinctive reaction was to cover himself, to hide his nakedness from the crowd, but his hands were pulled away, his arms held fast by his side, and suddenly there was something warm and wet over his cock. One of the women had taken him in her mouth. Another was forcing the end of a bottle to his lips, cradling his head in her hands and pouring the liquid in. Paul sputtered, then drank, feeling a warm glow as the thick honey-sweet liquid flowed down his throat. He couldn't take his eyes off Barbara, still groaning in front of him, wanking, sucking, being fucked hard and loving it.

Paul was hard now, his cock thickening and lengthening under the woman's agile tongue, and she cupped and squeezed his balls, letting out a moan of appreciation at his firmness. She lifted her head off his cock, then cried out, 'He's ready!'

There were more cheers, and arms around his shoulders lifted him up until he was sitting. Other hands scrabbled at his head, and he sat there dazed, one of the women wanking his cock slowly, keeping him hard, while something heavy and cumbersome was fixed to his head. As soon as it was on, the others moved back, and he put his hands up to feel the antlers, furry under his fingers and huge.

Hands were gently prodding him and he could see the men around Barbara moving away, keeping their hands on their cocks all the while. Then the man in the wolf mask pulled out, and Paul heard Barbara's groan of disappointment as the wolfman withdrew. There were cries of 'Go on, then!' and 'What are you waiting for?' and Paul stepped forward and took her in his arms.

She opened her eyes again, and he searched them for some sign of recognition. There was nothing, only an urgent pleading in the dilated pupils as she whispered to him, over and over again, 'Fuck me. Fuck me.'

He'd never been so hard. He took her thighs, feeling the slickness of her excitement and the slime of the other men, then felt his cock twitch as it touched her, the thick head pushing inside her red, swollen hole. She moaned, pushing herself down onto it, and he pulled back, wanting to prolong the moment, grabbing the base of his cock and rubbing it up and down her slit, noticing how hard her clit was, how she shuddered when he flicked his cockhead over it, fast.

But then Paul couldn't wait any longer and had to plunge it in. Barbara was wet, almost too wet, but tight, and he could feel her muscles gripping him, trying to hold him deep inside her. But he pulled out, to hover with the tip of his cock at the edge and fuck her hard again. He hadn't done it like this for years; he wasn't sure where the energy was coming from and he didn't care. He felt rejuvenated, hardly himself any more.

The other men came closer now and again Barbara was surrounded by hard cocks, animal men tugging on them and offering them to her hand or mouth. The wolfman was there too, a grotesquely oversized cock protruding from his crotch with a hairy hand pumping away at it. But Paul hardly cared now, his full concentration focused on the sensations running up and down from the base of his skull through his spine and out from his cock.

Barbara was still mumbling, 'Fuck me. Fuck me, as he pounded her hole. She alternated her moans with an occasional squeal if he sped up or ground himself deeply into her. Some of the other women had come up behind him too, and were stroking his back, down to his arse, then his balls, stroking or squeezing them as he pumped away. Then Paul's arse cheeks were being pulled apart and he felt something hot and wet

35

trail down to the centre. He paused, deep inside Barbara, and felt a hot tongue burrow down into his dark hole. His ring clenched on it, then relaxed, letting it in – and suddenly it was too much, the forbidden sensation combining with everything he'd seen Barbara do, and as he came he stared at her: the image of her face covered in come, her lips bruised and swollen, an ecstatic glow in her cheeks, burned into his mind, his cock pulsing jet after jet of thick come deep inside her, his hands mashing her breasts, the tongue burrowing further into him as white light boiled behind his eyes, until it was over.

He softened and slid out of her. The other women moved back, and he stepped away, bewildered. Gently they took the horns from his head, and he watched as the wolfman took his place between Barbara's legs again, plunging in and making her eyes pop open in astonishment. Paul turned and saw the pile of his clothes, then started to dress himself again, left alone by the crowd now, the sound of Barbara's squeals burning in his ears. Someone passed him a bottle, and he took a long draught of the sweet liquid, then passed it on and pushed his way through the crowd, unwilling to turn and see what had made Barbara's moans so high-pitched and frantic, barely knowing what he was doing, until finally he was clear of the crowd, and in the other room again.

Paul made his way back to the pub in a daze. The back door was unlatched and he climbed the stairs to the bedroom, then collapsed on the bed, hoping against hope that Barbara would join him. He was exhausted, but he slept only fitfully, reaching out an arm for Barbara and half waking when he found her gone, the memory of what had happened flooding back into his mind. He dreamed, too, a vivid, confused jumble of images: stags shifting into men wearing antlers, men with furred legs that bent the wrong way, dancing through woods as he searched for something, something he'd lost.

Emma peered out of the door. It was busy, even for a Friday, busier than she'd seen it for a while. She gazed out at the expectant faces wreathed in smoke, all turned to the stage. Wolf whistles and lewd shouts were clearly audible above the thud of the dancer's music. She closed the door and turned back to Miriam.

'It's pretty busy out there.'

Miriam didn't look up but just carried on lacing up the rubber boots that hugged her legs to her lower thigh. Once again Emma felt glad that Mike, the pub landlord, didn't want both of them in that get-up: she'd tried the boots and had only been able to teeter around in them, while Miriam moved gracefully, even in the positions she was encouraged to hold. Emma was no fan of the rest of the gear, either – rubber made her sweat in general, and she hated the struggle to get into it, the way it pinched the skin. And there were specific things she disliked about Miriam's outfit, too: the studded collar she found constricting, the corset and pants uncomfortably tight, even if the eyemask might have helped preserve some anonymity. Miriam had told her once she found it like a second skin; well, she was welcome to it.

Miriam hadn't said a word to her since their lunch, and Emma had almost had regrets for what she'd done – but only almost. The looks on Miriam and Cavendish's faces had been worth it.

A drum roll announced a switch of dancers and Emma checked her outfit once more: a gold lamé bikini with a thin orange shift like a baby-doll nightie attached above her top, and a pair of gold kitten heels. It had been Mike's idea to dress them differently, and he'd even done a corny pitch for it, too, advertising them on flyers as 'Fire and Ice' – cheesy as hell, but it seemed to draw the punters in, and it gave the girls more of a distinct image than most of the other dancers. It also suited their colouring, with Emma's lightly tanned skin and tawny hair contrasting with Miriam's milk-white flesh and lustrous straight black locks.

Emma was on first, and gave a nod to Miriam, who finally met her gaze, before walking out into the pub. A couple of the men cheered, and she heard one call out, 'Come on, love, we haven't got all night!' The other dancers, one sweating and another clutching a pint glass full of pound coins and notes, grinned at her as she walked past and climbed up onto the small stage.

Emma peered through the smoke to the bar and nodded to Mike, who switched on the music. As the backbeat kicked in before the big-band brass section blew the first few chords, she turned away from her audience, row upon row of eager faces staring up at her, and began to shimmy from side to side, letting them get a good view of her arse through the shift before she turned to face them again. She knew all the tricks and recognised the regular punters. She knew how to look someone in the audience in the eye while she was touching herself, rubbing her hands along her sides, lifting her breasts, and she knew how to lick her lips suggestively while maintaining eye contact.

It was what the punters wanted, and it was what she was happy to provide. The money was important, sure, and she checked to see that Miriam was out there now, in her full kit, but it wasn't the only thing: she wasn't about to tell Mike about it, as he'd just see it as an excuse to cut their bar earnings, and she wasn't even sure about talking about it to Miriam. But the truth was that she enjoyed showing herself off, turning the men on, getting them excited, even if she preferred to take girls as lovers herself. It still got her excited, and she knew they knew.

Without missing a beat, Emma unclipped the shift and let it drift to the ground. She stuck a finger in her mouth, ran it over the full, glossy lips, then eased it under the top of her bikini and pinched a nipple. A murmur of appreciation came from the crowd. She reached up and unhooked first one shoulder strap, then the other, and leaned forward and pressed her upper arms against her chest, displaying her full cleavage to the front row of men.

Then she turned away from them again and tugged the front of the bikini down so that it pushed her breasts up, her nipples already stiff and poking out. She covered them with her arms and turned back to face the crowd, giving them a coquettish look. Holding the gaze of one of the men in the front row, she dropped her arms slowly, exposing the taut pinkness of her nipples. She could feel a wave of energy coming off the crowd at the exposure, a melting between her thighs at the thought of the power she had over them, but the eyes of the man she'd selected, dilated now, held her transfixed, and it was only with difficulty that she managed to break away from them.

Looking around the rest of the crowd, Emma dipped two fingers into her mouth then trailed them down over her breasts, pushing into the soft flesh with her hard red nails, then across her belly to slip them under the bikini bottom. She squatted down, slowly, spreading her legs as wide as they would go, listening to the appreciative groan from the audience, then tugged the bikini material to one side and turned slowly through a half-circle arc, showing off the shaved lips and oily pink crease to the crowd. The men were louder now, some thumping on the pub tables with their pints.

She stood up again, then turned away from them and bent down, grabbing her ankles, to sashay from side to side, the bikini bottom still yanked to the side of her pussy, now making the thick swollen lips bunch together and squeeze out juice. Still with her back to the crowd, she hooked a finger around each side of the bikini bottom and, wiggling her arse sensually, tugged it slowly down. The noise intensified as her arsehole came into view, and then grew even louder as her sex was fully exposed, her excitement clearly visible. Turning to look over her shoulder, she popped a finger in her mouth and then reached back to run a nail along and into the crease, opening it just enough to give a full flash of pink to the punters.

Then Emma knelt down, sticking her arse as far up as she could, and walked back on her knees until she was nearly touching the men in the front row. They were going crazy now, pounding on the tables, and her excitement was mixed with fear at her exposure, her vulnerability. She trusted the bouncers there, trusted Mike not to let anything happen to her or Miriam, but she'd never quite got used to the sexual energy, the charged testosterone atmosphere.

Her track would finish soon; she knew it back to front. Just time, then, for a final touch, something to make the punters dig a little deeper in their pockets for her next dance. She ran another finger into her crease, and dipped it in a short way, covering it in grease. Then she dragged it up, pressing against the slit all the way, until it rested on her arsehole. A few of the men were shouting at her, calling her a filthy bitch, telling her to stick it in, and she smiled to herself as she eased the tip of a finger inside her arsehole and wiggled it from side to side, feeling it hot and tight in there as she thought of what she'd told Dr Cavendish earlier.

As the music drew to a close, trumpet flourishes and snare rushes signalling a climax, Emma pulled the finger out and turned back to the audience, then gave them a broad wink. There was a fierce round of applause and table bangings when the music stopped, and she turned to pull on her bikini again, watching as Miriam walked towards the stage. The pint pot that Miriam gave her was almost full of coins and notes, and Emma felt a hot flush when Miriam returned her grin as she passed her the pot.

As she walked over to the bar to put the first of the night's earnings in secure keeping, Emma heard Miriam's music begin. It was darker, more modern than Emma's choice, in keeping with her outfit, some doomy industrial-tinged techno, but not so abrasive it would put the punters off.

Miriam's act, in its early stages at least, revolved far more around the pole that Mike had had installed a couple of years ago. As Emma passed the pint pot around, cheerfully acknowledging the comments of the men who'd just watched her, she could see Miriam moving up and down the pole, one hand on it to steady herself, her legs wide apart and the rubber between her legs rubbing against it.

Miriam moved well to the music, her hips giving little shimmies to each beat, her eyes roving over the audience, making eye contact with each of the punters in turn. Emma knew that most of the punters who hadn't been there before would consider what was happening now the climax of the act, as Miriam slowly pulled the zip of her rubber pants down, then up the other side to bare her arse as well. Emma kept her pussy lips shaved, but had a tuft of hair on top; Miriam had shaved the whole thing, partly, she maintained, so that hairs wouldn't get caught in the zip of her tight rubber outfit. But Emma had long suspected it was more than that, as she'd more than once found Miriam squatting on a mirror, a bowl of warm water, a razor blade and a can of shaving foam in front of her, bringing herself to a slow, shuddering orgasm. Evidently Miriam's motives for shaving herself weren't exclusively professional.

Still, it did the job well enough here. Miriam was spreading her legs around the pole again, this time with her sex wetly exposed, and the men were craning forward for a better look. She was only too happy to oblige, moving away from the pole and squatting in front of them, her legs wide apart just as Emma's had been, the raw redness of her bare sex lips in stark contrast to the porcelain whiteness of her skin and the shiny black rubber.

The music seemed to be drawing to an end, and as Miriam stood up Emma knew that some of the men would be starting to turn away, thinking of ordering another pint, checking the football scores or consulting their mobiles. But the regulars were still staring, knowing there was more to come, their gazes hungrily expectant as Miriam stood close to the front row and tugged down her corset, exposing her breasts.

The noise among the men, which had been growing steadily louder for a few minutes now, quietened again as the audience realised that the show wasn't over yet. But it probably wasn't clear to most of them why Miriam was bunching her breasts in her hands, massaging them hard and tugging on the nipples, pulling them out and then squeezing the breasts again – until the thin bluish milk started to spurt out, long jets of it spraying over the faces of the men in the front row, some of them letting out gasps of shock or annoyance even as others raised their faces to let the warm spray cover them. A riotous sound of table thumping drowned out the music as Miriam, a dreamy smile on her face, emptied the last of her milk over the punters.

On Saturday morning Paul felt listless, on automatic pilot, as he washed and then went downstairs for breakfast. He wasn't hungry and just opted for cereal rather than the full cooked meal, but he drank a couple of cups of coffee to try and put his thoughts in order and make sense of what had happened. A place had been laid for Barbara, and he stared at the empty space where she should have been sitting, feeling numb. Fortunately, apart from a quizzical glance from the landlady, nobody mentioned her absence to him, or indeed spoke to him at all, save to wish him a good morning, to which he could only mumble and nod.

After retrieving his coat from the room he went out, to retrace his steps back to the hall. It was easy to see the church steeple in the daylight, although he realised for the first time that it badly needed renovating, and the streets seemed more normal now, not as narrow or threatening in the crisp, clear light of day. The green looked innocuous enough, too, as did the hall, although the doors were closed. Paul wasn't altogether sure what he'd expected to find here, but he'd imagined there'd be *some* sign of what he'd seen. Instead there was nothing: no empty bottles or the usual drinking detritus, let alone antlered youths nursing hangovers. He stepped up to the reinforced glass windows on the doors and tried to peer inside, but his eyes couldn't penetrate the gloom; he took hold of the handles of the doors and rattled them, but they were locked.

'Wanting to get in, are you?'

The voice, coming as it did out of nowhere, so close to his ear, gave Paul a start, especially as he'd been feeling self-conscious enough anyway about trying to get into the building. He turned to the speaker and saw a severe-looking woman with prematurely grey hair tied back tightly. She was wearing a long grey coat. He tried to smile at the woman, but she just stared back at him.

'It's just – I was here last night, and I left something behind,' he started.

'Oh aye? You don't seem the sort. What was it you left behind?' the woman demanded.

'Oh, never mind,' Paul replied, suddenly embarrassed by the encounter and trying to walk past her. 'It doesn't matter.'

'No, wait!' The woman put a hand on Paul's sleeve. 'Was it your wife you were looking for?'

Incredulous, Paul turned to stare at the woman. 'My wife?' He was on the verge of denying what had happened before he realised that this woman might be able to help him get Barbara back again.

The woman hadn't released her grip on his coat. 'Aye, your wife. Your name's Paul, isn't it? We don't get many incomers here, and it's easy enough to keep an eye on what happens to them. That said, I don't know just what went on in that building last night, and I'm not sure I want to know; something ungodly, no doubt. But tell me –' she gripped Paul's coat sleeve harder '– are you one of them?'

Paul stared at her in bewilderment. Her eyes were fixed in a crazed glare. 'I'm not sure I understand what you mean,' he replied, trying gently to pull away from her.

'Aye, yes, you do, of course you do! Are you one of them, or are you with us, God's people?'

'Well, of course, I'm a Christian,' Paul said, involuntarily puffing out his chest. 'But I don't see that it's important now. You see, I have good reason to believe that these people kidnapped my wife.' The image of Barbara as he had seen her the night before, her face dripping with other men's come, flashed before his eyes, and he took a second to compose himself. 'If you know anything about it, anything at all, I'd appreciate it if you told me.'

'Come with me.' The woman tugged at his sleeve, and he started, reluctantly at first, to walk with her. 'You're not alone. There are others who've lost people, too. We won't stay in the village much longer, to be tainted by their filth, but there's a meeting going on by the church.'

Paul allowed himself to be led through the warren of streets, passing a few people who either turned away from them, refusing to make eye contact, or greeted the woman with a 'Good morning, sister,' until they reached the church. He hadn't realised how ruined it was until now, and he gaped at the sagging roof with the bare beams exposed below and the smashed slate tiles underfoot.

'What happened here?'

The woman shuddered, and glanced up at the castle on the hill. 'They've taken over the village now, but not for long, mark my words. Come on inside, then – you can meet the others.'

She pointed him towards a low dilapidated structure to the side of the church. Paul opened the door and found himself facing a room similar to the one he'd been in the night before – a function room, entirely bereft of grandeur, with two trestle tables running along the far side carrying flasks of tea and plates of biscuits. To his left was a small podium where a bearded man with wild flashing eyes was addressing an audience of about twenty people, men and women, some dressed in a similar way to the woman who'd brought him here, others in less drab outfits. He turned to look quizzically at the woman and she nodded pointedly to one of the chairs. He shrugged and sat down, the chair squeaking on the lino floor.

'I thought I'd done everything,' the man at the podium was saying, his voice passionate, his face red with effort. Paul realised with a start that the speaker was close to tears. 'I'd locked all the doors, barred all the windows, everything you'd do if you heard it close to the house.' A murmur of agreement ran around the room. 'But then my wife came and found me, and –' he choked back a sob '– and I found that it had got into my daughter's room. The worst thing is, she let it in. She wanted to be with it. And then I saw –' But this was evidently too much for him, as his huge shoulders began to shudder with sobs. A man dressed in a grey suit stepped up to him, whispered something in his ear, then led him back to a seat.

The woman who'd brought Paul there then stepped up to the podium. 'The Order of Sanctity thanks Brother Joshua for sharing his tale with us. We know how difficult it is to tell the story, but each of us have a story to tell, and through sharing we grow stronger.' She paused, and looked directly at Paul. 'Please welcome to the Order a new arrival, Brother Paul.' There was a loud squeaking as the audience turned in their seats to face him, and Paul looked around at the faces, some welcoming, some distrustful, some expectant. 'Brother Paul?' The woman's voice made him look up at her on the podium. 'You'll share your story for us, will you not?' Scarcely able to believe what he was doing, and knowing full well that he couldn't reveal to these people what he'd actually done, Paul stood up.

'Take a look at what you're missing, preacher!'

He spun round, startled, half expecting to feel a pelt of mud hitting him between the shoulder blades. The children had attacked him like that before, when it had just begun. But there was only a girl – Mary Beth, he had taught her in Sunday School, in what seemed now like another age – grinning at him and lifting up the hem of her white dress to expose the triangular black bush between her legs. He took in the sight, then looked away, his cheeks burning.

'You'd like some of this, wouldn't you, preacher?'

He shook his head and started to climb the steps to the church doors, one hanging off its hinges, muttering a half-formed prayer under his breath.

'No point denying it, preacher, everyone knows about you and that girl!'

He turned back, alarmed, but Mary Beth was walking away now, giggling, hand in hand with a boy. He stared after them. Seventeen years old and already displaying herself so wantonly, abasing her purity for the sins of the flesh. And she knew about the girl; which meant they'd all know. His jaw set with grim determination, he stepped through the threshold of the church.

He hadn't come here since May had arrived, like a foundling left on his doorstep. That was five days ago; she still hadn't spoken, and tore up the clothes he dressed her in, his own, as he had never had wife or daughter. He didn't know if she was mute, or somehow beyond language, but one of the sounds she'd made when he pressed her for information sounded like 'May', and the name had stuck. He hadn't liked to leave her alone. It might be dangerous, he reasoned: he had seen her change, once, his frantic, panicked slapping at her skin apparently the only thing that had stopped her from going all the way, and he knew that he had invited a wolf into his house. But he knew also that he had become fascinated by her, by the possibility of saving the poor child from damnation.

The devastation inside was worse than he'd feared. He flicked the switches, peering into the gloom, but there was no light apart from the sunbeams illuminating the central aisle, dust swirling lazily in the bright shafts cutting through the darkness from the hole in the ceiling, the jagged edges of broken rafters leaving crazy shadows on the floor.

Glass crunched underfoot as he began to walk down the aisle, his eyes adjusting to the dimness. The stained glass had been shattered, its lead framework twisted by the rocks he now stumbled over, while the pews were littered with the torn pages of hymn books and the larger gilt-edged pages from the church Bible, its leather binding ripped back as it rested at the foot of the nave.

The walls of the church had also been defaced. Some of the vandals had merely written their names on the whitewash, daubed in bright red paint, but others had taken more care with their graffiti, depicting caricatured beasts standing on their hind legs, chasing fleeing maidens with outstretched arms. The beasts looked almost human, save for the grotesquely oversized phalli rearing from between their legs and the hair covering their bodies below the waist. He blinked, astounded at the obscenity, while an amused, diabolical thought ran through his mind: a memory of similar images, less sexualised, of course, but images of demonic lust nonetheless, in cathedrals all over Europe. As a student he had seen many himself. But no, these were hideous parodies, celebrations rather than warnings.

He turned away, to survey the wreckage of the church once again, but the image of the bestial legs returned to his mind. The hair was proof of the animal's nature, a sure sign of its wantonness; shorn, the animal would be closer to man, or man closer to God, cleaner, purer. An image seeded itself in his mind. Perhaps he could help May after all.

With renewed vigour he strode back to the exit, his mind going over the things he would need. As he emerged, blinking, into the sunlight, its rays warm after the chill must of the church, he saw that while he had been there somebody had left a figure fashioned from twigs and flowers on the steps, a female figure with enlarged waist and breasts, a pronounced slit between her legs. Grunting, he crushed it underfoot and walked on, determined to reach his cottage without being swayed from his purpose.

But the streets were almost deserted and he saw only a child playing outside an open door, a child who was pulled inside and the door slammed as he passed. To be honest he was glad not to encounter anyone but he was still curious as to their where-abouts – until he heard the distant sound of the horn and his skin crawled as he realised that the villagers had gathered in the woods again.

He let himself in through the back door of the cottage, half expecting to find May in the kitchen. She seemed to like it in there, huddling by the stove for warmth; he'd even let her sleep there, curled up in the corner on a bundle of rugs, as she didn't seem to like sleeping in beds: she'd kept him up all night in the spare bedroom, pacing around the bed like an animal, and after that he'd let her sleep wherever she liked. Except, of course, in his own bedroom.

She hadn't touched the food he'd left for her, either. The toast rack was still full, the butter shiny in the warm air. He called for her, then listened. There was no answering sound and he put the butter back in the fridge, then packed away the breakfast things and called for her again.

This time he could hear something, a squeaking noise, coming from upstairs. Perhaps she was still asleep and had decided to sleep in the spare room after all? He listened out for any other sounds as he mounted the stairs, but even the squeaking that he'd heard in the kitchen was inaudible now. He tapped on the door of the spare room before edging it open and peering round the side. There was nobody in there, and the bed was exactly as he'd seen it last time; it hadn't been slept in at all.

Curious, he called out for May again and peered into the bathroom, even checking behind the shower curtain. That left only his room. He'd told her not to go there; he had a right to privacy in his own home, and even if she couldn't understand what he said, surely he'd explained it to her well enough in other ways. He was angry by the time he reached the door, muttering imprecations to himself, so that when he flung it open he was entirely unprepared for the sight that met his eyes.

May was lying on his bed, naked, the squeaking sound, clearly audible again in here, coming from her bucking and writhing, the bed moving back and forth on the floor. She didn't seem to have heard him come in. Her eyes were closed, her legs spread, one finger holding the lips of her sex apart while the other cradled the large cross that had been taken down from its rightful place above the head of the bed, its tip nestling in the entrance to her open, wet vagina.

With a strangled cry he leapt across the room and grabbed the cross away from her, looking aghast at the smears of fluid marking the wood. Her eyes opened and she welcomed him with a sound halfway between a moan and a snarl. Already her muscles were bunching up, her feet quivering, the hair growing thicker on her forearms and between her legs; he'd seen it before, and looked wildly around the room for something, anything, to stop her.

His eyes fell on a belt, coiled in the corner of the room on top of a pair of trousers, and in one swift movement he'd grabbed its buckle and brought the other end cracking down over May's bare breasts, snapping the cold leather across her distended nipples. May sat up, yowling with pain and rage, one arm snatching across her chest, the white mark of the belt slowly reddening and swelling, but he cracked it across her skin again, marking her inner thighs, bringing a choked sob from the girl as she attempted to defend herself against more blows, bringing her knees up so that the plump lips of her sex, the curls damp with her excitement, were squeezed together before him, the puckered whorl of her anus clearly visible beneath.

He could feel himself growing excited at the sight but tried to resist the thoughts that rushed unbidden into his mind and to concentrate on the rest of her appearance. Her muscles seemed to have relaxed, the quivering anticipation of a change nowhere to be seen, and he thanked the Lord that he had returned in time, his swift actions preventing a worse fate.

May had stopped cowering away from him in fear now, and looked from his face down at his crotch with shrewdly narrowed eyes. As he watched her,

51

uncertain of what she might do, she lunged towards him, reaching a hand for the bulge behind his robes while smacking her lips. He moved abruptly out of reach and brought the belt down again, hard, between her legs, the leather smacking wetly against the greasy skin, and May froze, an agonised gasp on her lips.

There was no time to lose. Reaching into the wardrobe, he pulled out a handful of ties. With feverish swiftness, he secured first her wrists to the head of the iron bedstead, then her ankles to the other end, spreading her legs and inadvertently opening her sex, still puffy after the kiss of the belt.

Once he was sure that she could not move he left the room and fetched a bowl from the kitchen, then his shaving materials from the bathroom, where he let the hot tap run until the bowl was full of steaming water. Carrying these items back into his bedroom, he stared at May, who regarded him uncertainly, a hint of fear in her eyes.

The hair on her head was lustrous and thick, framing her face in long, gentle curves. It would be an offence against God to rid her of it, he realised, and his eyes moved as though of their own volition down her body, taking in her reddened breasts and the swell of her belly, down to the matted curls surrounding her slit.

He knelt by the side of the bed and smeared the shaving soap over the swollen flesh, which gave slightly under the pressure. Trying to ignore her moans and cooing sounds as he paid attention for the first time to her sex, he wetted the shaving brush in the warm water and began to rub it over the hair, working up a lather, flinching when he inadvertently grazed the hard nub peeping out between the inner lips and felt May stiffen.

By the time he'd worked up a good lather May had begun to rotate her hips, pushing herself towards him and sighing gently. He dug a hand into the soft whiteness of her inner thigh, a warning to her to be still, then opened the razor and touched it to the foam. She stiffened again at the touch and remained still as he scraped the blade over the coarse fur, reaching down after every pass to clean the razor in the water, the bristles floating with the soap bubbles on the surface.

As he removed the hair, working with minute precision to ensure that every last wisp was taken, his eyes were drawn to the nakedness of the skin beneath, both red raw and enticingly soft, and the line of greasy pinkness in the centre that seemed to grow wetter with every stroke of the blade.

He moved further down, his knuckles nudging against the warm oil as he scraped the hair away, and he could feel May's body tensing still further. As he continued to shave her he put her shivers down to fear, an awareness of what he was doing, but then she began to pant, shifting her crotch down so that his knuckles pressed against her, and he looked up from his work, alarmed, to see her tensing and relaxing, the muscles bunching as though in anticipation of another change.

He dropped the razor and stumbled back, almost knocking over the water as he took in the feral cast to her face, her arms pulling against the bonds, the muscles of her feet seeming to jump and twitch beneath the skin. He ran from the room, hurtling down the stairs to the kitchen where he rummaged around in a drawer until he found what he needed.

Praying breathlessly that it would be enough – he wanted to finish what he'd started, and couldn't have her bucking under the sting of the belt – he hurried back up to the room, looking appalled at the arch in May's back as she strained against her bonds, the change imminent now, and clamped the pegs over her stiff nipples. She screamed at the top of her lungs and he pulled on the pegs, stretching her nipples away from the breasts, watching in desperation for the symptoms to subside, even twisting the pegs when no effects were immediately visible.

Then May seemed to relax, the bunched muscles smoothing, the feet and hands losing their stretched rictus quality, her hips returning to the bed. Leaving the pegs on her nipples, relieved to have found a simpler way of controlling her transformations, he returned to his task, realising that he'd have to work quickly, that the attention was exciting her. He couldn't deny its effects on himself, either, but tried to ignore the tight fullness in his crotch, the way his balls hugged the base of his straining cock, and focused on removing the last of the hair.

The left side finished, he had to pull the right lip to spread the skin for shaving, his knuckles again sinking into the wet warmth at the centre. As May's groans began again he tried to finish the job as methodically and effectively as he could, tried to ignore the pull of the wet crease, the excitement clear in May's panting breath, mirroring his own forbidden, growing lust.

Finally it was over, the razor washed for the last time, and he dipped his fingers in the water to clean away the last of the soap and bristles from her sex, marvelling at the cleanliness of her now, the naked lips looking somehow purer, more innocent without the bestial hair that had covered them before. And as he congratulated himself on having brought May closer to godliness, he leaned his head forward to plant a kiss on the denuded lips, unable to resist any longer, knowing that as he had succeeded he had just as surely failed, filled with the trembling understanding that as soon as he had touched her there with his tongue he would not be able to stop.

Three

Swallowing her nervousness, Miriam rapped on the door. There was no answer and she peered at the plaque, marked DR R CAVENDISH, as though to see through it to what was on the other side. She knocked again, then pressed her ear to the door. She could hear nothing.

Experimentally, she tried the handle. To her surprise it moved and the door opened. Looking both ways down the corridor and finding nobody there to see what she was about to do, she pushed the door slowly open.

'Dr Cavendish?' she called out.

He wasn't in the room, she could see that at a glance, and Miriam's heart lurched as she stepped across the threshold, pulling the door to behind her. The room was large, with light flooding in from a window to her left, and long, heavy curtains tumbling to the floor on either side. The only furniture in the room was a chair and desk to her right and a sofa by the window, but bookcases covered most of the walls, with racks of untidy shelves behind the desk. She'd never been in here before, and wasn't quite sure why she'd come now. If Emma hadn't spoken to Dr Cavendish the day before she wouldn't have dared, but now everything had changed.

A thrill coursed through her, a sense of exploring the forbidden that she'd last felt at school, breaking into the headmistress's office. What could she say if she were caught here? That she wanted her knickers back? She stifled a nervous giggle, and walked over to the desk. It was covered in papers and journals, and Miriam ran a hand lightly over the top of the mess, careful not to dislodge anything, then crossed over to the other side of the room and sat on the sofa.

She closed her eyes and breathed deeply, drawing in the professor's smell, mingled with the rich leather musk of the sofa and the mustiness of his old books. There was a hint of perfume there too and she felt a pang of angry jealousy as she imagined another woman in here, sitting just where she was now. Was it a student? She hadn't seen Cavendish being overly friendly with any of her peers. But then, if anything *were* going on they'd be careful to keep it to themselves. Maybe he was fucking that skinny blonde girl, the model, the one all the boys fawned over. She'd seen her staring at him, the slut, and the image popped into her head of Cavendish grunting over her, bent over the sofa, his cock up to the hilt in her cunt, grinding around . . .

Suddenly there were voices outside the door and the handle was turning. Miriam leapt up, panicked, and pulled herself behind one of the curtains just as the door opened.

'. . . long have you been working for the student paper, Miss . . . ah . . .'

Miriam recognised Cavendish's voice.

'Hoban, Dr Cavendish. But you can call me Julia.'

But not the other one.

'Would you like something to drink? Tea, coffee?'

The professor's voice was moving away from her now, but Miriam could sense, even through the curtain, that the woman was still close. They hadn't seen her. She started to breathe again, slowly.

'Nothing, thanks, Dr Cavendish. If we could proceed with . . .'

'Of course, of course. Please take a seat.'

Miriam heard the sofa squeak as the woman sat down.

'I must say I'm flattered to be considered worthy of an interview by the student paper. But I do hope it's not going to be one of those "Is your tutor a witch?" hatchet jobs.'

The woman laughed. 'No, nothing like that. The students have been very impressed by your courses.' She paused. 'You've had another guest here recently? A woman?'

'Um, no. Not that I know of. The cleaners come in here every so often. Why do you ask?'

'No reason, I just didn't want us to be disturbed during the interview.'

'Well, I shouldn't think there's any danger of that. Shall we begin?'

The sofa squeaked again. There was a long pause, during which Miriam could only hear the sound of heavy breathing.

'That's a very – uh – distracting position you're in, Julia.' The professor's voice sounded heavy. 'I'm not sure if it's entirely appropriate.'

The woman chuckled. 'I'm sure you won't mind, Dr Cavendish. After all, whatever happens in this room won't go any further than the two of us.'

The professor cleared his throat. 'I'm glad to hear it.'

Miriam, desperately curious to see what was happening, inched her way to the side of the curtain. She could see the back of the woman's head against the top of the sofa. Her hair was very dark brown, almost black, and she seemed to be slumped down.

'Enjoying the view, professor?' The woman's voice was flirtatious now.

There was a pause, then a muffled 'Yes.'

'Then why don't you come closer for a better look?'

Miriam heard a creak, then the sound of heavy footsteps.

'Sounds like you're having trouble walking easily, carrying all that around. Would you like me to help you?'

Again Miriam heard an indistinct 'Yes,' then saw the woman's head lift off the sofa. She heard a sharper pattern of steps, as though someone was now walking in heels across the floor.

'No – wait, I –'

The woman chuckled again. 'You don't want to do without the view? Well, if I pull this up, then bend down here –' her voice tightened, as though with an effort '– you can see what you like, and I can give you a suck.'

Miriam started, then leaned back from the curtain, terrified that she'd given herself away, but the others seemed engrossed in what they were doing. She heard the sound of a zip being pulled down and crouched to slide behind the sofa, her heart pounding violently. She mustn't be caught. But she had to watch.

Still hidden behind the curtain, she lifted her head to peer over the top of the sofa. A woman wearing a flouncy ruffled black skirt, black heels and a red shirt was squatting in front of Dr Cavendish. His head was tilted back, his eyes closed, and he was groaning softly. The woman's head was level with his crotch and from the sight of her head bobbing up and down Miriam was left in no doubt as to what was going on. One of the woman's hands was cradling Cavendish's balls while the other was working away between her legs, deep in her own sex. As Miriam watched she could feel herself getting wetter and instinctively clamped her thighs together, rubbing them against each other to get a little friction.

So this was the kind of relationship Cavendish had with his students. Miriam was half relieved; it would make her own needs that much easier to satisfy. The woman had pulled her head away from his cock now and taken it in her hand. As Miriam watched, a long line of spit caught the light as it dangled from his cock, then broke off and fell to the ground. The woman pumped his cock, which Miriam noted with a sharp pang of excitement was large, thick and veiny, with an angry-looking plum-shaped head.

'You want to feel it inside me?' the woman asked him breathlessly. He nodded. She pushed him back until he was lying on the ground, then stepped over him so that she was straddling him. He began to sit up, to lift his head between her thighs, but she raised a heel and pushed it down on his chest, grinding it in.

'Stay there,' the woman ordered, and Miriam heard a murmur of assent from Cavendish. Then the woman lifted her skirt, knelt on either side of the professor, her back to Miriam, and sat down on top of his cock, slowly easing it inside herself, using her weight to drop down onto it until she was fully impaled.

As Miriam watched, astonished, the woman raised herself up, then sank back down, and began to bounce on Cavendish's cock, all the while rubbing at herself with one hand. Miriam stole a hand down to her own sex to find it hot and swollen, ready for attention, and began to rub it in time with the woman's bounces, giving it long, slow strokes at first. Then, feeling the bud come out of its hood, she rubbed her grease over it from side to side, building up a steady wave of pleasure.

The woman was bucking now, something unnatural in her movements, shaking her head from side to side, muttering something. Cavendish began to sit up again but she pushed him back. Miriam thought that she might have been coming but she didn't cry out, just leaned forwards and down. Cavendish screamed, a piercing cry quickly cut short as the woman pushed a hand over his mouth, and Miriam froze, her hand still between her legs.

Cavendish's feet twitched and the woman's body seemed to stiffen, then jerk, her head level now with Cavendish's shoulder. Miriam stared, unable to believe what she was seeing, as the woman's legs seemed to lengthen, muscles bunching and spasming under her skin, which was now covered in a light fur. But only when the woman's head came away from Cavendish's shoulder, her mouth grotesquely elongated and lengthened into a snout, red with Cavendish's blood, did she in turn cry out, straightening up behind the sofa.

The last thing Miriam saw before she passed out was the thing on top of Cavendish turning to face her.

'Wolves?'

'Yes, I know. Pretty peculiar, isn't it?' Peter Hillcoat took off his glasses and massaged his eyes. He looked tired, the lines around his eyes deeper than normal. There were papers strewn all over his desk, the corners of some lifting in the current of air from the fan.

'So how far has he got?' asked James White.

'Oh, he's just made the suggestion so far. You may remember we ran this story.' Peter tossed a folded-over newspaper at him, further disturbing the mess of papers on James's side of the desk.

James leaned over to take a look. 'WOLVES TO BE REINTRODUCED ON SCOTTISH ESTATE.' He quickly scanned the text: a Lord Garner, pictured in a black and white photo as a young man with a stern face and piercing eyes, had proposed reintroducing wolves onto his land. According to the article there was some support from ecologists for the idea, although local farmers were less impressed: as the writer of the article pointed out, if wolves were introduced on the estate, it would only be a matter of time before they spread over the surrounding countryside. James put the paper down and looked questioningly at his editor.

'I know what you're thinking,' Peter said, holding his hands in the air. 'Not much of a story by itself, is it? The thing is, there's more. Possibly a lot more. We've had reports filtering down, odd snippets of stories, really, not much more, about pagan activities near Ardegan, the village closest to Garner's castle.'

'Well, they're all up to it up there, aren't they? I've seen *The Wicker Man.*'

Peter smiled. 'We haven't had any accounts of human sacrifice. Not yet, at any rate. No, this stuff's more like a bunch of morris men gone crazy – dancing round the maypole, that kind of thing. I don't know what to make of it, to tell you the truth, and I wouldn't give it a second thought if it weren't for a couple of other stories that have come down too.'

James raised an eyebrow quizzically.

'First off, something funny's happened to Ardegan itself. It looks like nobody's going there and nobody's coming out. The roads are blocked, or they've fallen into disrepair, or something. Secondly, and this has been confirmed by local police, there have been a number of arson attacks on shops in the region. The police suspect some nationalist group is responsible because they haven't gone for anything locally owned, just chains. But still, that makes for a lot of shops, and retailers are getting edgy, asking for more police protection and so on. Some of the towns near there look exactly the same as the ones down here – rows of Boots, Snappy Snaps, JD Sports, you name it – and they all think they're going to be next.'

'So what's that got to do with the morris men?'

'On the face of it, nothing. It's just that they both started at around the same time.' As James shrugged and held his hands out, Peter continued, 'I know, I know, there's probably not much in it. But there are a couple of other things too. You'll probably think I'm crazy for even mentioning it, but this happened a week ago.' He tossed another folded paper across to James, who read the story:

ANCIENT BRITISH WOLF AMULET STOLEN FROM BRITISH MUSEUM

Shortly after closing time on 3 April a brass amulet representing a wolf's paw was stolen from the Ancient Britain rooms of the British Museum. A guard was knocked out in the robbery, in which a dark-haired young woman purporting to be a student acted as a decoy. A spokesperson for the museum stated that 'This theft represents a serious loss to the museum's collection. However, unlike other items in the museum, this has limited resale value in itself, and is likely to have been stolen to order by a private collector.' The police investigation is ongoing.

James tossed the paper back. It didn't seem like much, but he was beginning to share Peter's enthusiasm: there was a story in here somewhere.

Peter shifted uncomfortably in his chair. 'I've saved the best till last. Most of the local papers and news services haven't been reporting this – they obviously think it's as crazy as a piranha with tits – but I've come across the stories concerned from various sources, and it's one more reason why I want you to go up there and check it out.'

'Yes?' James asked, his interest piqued.

Peter cleared his throat. 'There's been a resurgence of belief in – uh – shape-shifters in the area.'

James coughed in amazement, then started laughing. 'What, you mean frogs turning into princes when they're kissed by a beautiful woman?'

'No,' Peter went on, smiling sickly. 'I mean were-wolves.'

Still laughing and shaking his head, James closed the door behind him and turned to face Kirsty, who was smiling brightly at him. He grinned back. Peter's PA was cute, all curves, full lips and long, glossy brown hair, even if she was slightly more petite than James's ideal shape.

'So what is it now for our intrepid investigative reporter?' she asked coyly, toying with a pen in the corner of her mouth.

James's grin spread. 'Oh, I've just got to go up to the Highlands and look for some big dogs.'

Kirsty looked puzzled. 'Doesn't sound up your alley at all. But I suppose it'll keep you out of trouble. Won't you miss all your friends down here?' she asked, swivelling her chair round to face him and giving him a good view of her crossed legs sheathed in glistening opaque stockings as she bounced one foot up and down.

James drank in the sight, then returned his gaze to Kirsty's face. He'd always been impressed by her clothes and their flirtation had progressed from furtive smiles and winks to a bolder assessment of each other's charms. Still, nothing had come of it; James knew Kirsty had a boyfriend somewhere and suspected that Peter wouldn't approve of a fling, while he himself had always been opposed to the idea of mixing business with pleasure. Still . . .

Holding his gaze, Kirsty murmured, 'Well?' and uncrossed her legs, sliding forwards slightly in her seat. James automatically looked down and was rewarded by the sight of the tops of her stockings and an enticing glimpse of the pale flesh above. The rest was wreathed in shadow. He looked guiltily back up into her eyes, fully aware that he'd been caught peeping at her but knowing as well that she'd wanted him to, or at least that she'd been testing his interest. She didn't look upset, at any rate; if anything she looked excited. Kirsty moved the pen suggestively in and out of the corner of her lips, which seemed fuller now, more swollen.

'See anything you –' she began. Then Peter's door opened and the editor's stubbled face poked out. He saw James, muttered, 'You still here?' then turned to Kirsty. 'I have some letters, Miss Beck, if you're *quite* ready.'

Kirsty surreptitiously pulled her skirt down over her stockinged thighs, threw James an apologetic glance and followed Peter into his office. James sighed. Scotland it was, then.

David beat her to the door, up and off the sofa in a flash even as she ran down the stairs in response to the thunderous banging. Ever since they'd heard the horn that morning they'd known the visitors would arrive. Jess hadn't mentioned it to her husband, nor to her daughter, but the atmosphere in the house had been electric with anticipation. David and the women had by turns urged each other to leave the house: the women would normally have gone out shopping on a Saturday, leaving David in to watch the sport on TV, but they'd made feeble excuses today for why they had to stay in; David, while he obviously knew why they wanted to stick around, wouldn't admit it to them and sulked instead in front of the TV.

Since breakfast they had hardly said a word to each other. But each, Jess knew, was full of their own hopes: David, that the visitors would be too drunk and tired to insist on anything more than a simple offering, while Jess hoped for exactly the opposite. The year before, when it had happened for the first time, Katie had been too young to take part; she was old enough now but she hadn't discussed it with her mother. Jess's mind was a whirl of emotions, worry about how they might treat her daughter mixed with an undeniable jealousy that she, Jess, was no longer the sole woman of the house.

She peered over David's shoulder, already trembling with excitement. He'd only opened the door a crack but the smells of fresh sweat and cider were beginning to fill the hallway and a leather boot was jammed in the door.

'David Scott, we demand entry. We have a right to expect kisses from the women of the house,' a voice slurred from the other side of the door.

David was pushing the door against the foot now. 'My wife is ill, you've no right to come in. And my daughter isn't here – she's gone shopping.'

Jess moved behind him to make herself visible to the men outside. She could see only one of them, his bright eyes shining through the holes of the wolf mask that he wore, but when she smiled at him she could see the answering glint in his eyes. He gave an abrupt shove, David fell back, and suddenly the hall was filled with men, three, four of them, all dressed in the same tunics and short trousers, all wearing the wolf masks. One played a triumphal run of notes on a wooden flute, and another accepted the flagon of cider proffered by a third. Jess suddenly had a rush of fear, mingled with excitement: there had only been two of them last year and this bunch looked like they'd been drinking a lot; things might get out of control. She squeezed her thighs together at the thought.

As David offered them money, more spirits, anything, if only they'd leave, the one who'd spoken first stepped close to her and put a hand to his crotch to adjust himself. Jess stared at him, unconsciously licking her lips as she saw the long lines of his cock and the bulge of his balls outlined against the cloth of his trousers. But she was entirely unprepared when he reached forward and tore her blouse open, spraying buttons all over the hall.

The others cheered giddily, the one with the flute putting it to his lips again and playing as he hopped from one foot to the other. Jess put her hands over her breasts, the soft fat flesh spilling out over the top of her bra. But the man pulled her arms away roughly, then ripped the bra down too, leaving her exposed in front of all of them. Her stare met David's and she saw the weary despair and disgust in his face, mixed with something else. As she gulped, then looked back at the man who'd exposed her, cupping her full breasts for him, the nipples already long and hard, holding them up for his inspection, she saw that David had put a hand to his crotch in turn.

The wolf boy buried his head in her chest, the hinged jaw at the bottom of the mask allowing him to leave scarlet bite marks on the tender white flesh and bite and suck on the sensitive nipples. She caressed the back of his head, feeling the edge of the mask, and another boy came forward to burrow his snout into the side of her neck and kiss her there. Then the second boy ran a hand down her back to rest on her bottom, which twitched as he pushed his fingers under her skirt to feel the knickers she wore, silky and frilly, put on specially this morning. He delved a finger under those too, to touch lightly on her anal bud, making it clench before pushing on into her crease. Jess gave a sob. She knew that she was soaking; her juices had dampened the front of her knickers as soon as she'd heard the banging on the door. There was no escape from what would happen now.

The boy lifted his finger and made an elaborate show of sniffing at it with the long snout of his wolf mask. He turned to the others. 'This one's ready. Mr Scott's been keeping a treasure to himself here.'

There was a movement at the top of the stairs and the wolf boys turned their heads to look. David turned too and made frantic gesturing movements with one hand. But when Jess looked in turn she saw her daughter coming down towards them, biting her lip, her eyes wide with fear and excitement. She'd obviously prepared for them, wearing the nearest clothes she had to the robes most of the women wore during the festivities on the village green, in her case the soft cotton nightie covered in a teddy-bear print that Jess had bought for her a few years ago when she'd still been a little girl.

The wolf boys had been silent until now about Katie's appearance, but the one who'd approached Jess first and still held her breasts in his hands whistled. 'Well, what do we have here? A girl who's meant to be out: Katie Scott, if I'm not mistaken, coming down to join in the fun. Well, you're most welcome, Katie Scott. And shame on your father for keeping another treasure out of the way.'

David flushed, and half-heartedly tried to stand in front of one of the boys as he stepped up to Katie, who stood now on the bottom step of the stairs. The boy pushed him aside angrily then put his hands up to Katie, who instinctively hugged her chest and moved back a step. The boys laughed, the one closest to Katie suddenly reaching out and grabbing hold of her bottom before turning to the others.

'She's ready too, this one. Like mother, like daughter. She's not even wearing any knickers.'

The boy holding Jess's breasts laughed. 'Let's take them through in the kitchen. You needn't follow, Mr Scott. Go on, lead the way,' he told Jess, slapping her hard on the rear.

Mutely Jess obeyed, trembling still. As the leader of the wolf boys pushed her forward, his hand fondling one bottom cheek, she turned, to ask him in a quavering voice, 'You won't be too hard on her, will you?' Already behind him she could see the other boys reaching for her daughter, handling her roughly, pinching her nipples through the thin fabric of her nightie and bouncing her back and forth between themselves.

The boy laughed again. 'Any girl who comes down dressed like that, not even wearing any knickers, when they know we're about ... well, she knows what she's letting herself in for, doesn't she?'

They'd reached the end of the passage now and Jess opened the door to the kitchen. The boy who'd been pushing her moved past and with a wide sweep of his arm pushed all the papers, magazines and diaries off the table, leaving a clear surface.

The others came in as well and Jess turned to see her daughter's flushed face, bite marks on her neck and her small hand squeezing the crotch of one of the boys. Jess swallowed, staring at her, and Katie stared back, insolence mixed in with arousal, then squeezed harder. One of the boys gave Jess a shove.

'Go on, Mrs Scott. You know what to do. What are you waiting for?'

With a sob Jess climbed onto the table and lay back, lifting up her skirt. From the other room she could hear the TV come back on, the volume turned up to drown out any other noise, and she began to spread her legs, slowly, until one of the boys reached down and wrenched them apart. Jess felt her pussy begin to pulse in anticipation. Then there was a movement to her side and one of the boys had taken his cock out, an ugly, thick and veiny thing that he thrust towards her mouth. As Jess reached up, balancing herself on one arm to take him in her mouth, she felt her knickers being ripped off. She groaned, regret at losing her finest knickers lost in her mounting arousal.

Then another cock had been pushed inside her, sliding easily into her wetness. Her thighs were gripped hard and before long the two men using her had begun to rock her back and forth between them, stuffing her full of cock at both ends.

Jess could see her daughter watching her from the other side of the room, her eyes wide, her hand still absently stroking the cock of the nearest boy. But Jess didn't care any more, the sight even spurring her on, making her show off her sluttishness. She took the cock out of her mouth to rub it all over her cheeks, greasing her face with the stickiness leaking out of the tip, then pushed it up to lick at the boy's balls, a tight sac smelling strongly of come.

Then the man fucking her had pulled out and she gave a squeal of disappointment, pushing herself towards him, spreading herself still wider open. He chuckled and pushed her thighs further back, exposing more of her bottom. 'You're just too wet in there. Time to try something new.' And with that he put a thumb into her sex, making her wiggle her hips again, then pushed it downwards so that it slid easily into her anus, greasy and relaxed from her arousal. Jess squeaked, pulling away from the cock bumping against her mouth, and tried to push her thighs down, protecting herself. But it was too late: the man had felt how greasy she was and, taking a firmer grip of her thighs, he put the hard end of his cock to her anal bud and pushed.

She gasped at the pressure, only for the man she'd been sucking off to wrap a hand in her hair and push his cock into her mouth again. The other man groaned as her tightness gave. He slid himself in, inch by inch, until Jess felt an unfamiliar sense of fullness, of being stretched to the hilt.

As he began to pull out and then push in again, buggering her with slow, even strokes, she felt her anal ring pull out and push in against his cock. The sensation felt like she was burning and her pussy felt empty. But it was still swollen and so sensitive and she put her free hand down to touch it, to feel how greasy she was, that the man should have chosen to fuck her arse rather than her cunt. Then she'd done it: she'd touched herself in front of all of them, in front of these masked men, in front of her daughter, with her husband in the other room, touched herself because she was turned on by having one cock forced in her face and another stuffed up her bottom, somewhere it should never have gone, somewhere her husband would never have dared to stick it, but where this boy had put it without even asking her.

Jess was stroking her clit hard now, rubbing the stiff bump and pinching it between her fingers as the pace of the buggering increased, the man's fingers gripping still tighter on her thighs. She was still sucking hard on the cock in her mouth, which now pulled out, the man moaning as he erupted onto her face, long streamers of sticky come spraying out to cover her. Some went in her hair, some ran down her cheeks, the rest jetted into her open mouth where the taste of it was enough to push her over the edge so that her anus began to contract, clenching on the cock buried deep in there, her pussy twitching under her busy fingers as she began to come . . .

But the man buggering her had pulled out, leaving her arsehole closing on nothing, and Jess was pushing herself down again, desperate to be filled, to have the burning, stretched sensation as she came – only to see her daughter drop to her knees, her eyes wide with anticipation, one hand burrowing between her legs under her nightie, and take the man's cock, fresh from fucking her mother in the arse, in her mouth.

Four

Birdsong was the first thing Miriam was aware of as she woke up. The sound was so restful that the full shock of being awake didn't dawn for a few seconds as she lay on the bed with her eyes closed. Then she sat bolt upright and stared around her.

The room was totally unfamiliar. It was large, and well lit from a long window at the end opposite the door. Miriam was in one of six beds – three along opposite walls, the one closest to the window – and after having taken in the furnishings (slightly Spartan and functional, but not uncomfortable, the room painted a pale cream, the bed linen fresh) she stood up, a little unsteady on her feet, and moved to the window.

It was open at the top and the air coming in was gloriously clean, fresh and with a slight nip to it. Miriam shivered and hugged herself. She had no idea where her clothes were; someone had dressed her in a long nightie, not her own, and it was certainly too cold to be wandering around out of bed. She peered out of the window, hoping for some clue as to where she was, but could see only an expanse of lawn, gently rolling down to a line of thick forest. There was nobody in sight to either side, although if she peered round far enough she could see other windows. The building looked old on the outside, too, older than it did inside, all mossy, time-worn stone; and there was a tower to her left, a peculiar squat thing with gargoyles visible at the two corners she could see, round-eared spouting heads that looked like those of bats.

The muddy feeling in her head had started to clear now and she looked around with more alarm. Where the hell was she? Where were her clothes? The last thing she could remember was passing out in Cavendish's office after witnessing some kind of grotesque attack. She felt something twinge on her neck and put her hand up to touch the skin, only to take it away again as though she'd been scalded. There were marks there; she'd been hurt. She fingered the marks again: small puncture wounds – they didn't seem very deep but they hurt.

Confused, Miriam sat back down on the bed, one hand still clasped to her neck. What had happened to her? Then she stood again, sniffing at the air, suddenly irrationally happy. She knew she shouldn't be feeling good; she should be panicked – she'd been kidnapped, wounded, she didn't know where she was. But instead she felt elated and she moved over to the window again to scan the lawn, to stare into the forest beyond, feeling her heart beat and her muscles quiver in anticipation. What the hell was wrong with her? She should be screaming for help, not grinning like an idiot as she stared at some trees. But she couldn't wipe the smile off her face. She'd never felt this good before.

There was a sound behind her and she turned to see the door open. A woman walked in, about Miriam's age and with dark shoulder-length hair, carrying a bundle of clothes. She noticed Miriam and started.

'Oh! You're up! You gave me a fright.' She grinned

broadly at Miriam and walked towards her, putting the clothes down on Miriam's bed.

Miriam stared at her. The woman was dressed strangely, in a low-cut tunic, her full breasts, encased in a white shirt, jutting out in front of her. The first few buttons of her shirt were undone and Miriam could see, even in the shadows, that she was covered in colourful designs that were visible on her legs too, underneath the tunic dress, which reached to the top of her thighs. Her face was untouched, but there was a mark on her neck that Miriam had taken at first for a birthmark but now saw was a tattoo: three broad black streaks.

The other girl, noticing Miriam's attention, touched her fingers to her neck. 'It's not where most of us have it but my shoulders were covered already.' Prompted by Miriam's uncomprehending stare, she continued, 'That's where yours is, isn't it?'

Miriam felt herself pale and peered over her shoulder, lifting the nightie up to look under the material. Sure enough, she had identical markings on her left shoulder. The skin around them was still sore and raised. She turned back to the girl, suddenly brimming with questions.

'What is this place?'

The girl looked at her kindly. 'Don't you know? You've come to the castle.'

'But –' Miriam sat down heavily, one hand still on her tattoo '– I didn't want to come here. I mean, I didn't ask to. The last thing I remember is being in London, and seeing –'

The girl broke, in looking pointedly at the wound on Miriam's neck. 'You've been marked. That only happens to the special ones. You should count yourself lucky. You can see that I don't have anything here.' She craned her neck for Miriam to look. It was true: only the tattoo marred the creamy whiteness of the girl's neck.

'So what does it mean?' Miriam asked, her voice almost a whisper.

The girl laughed delightedly, the touch of sorrow from a moment before apparently forgotten. 'You really don't know? Well, I'm sure the mistress will be happy to tell you everything soon. In fact, as soon as you're dressed I'm to take you to meet her.'

'But I don't have my clothes with me,' Miriam blurted out, aware all the while of the patent absurdity of the situation.

'That's what I've brought you here.' The girl smiled broadly and patted the pile of clothes that she'd just brought in. 'Oh! I almost forgot. We're going to be working together, and probably living together for a while as well, so I should introduce myself, shouldn't I? I'm Alice.' She held out a hand, her head cocked to one side.

Miriam took Alice's hand and shook it falteringly, replying, 'Miriam,' feeling herself buoyed by the other woman's enthusiasm, even in her confusion. 'Working together?' she echoed. 'I'm sorry, I don't know . . .'

'In the circus,' replied Alice, busily laying the clothes out on Miriam's bed. 'Lord Garner's circus. What's your speciality?'

'Sorry?' asked Miriam, utterly bewildered now.

'You know,' Alice urged her impatiently. 'What act are you going to do?'

'I didn't know – I mean, I haven't spoken to anyone about that. Or about anything. I don't even know where I am!'

Noting the rising note of panic in Miriam's voice, Alice put her hands on the new arrival's shoulders. 'Shh, calm down. It'll be OK. Guess what I'm going to be?'

Miriam shrugged helplessly.

'The tattooed lady!' Alice struck a pose and then shook her head as Miriam stared at her, dumb-founded. 'I'm covered all over, you know,' she continued. 'So you must have a speciality too. What's it going to be?'

'I'm a dancer,' Miriam said.

'What, in clubs and that sort of thing? Or ballet?'

'Neither.' Miriam astonished herself by blushing slightly. 'Exotic.'

'Oh, you're a stripper!' Alice grinned at her. 'Well, it was never going to be a normal circus. And is there anything special you do during your act?'

'No.' But even as Miriam lied, she could feel herself flushing a deeper red and knew that Alice wouldn't believe her. 'Well, actually, there is one thing.' Alice looked at her expectantly. 'I – I can make milk come out of my breasts.'

Alice looked at her in surprise. 'Show me.'

'No!' Miriam shook her head, embarrassed, and turned away from her.

'Don't be ridiculous,' Alice snapped. 'I'll see a lot more than that of you. And if you've been showing it to men, total strangers, then you can show me.' Miriam hesitated, uncertain of how to proceed. 'Listen: if I do my act now, put on a private display for you, will you show me?'

Miriam turned back to Alice. She was attracted to the woman, she couldn't deny it, and there was something tempting in her offer. And although she'd blushed, had been acting coy, if Miriam was honest with herself she had to admit that some of her shyness had gone. She felt more at ease with herself now, bold in a way she'd never felt before. And the room was crackling with sexual energy, a fast-building sense of lust, stronger than she was used to. Suddenly excited,

77

she nodded to Alice, whose eyes widened in anticipation.

'OK, then,' the tattooed girl breathed. 'I don't have my costume with me, so I'll have to improvise a little.'

As Miriam watched, Alice took the hem of her tunic skirt in her hands, smiled coyly at her and then began to lift it up. She was wearing no underwear and her sex was shaved completely bare. Miriam could see already that there was a broader pattern to the design of Alice's tattoos: her left side was covered in representations of marine life, impossibly rich renditions of colourful tropical fish swimming through coral, bizarrely shaped sponges and fans; eels wrapped around her thighs, their tails pointing up towards the enticing space between her legs. Alice saw Miriam staring and mistook her look of amazement for one of concern. She leaned forward and whispered suddenly in Miriam's ear, still holding her skirt up. 'We don't wear underwear here. Lord Garner doesn't allow it.'

And then, as though she had never paused, she continued to lift up the tunic until it was raised over her head, then discarded it. She had shaved her armpits too and even these had been tattooed. A sea urchin nestled in the greyness under her left arm, a hedgehog under the right. As Alice unbuttoned her shirt, Miriam marvelled at the designs further up her body, giant octopus arms wrapping themselves round her side, tentacles reaching up to cup her full breast; a sea horse, its face full of melancholy, coiled its tail around her nipple; the tail of some larger grey fish marked out the rest of the breast, its body vanishing around to her back.

At the centre of Alice's body, dividing her from head to crotch, was a line of clear skin, which appeared brilliant white in contrast to the riotous colours exploding elsewhere. The marine side ended in a wobbly line of surf, as though the tide of creatures was about to be washed away again, dragged back across her skin. But the surf ended above her sex, where fronds of seaweed lapped at the edges of her lips, while on the other side mosses and ferns were marked in minute detail on her swollen skin.

The marine theme entirely covered the left side of Alice's body. The right side, Miriam's left, was given over to land. Its creatures were at first more difficult to make out, partially hidden behind rich green vegetation. But as Miriam scanned Alice's skin animals began to emerge: a jaguar peering out from behind a tangle of lianas on Alice's thigh, with a gorilla's solemn face not far above, and violently coloured birds, a rainbow of primaries against the emerald of the jungle that covered the skin of her legs.

Further up, above the hip, the vegetation changed both colour and shape, to the more familiar forms of woodland: oak leaves and holly, a barn owl staring from its roost on a branch; further up a stag, its antlers full and proudly raised, the bright reds and blues of butterflies providing a counterpoint to the dark greens and browns of the woods; the tail of some wild cat Miriam didn't recognise, its expression too savage to be domesticated, curled around Alice's right nipple.

Further up still, above the breast, across the collarbone and on the shoulder, the vegetation thinned out, pine branches stark against the milky whiteness of Alice's skin, which had been highlighted, impossibly skilfully, with blue tints to give the impression of snow, offset by the spotted red of reindeer and the wise, ancient face of a wolf.

Miriam felt herself being drawn in closer to see more, the skin seeming full of endless promise, each scene unfolding to show something different, then something else again. As she approached, her stare darting over Alice's body, the tattooed lady began to move, subtly at first, animating the figures covering her so that they seemed to shift, lifelike, real, hiding behind trees or fronds of aquatic plants, emerging then vanishing again as others pressed themselves onto Miriam's sight.

Miriam drew closer still until she was only an arm's length away from Alice. 'I want to see you,' said the tattooed lady simply.

Miriam, hypnotised by the undulating patterns on Alice's body, the wind that seemed to ruffle the leaves and ferns, the currents that swayed the seaweed, exposed herself, trusting in the other's gaze, lifting up her nightie, her body seeming impossibly bare compared to the other girl's decorations. The garment snagged on her nipples, stiff and long now, and she pulled it harder, up and over her head, then let it drop to the ground.

'Show me,' said Alice. But Miriam shook her head, smiling dreamily, and took Alice's hands to place them on her breasts. As Alice began to massage the heavy globes, gently stroking and squeezing them, Miriam marvelled at the life on Alice's arms, white birds flitting across snow-laden pine forests, curious deep-sea creatures snapping after invisible prey. As Miriam felt her nipples distend further, her breasts growing heavier, fuller, ready to give milk, she touched her fingers to Alice's breasts, almost scared to touch them in case the creatures that protected her might lunge from their positions to crawl all over Miriam.

Alice, spurred on by Miriam's attentions, stroked Miriam's nipples lovingly and began to pull on them, making them even longer, harder, caressing the tiny buds around their base, then pinching them until the first spurt of bluish milk spattered onto her varicoloured skin. She gave a little gasp, then rubbed the milk, a thin line running down between her breasts, across her soft skin, massaging it in until her animals gleamed with life.

Wordlessly, Alice took Miriam by the hand, holding her gaze, and moved back until the backs of her legs touched Miriam's bed. Then she sat down, her stare still locked with Miriam's, and slowly spread her legs, her lips peeling apart wetly.

Miriam knelt down in front of her, resting her hands on the insides of Alice's thighs, and stared at the centre of Alice's quim, even as the jungle and reef seethed with life under her fingers. The tattooed lady seemed to be able to move even this part of her body, the lips of her sex quivering, undulating, so that the rich wet pinkness within was gently brushed by mosses and ferns on one side and lapped at by fronds of salty seaweed on the other.

Mesmerised, Miriam leaned her face in and darted her tongue out to taste Alice's juices. Emboldened by the other girl's gasp of pleasure, she let Alice's oil pool on her tongue, then licked the length of her crease, pressing her tongue into the hard bud of Alice's clit. Alice groaned and reached her hands down to wrap her fingers in Miriam's hair before twisting it and pulling her face closer in. Miriam needed no further encouragement and began to lick in earnest, hearing Alice's breathing grow fast and shallow as she alternated between long, slow laps, like a cat cleaning itself, and little darting flicks of the tongue, pressing hard on the clit.

Alice was so greasy now that the whole area around her sex was glistening with juice. Miriam ran her right hand down Alice's thigh until she could peel the seaweed-decked lip to one side, to give herself better access. Then she pushed Alice's legs further up so that her bottom swung closer towards Miriam. Alice gave a little gasp of surprise as Miriam, her chin oily with Alice's excitement, pulled her head back to gaze at the tattoos around Alice's sphincter. The tattooist had excelled himself here, blending the delicate tentacles of an anemone with the coarse bark of a wood bole in a ring around Alice's anus, which was twitching with anticipation now.

Miriam leaned forward and darted a tongue in experimentally. She tasted Alice's juices, which had run down from her quim to moisten the ring. She licked it again. Then, looking up at Alice and drinking in the tattooed lady's heavy-lidded expression of excitement mixed with nervous anticipation, she put her hand up to Alice's face, her fingers hovering over Alice's mouth.

Alice understood what she wanted immediately and sucked Miriam's thumb into her mouth, running her tongue over it and giving it a little nip, which brought a fresh wave of juices to Miriam's pussy. She pulled her thumb away and pressed it against the star of Alice's bottom-hole. Alice's buttocks clenched once, then relaxed, and the thumb slid in all the way, gripped by the warm elastic walls of the tattooed lady's rectum.

Miriam returned her attention to Alice's clit, licking it hard now, flicking it from side to side with her tongue, building up a rhythm with her tongue and her thumb, which she used to fuck Alice's arse, pushing on her thigh with her other hand to keep the girl in place. Alice's moans gave way to little squeals, faster and sharper every minute, until Miriam felt the contractions begin on her thumb, once, twice, the muscles of Alice's rectum spasming as she sucked hard on Alice's clit. The other girl screamed, her body bucking up from the bed, her hand pulling hard on Miriam's hair and forcing the new arrival's face hard against her crease. Miriam kept on sucking as Alice's ring contracted tightly against her thumb, then relaxed as she felt the waves of pleasure coursing through Alice more softly now. She released the tattooed lady's clit, lapping around it with gentle strokes of her tongue, feeling the grip on her hair relax until Alice was stroking it, cooing softly to her as she pulled her thumb out of the other girl's anus and brought it up to her lips.

They could see the supermarket from a mile away, lit up and glowing in the night sky, surrounded by icily illuminated parking spaces and a winding access road. There were hardly any other lights nearby but the swollen moon swathed the land around the structure in a silvery light.

One of the girls had pointed it out as the carriage traversed the woods on the slope above the new development. But nothing was said until they had descended and were waiting in a small clearing at the edge of the woods near the road.

Alice had made good on her promise to introduce Miriam to the mistress, a dark-haired woman of around forty with an imperious gaze and a faint Middle European accent. She'd answered most of Miriam's questions equably and had confirmed that Miriam would work in Lord Garner's circus. The acts would debut at the great feast planned for a few weeks hence. She even encouraged Miriam when the new arrival asked if she could invite her friend, another dancer, to join the circus. But when Miriam had asked her about what she'd seen in Cavendish's office and shown her the puncture marks on her neck, the woman had simply smiled, commenting that while the trophy she'd received was a blessing indeed the ritual that would precede the full transformation had yet to be arranged. She ignored Miriam's obvious bewilderment. It would not happen tonight, the mistress assured her. Tonight she had something different in store for Miriam.

The mistress, clad in the furs that she'd been wearing when she'd spoken to Miriam, climbed down from her seat at the head of the carriage and beckoned to the others to join her. She turned to face the building, a giant block of blue and yellow light, luminous and unreal against the surrounding woodland and farms.

'This site is sacred and its energies have been turned against the land.' She nodded to Miriam and Cavendish. 'You are new to us and must show your allegiance. Burn it down.'

Miriam felt her heart quicken at the order. 'How?' she asked.

The woman in furs turned to Cavendish. 'You have been supplied with certain tools. And you will find everything else you need there. The shop has not yet been opened; that was to happen in two days. But most of the stock is on the shelves. There should be no people inside but you may encounter security guards outside. You'll know what to do.' With that she gave a curt nod to them and stepped back onto the carriage.

Cavendish turned to Miriam and she could tell that he was smiling, even if she couldn't see him well. She felt the excitement too and knew why he smiled. A broad grin broke out on her own features. Then he turned away and moved down the path leading to the road.

One of the wolves behind them whined and pawed at the ground and she glanced at it before following

Cavendish down the path. Ever since she'd seen him being attacked in his room she'd ceased to be surprised by what had happened to her. He'd been bitten by something; something that wasn't human. That much she knew: she'd seen it with her own eyes. And it had changed him. She knew that because she'd been bitten herself and it had changed *her*. She felt more alive now, more than she'd ever done before.

Miriam's conversations with the mistress – nobody seemed to use any other name for her – and Alice had cleared up some of her confusion. She knew that she was in Scotland now, although she wasn't sure exactly where; that she lived in a castle, where she shared a room; that the castle belonged to a Lord Garner, whom she had yet to meet; and that the people in the castle appeared to worship wolves. Miriam knew that it was preposterous, that in her former life she'd have scoffed at the very suggestion, would have considered such activity credulous at best and at worst actually insane. She'd wondered idly at one point whether she was free to go, but the thought seemed ludicrous: there was nowhere else she wanted to be now. This was her home. Her former life seemed like a dream she'd just awoken from, with Dr Cavendish as the only reminder. But he'd changed as much as she had: she could see the fire gleaming in his eyes, free of glasses now, the happiness brimming over, and she knew that he felt the same way. She also knew from the way he'd been watching her that what Emma had told him had hit home, and that before the night was over the dreams that had made her cry out at night would finally be given life.

She was running after him now, loping along in long, strong strides. But her heartbeat was still slow and steady, her breathing natural. She was fitter, far fitter than she'd been before, the testing of each muscle intensely pleasurable. Even sprinting left her feeling scarcely more tested than she did now.

They were close to the supermarket and Miriam followed Cavendish as he ran across the newly laid turf to one side of the access road, out of reach of the sodium lights. But her nostrils picked up a scent, something unexpected, out of place, and she slowed as she sniffed at the air and looked around, allowing Cavendish to pull away.

Then she saw one lone security guard, standing by a blue Portakabin, smoking a cigarette and rubbing his hands together. Miriam grinned. The mistress had been right: she knew exactly what to do. It would be easy. She circled round, to approach him from behind and leave it to the last minute before he saw her. She didn't need to prepare herself; she was hungry now, excited, her nipples already stiff beneath her tunic.

'Excuse me?' she began, in her best little-girl-lost voice.

The man spun round and the expression of fear on his face changed slowly to an uncertain grin as he took in Miriam's face and her clothes, the thin tunic she'd worn since meeting Alice.

'God, you gave me a fright there! What is it you're after?' He stared pointedly at her clothes. 'Looks like you've just stepped out of a history book. What's with all that get-up, then?'

Miriam giggled and looked at him with her head bent forward, biting her lip. 'I was just walking towards Porthness, but I was lonely and bored. Then I saw you just standing here and I thought – well, I'd come and say hello.'

'Oh, aye?' He looked at her critically, then his face softened. 'I suppose you're not some ghost, then? Chances are you're not, with nails like that.'

Miriam stretched out her fingers and flexed her nails, digging them into the fabric of her tunic. Then she looked up at him again. He couldn't have been older than twenty-five. 'Is there somewhere we can go inside to talk? It's cold out here,' she pleaded.

The guard looked doubtful. 'Well, you see, I'm on duty here, and I shouldn't really –'

Miriam interrupted him. 'Please?'

He sighed, shaking his head, and moved towards the door of the Portakabin. 'I suppose making you a cup of tea wouldn't hurt. Come on, then.' He opened the door and beckoned her inside. She marvelled at the ease with which she'd been able to tempt him.

'Make yourself at home,' he called to her, having already moved through into a smaller room at the end of the cabin. She heard the rush of water as he filled the kettle. 'Tea or coffee?'

'Oh, I'll have some tea, please.' The cabin was a tip, full of empty cigarette packets, yellowed tabloid papers and old milk cartons. There was a bunk running along one wall, next to a table with a radio and a bank of four TV screens on it, the monochrome pictures flashing between images inside and outside the supermarket.

'Must get pretty bored in here. Not much to do, eh?' she called to the guard as she peeled back the rug on top of the bunk.

'Oh aye, well, it's work, and there's scarce enough of that around here.' He was still busy in the kitchen. 'Milk, sugar?'

'Hmm, no milk, one sugar, please.' Strewn on the surface of the bunk were a clutch of garishly coloured magazines – cheap British top-shelf publications, she could tell at a glance. She grinned again and leaned over to flick through the closest one. The magazines didn't look old but they'd already seen a lot of use –

the staples were loose and some of the covers were missing.

The guard turned and came out of the kitchen, only to stop dead in his tracks when he saw what Miriam had found. 'Ah,' he said, putting the cups of tea down. 'They're old Jake's. I expect he gets lonely in here nights. You'd better leave them be.' He took a step towards Miriam.

'But I like looking at these,' she protested, turning to him and very deliberately licking her lips. He paled and looked a little unsteady, but she could tell that he was excited. 'Which one's your favourite, eh?'

'I – uh – I don't have a favourite. It's like I told you, they're not mine, they're Jake's.' He cleared his throat as she moved closer to him. 'Tea?' he offered, his voice faltering. But she was standing in front of him now, looking pointedly down at his crotch where a visible bulge was growing.

'I used to be a dancer,' Miriam told him. 'Would you like me to dance for you?'

The young guard simply stared at her, dumb-founded, his mouth open in shock, as she began to sway from side to side, stepping back from him and running her hands up and down her sides. She spun around and bent over slowly for him, catching a glimpse on one of the TV screens of Cavendish, inside the supermarket now, pouring liquid from a can all down an aisle, before the camera switched to an outside angle. She grinned to herself. Cavendish needn't worry: she'd keep the boy's attention fixed well enough.

Her clothes weren't ideal for stripping but Miriam didn't think it'd matter too much. She turned back to face him and began to squeeze her breasts together, leaning forward to draw his stare deep into her cleavage and shimmying her hips, watching him all the while. The bulge in his trousers had grown noticeably larger and his eyes looked glazed as he watched her. Her stiff nipples poked through the fabric and she let out a groan as she tugged on them, rolling and pinching them between finger and thumb. She then turned her back to the guard again, but watched him over her shoulder as she swung her hips deliberately from side to side. Then she bent down, taking hold of the hem of her tunic skirt and pulling it slowly up, exposing inch after inch of bare white flesh, pausing just where she knew he'd be most excited. As her neatly trimmed sex was exposed, already greasy and swollen with excitement, she reached back to clutch her bottom cheeks and pull them apart, giving him a good view of the brown star of her anus.

Miriam heard the guard gasp and she grinned at him from between her legs as she bent further down, pulling the tunic higher until it was wrapped around her shoulders. Then she tugged it over her head and dropped it to the floor. He had his hand wrapped around his crotch now, rubbing at himself through his trousers. She held the position for a few seconds, letting him drink in the sight of her fully exposed and ready for him, half expecting him to lunge forwards and bury himself inside her. Then she slowly stood up and turned back to face him, unbuttoning her shirt so that his eyes were drawn to the full roundness of her breasts.

'Can I –' the guard asked uncertainly, his stare searching Miriam's body from her face to her crotch for some sign that he could approach.

In response she simply cupped her left breast in her right hand and squeezed, pinching the hard nipple between thumb and forefinger until a thin stream of bluish-white milk began to run from the tip and slide down her belly. She squeezed it again and again, loving the feeling of freedom, of satisfaction that it gave her, feeling the fluid pool in her belly button and then gather in the small tuft of hair above her sex. When she felt it there, thick and heavy in the tight curls, she reached her hand down and began to rub the milk into her crease, dipping her hand up and down the length of the slit then circling her clit.

The guard gulped audibly, his hand frozen on his crotch, as Miriam approached him and dropped to her knees in front of him. She unzipped his thick blue uniform trousers and released his cock, which bounced up in front of her face. She licked the drop of pre-come from the tip, then dug inside his pants and brought out his balls, already tight against the base of his cock.

She leaned forwards to sniff at them, revelling in the heady scent of come her heightened sense of smell brought her, then cupped them in her long red nails and squeezed. The guard groaned, his cock bucking, then looked down at her, his expression torn between delight and panic.

Miriam circled the tip of his cock with one finger, wiping off the fluid that continued to pool around his hole, then reached down between her legs and touched herself again.

'Bet you like thinking about stuff like this when you're wanking yourself off in here, don't you?' she taunted him. He groaned again, his eyes widening as she began to slap at her sex, rubbing it hard and pinching at the clit.

'Gets you all hard, having a dirty slut rubbing herself and sucking on your cock, does it?' And she wrapped her lips around the head of his cock, sucking hard, then began to bob her head back and forth on it vigorously while squeezing his balls and slapping at her clit.

The guard didn't last long. Miriam felt the contractions in his balls first, then his cock twitched, his breath caught and the first spurts hit the back of her throat. The salty seed had made her gag in the past but now she buried the cock further into her mouth, gobbling on it greedily, wanting to get all of it inside her. She squeezed his balls and sucked harder, draining his cock of all its come, then let it fall out of her mouth. It was softening already as he staggered backwards. Miriam looked up at him and opened her mouth, letting him see the pool of seed she held at the back of her tongue before she swallowed it slowly, relishing the taste, and grinned broadly at him.

As she got up the guard stood unsteadily in front of her, his cock still hanging out of his trousers. 'Do you need –?' he'd started to ask her when she cuffed him hard across the head. He crumpled heavily to the ground, spent and unconscious.

It only took a few minutes for Miriam to dress, leave the cabin and find the door that Cavendish had jimmied open. She ran down the brightly lit aisles, calling his name, already smelling the solvents with which he'd drenched the floor and shelves. She finally found him in a small office to the side, filled with electrical equipment.

'What are you doing?' she asked after watching him for a few seconds.

'Disabling the alarms.' Cavendish grinned at her. 'How'd you get on?'

Miriam smiled back at him and licked her lips. 'Unexpected treat.'

He turned to face her. 'That's done. I wanted to wait for you before starting it off and I didn't want anyone coming along to stop it. It's ready now.'

He stood and moved through the doorway out into the bright light of the shop floor, Miriam close behind him. He threw her a box of matches. 'Why don't you start that end,' he suggested, 'and I'll do this one. We'll meet outside.'

Miriam nodded, excited beyond all measure now, then turned and ran to the other end of the supermarket. She knew they wouldn't be able to spend long in here: the fumes would be horrific, especially where she now stood, by the racks of cheap imported clothes, some spattered with fluid where Cavendish had primed them.

She struck a match and gazed at it as it flared and hissed before subsiding to a more stable flame. After waiting for a heartbeat, her blood coursing with adrenalin, she dropped it on the nearest rack of clothes. The effect was near-instantaneous as the rack went up in flames with a heavy crumping sound and a blast of heat that pushed Miriam back, singeing her eyebrows. The flames leapt to the next rack, then the next, and Miriam waited for as long as she thought she could, giving small jumps of glee until the heat grew too intense.

She ran down the next aisle. It was full of electrical goods and she spotted the boxes that Cavendish had doused with lighter fluid. She flicked a match at them, barely waiting for the *whoosh* of flame that followed. Already black smoke was billowing out from the clothes and she speeded up as she raced away, torching the stationery, unable to resist a glance back as the sickly teddy-bear exercise books became a raging inferno. Glass shattered in the heat of the kitchenware department, tyres exploded in the rack of bikes at the back. Miriam heard Cavendish whooping from the other end of the floor, clearly audible even over the muffled explosive thuds and the crackle of fire consuming everything. She screamed herself, letting all her exultation fill her lungs and then pierce the air until finally the smoke was too thick and she ran for the door that Cavendish had opened. She blinked her way through the smoke that now filled the shop, holding her breath, her lungs starting to scream, until she was out, away from the door, her feet sliding on the dewy grass. She took in great gulps of air, the smell of roasting food now mingling with the acrid burn of smoking plastic, the moon smiling down on her as the flames rose ever higher behind.

Miriam turned and saw Cavendish stumble out, coughing and laughing, and together they did a little dance on the grass, giggling. Then they held each other and hugged tightly before parting again and running towards the woods.

As soon as they had found cover, far enough away from the fire that they wouldn't be seen when the fire services arrived but near enough for the light from the flames to flash through the woods, striping them both in a strobing effect, they drew together again. Miriam could tell that Cavendish was as excited as she was, his eyes gleaming, and as she ground herself against him, her sex greasy with excitement, ready to be used, she felt him push his bulge against her.

She reached down to feel it, pressing it with her long red nails. Then she tugged his zip down and pulled out his stiff cock. Cavendish's balls were taut against its base and its engorged length quivered in the air, the head so swollen that it looked fit to burst. Miriam dropped to her knees, suddenly desperate for a taste of it, to feel him inside her mouth, to be able to give herself up to her lust, with none of the reserve she'd had to maintain earlier with the security guard. As she bobbed her head onto his cock, relishing the taste of man, Cavendish groaned and gripped her hair. She lifted her head away from him and looked up.

'Pull it. Hard.'

He responded by twining her hair round his fingers and twisting it until her eyes began to water with the pain. But the flashes of sensation it sent through Miriam's body were intensely pleasurable and she showed her appreciation by sucking harder on his cock. The feel of it in her mouth, the taste of it, only made her want to be filled all the more and she rolled back, away from him. Then she turned over and presented herself to him on all fours.

'Fuck me,' she whispered, glimmers of light dancing over her body. 'Fuck me like an animal.'

Cavendish paused, standing over her, then knelt and roughly pulled up her tunic. He sniffed at her, taking long draughts of her scent, then touched a finger to her swollen sex, already red and puffy from the evening's stimulation. Miriam whimpered, pushing her rear up to him, waiting for him to fill her. But he pulled her back abruptly, lifting up her legs and dragging her front along the ground before planting her across his lap with as little effort as though she were a doll.

She started to push herself up, confused, but he grabbed her wrist and forced it up her back, pushing her face into the leafy mulch. She tried to cry out, to fight against him, but he held her firm, and began to speak to her in a low, even tone.

'You liked giving yourself to that boy at the supermarket, didn't you, you slut,' Cavendish said, slapping the globes of her bottom with one hand while he pushed her arm further up towards her shoulders with the other.

'No!' Miriam cried as best she could with her face pressed into the soil. 'I had to do it!'

He increased the force of his blows, the sounds echoing round the woodland, cracks that mingled with the pops and bangs of the supermarket fire. She squealed and tried to wriggle away but he held her easily in place, reddening both arse globes in a rhythm that kept on increasing in tempo until her bottom felt huge, stinging hot and red. Then he paused and darted a hand between her legs, letting it linger slowly over the full sex lips before dipping a finger into her oily hole. Despite herself her hips gave a little wiggle, pushing back on his hand for more attention, the sensation a welcome relief from the pain of her reddened cheeks. 'Feel how greasy you are down here. It wasn't just work for you, was it? You loved sucking him off. I bet you swallowed, too.'

'No!' Miriam mumbled as his hand peeled her sex lips apart, exposing the pinkness to the night air that was slowly cooling the globes of her punished rear.

'You're nothing but a slut. A fuck toy. Only sluts like sucking men off as much as you do. And now look at you, pushing back on my hand, desperate for sex, begging for it.'

'No!' she repeated, but her body betrayed her, her hips circling against his hand, trying to push her swollen clit against his fingers.

'I want to hear you beg for sex. I want to hear you say you're a fuck slut, and beg me to stuff my cock in your hole.'

'No,' Miriam whispered once more, only for Cavendish to push her arm still further up her back. He started spanking her again, raining down a flurry of furious blows until the tears were rolling down her face and she was babbling, trying to put her other hand behind her to protect herself. 'Yes! I'm a fuck slut and I want you to stuff your cock in my hole!'

she blurted suddenly, all in one breath. He stopped spanking her then but caressed the hot cheeks for a few seconds. Then he flipped her off his knees and moved behind her.

Miriam began to moan with expectation, arching her back and pushing her hole, aching with need, up to him. But instead of plunging his cock into her he teased her with it, dipping the head into the mouth of her sex, then pulling back as she whimpered, until she was begging him in earnest, desperate to feel it inside her. 'Please fuck me. I'm a fuck slut and I want your cock inside me,' she gasped over and over as he covered his cockhead with her girl grease, pushing it up and down her wet slit, rubbing it over her hard nub and making her gasp.

Then Cavendish's hands had reached down and he was scooping the oil from her crease and rubbing it onto her tight anal bud, already slick with the juices that had pooled into it earlier. Miriam pulled away but his hands moved to her red buttocks, even the light pinches he gave making her jolt with pain. She groaned, her rectal muscles quivering, as he slipped a thumb in up to the hilt and started pinching and flicking her clit, his fingers sliding over the slippery pinkness.

She felt the head of his cock push again against the mouth of her sex and she clenched her internal muscles in anticipation of its penetrating her – only for the large bulb to shift upwards, smearing more juice around her anal ring and pushing against it. She sobbed, tensing, then relaxed and felt her anus stretch to accommodate his wide girth. He paused as her ring clenched around his cockhead. Then he pushed further in, reaching a hand round her leg to stroke her crease, until finally her resistance broke and he slid all the way inside her.

Miriam hadn't had anything much larger than a thumb in there many times before and she was still very tight. It hurt a little but the strokes and flicks that Cavendish was giving to her clit made the pain just heighten the feeling of dirtiness and the strange sensation of fullness in the wrong hole as her quim, aching with need, leaked its juices onto his hand.

He buried himself inside her, letting his tight balls rest against her slit. She put her weight on one arm and reached back to feel them, tightly furred and rubbing against her swollen lips. She dug her long nails into the compact sac, then, impatient, pushed his hand away from her slit and began to stroke it to her own rhythm as he pulled her bottom cheeks apart and slowly eased himself in and out of her.

Miriam could see the fire raging through the branches of the trees in front of her, the flames now mixed in her mind with the burning in her guts, the sense of invasion as Cavendish pushed repeatedly into her, holding her cheeks wide apart. She could hear the sirens of the fire engines arriving too, the flashing lights growing closer and closer until she could make out individual voices and shouts. Her fingers worked faster and faster in her crease as she felt the energy welling up inside her, a wave growing, building, then cresting as she squeezed her eyes shut, her rectum contracting rhythmically against Cavendish's cock. She was dimly aware of his groan over the sounds of fire crackling and water hissing. Then, before she'd quite come down, her anus still opening and closing, now on empty air, he'd pulled out and released her.

Miriam looked round, bleary-eyed and dazed, to find him beside her, his cock, smeared with her dirt, in front of her face. She didn't need to be told what to do. Taking his balls in one hand, rolling them around her palm and teasing them with her nails, she licked his shaft with long, urgent laps of her tongue, relishing the dark, bitter flavour as well as the depths to which she'd sunk so easily, until it was clean, then she sucked on it in earnest until she felt his ball sac contract and Cavendish pulled away to shoot his seed in spurt after spurt onto her face, great gouts of it landing on her cheeks even as she waited with her mouth open, greedy for the taste of it, hungrily gobbling on his cock again as soon as the jets had subsided and only a dribble of sperm came out. She stroked her cunt languidly as the fire raged behind them.

The first thing that Emma knew of Miriam's disappearance was when she didn't show up at the pub the evening after Emma had humiliated her in front of Cavendish. Mike just shrugged when Emma asked him if he knew where Miriam was and didn't seem particularly bothered that she'd have to go ahead with the show without her partner. Some of the punters had looked a little disappointed, though, and a handful of the regulars had asked Emma where her friend was.

She'd called up Annie, Miriam's flatmate, when she'd got home, but Annie hadn't heard from her either. Emma made her promise to call her if she heard anything. According to Annie it didn't look like Miriam had gone away for long: all of her things were still there and she hadn't left any kind of note.

Emma could only guess that she'd met someone and gone off with them for a few days. She felt slightly hurt that Miriam hadn't told her, although she reckoned that her friend was still upset over what she'd told Cavendish.

But the following Monday, when she tried to go to Cavendish's lecture, Emma discovered that he had gone away as well. He didn't seem to have let anyone know and the lecture hall was in disarray, full of confused students waiting for him. In the end one of the postgraduate students told the secretary at the faculty and Cavendish's classes were cancelled. Word soon filtered down to Emma that he'd vanished without trace, wasn't answering his calls, and had left no note to say he was going anywhere.

At first most of the students thought that he'd simply gone away for a few days – a city break, perhaps, or another academic appointment that he'd simply forgotten to let the faculty or students know about; it wasn't too unlikely, given his general air of absent-mindedness. But after a week the tone of the gossip about Cavendish changed. Miriam was known to have disappeared as well and because Emma had drunkenly confided in one or two of the other girls about her friend's crush on the professor rumours were quickly all over the university.

The most popular one had it that Cavendish and Miriam had eloped to start a new life elsewhere since the university authorities frowned on relationships between tutors or lecturers and students. Emma felt sick when she thought about this, particularly as she had begun to blame herself for initiating a relationship between the two of them; although if this were the case at least they were safe, free from any danger.

Mike lost no time in recruiting another girl for their 'Fire and Ice' routine. But he wasn't able to find someone else who could express milk, much to the punters' disappointment, and Emma took an instant dislike to Maria, the girl he'd found. She knew that as much as anything her dislike was based on the girl having replaced Miriam, which was hardly Maria's fault. But there was something about the new girl's brittle brashness and ambition that was hardly endearing, and soon Emma was just going through the motions with her act. The punters picked up on it too, and although for a while takings were up because they enjoyed the sight of a new girl Emma's despondency soon showed through and they began to stay away.

When Emma approached Mike with the idea of taking a break for a while, he nodded and told her that he'd been thinking of suggesting the same thing. He liked her, he said, and she was talented, but it wasn't the same without Miriam, was it?

When Annie called her up for advice, saying that Miriam's rent was overdue and she wasn't sure what to do, Emma paid it for her, sure that her friend would turn up again soon; but after a second week had gone by with no word from Miriam she considered calling the police. The only thing that stopped her was the realisation that they'd do nothing if she did: Miriam was an adult, after all, and as far as anyone knew she'd gone away of her own accord. The simultaneous disappearance of Cavendish made foul play even less likely and the thought of being ferried around from hospital to morgue to look at bodies, the most likely result of trying to report Miriam as a missing person, was too grim for Emma to bear.

She threw herself into her work, trying to fill the sense of loss she felt with wide reading and research. It worked, up to a point. One of her tutors even remarked on the change in her as she engaged him in discussion during a tutorial, having for once read the coursework unlike most of the other students. He was pleased but puzzled too, and he took her aside at the end of the tutorial to ask her if anything was wrong

and to recommend that she should consult a counsel-
lor if she couldn't speak to him.

Emma had almost burst into tears there and then
at his offer. But instead, filled with a shame and guilt
she couldn't find a source for, she hurried back to her
flat. As she opened the door she heard her flatmate's
voice saying, 'Oh! Hang on a minute, I think she's
just come back.' Then she saw Kelly leaning round
the end of the hall, calling 'Phone!' to her.

'Who is it?' Emma mouthed as she hurried down
the hall towards Kelly.

The other girl shrugged and mouthed 'Miriam'
with an uncertain turn of her lip.

Emma's heart flip-flopped. She grabbed the phone
as Kelly, unconcerned, went back to her room.
'Hello?'

'Emma? Is that you?' The voice sounded distant, a
little tinny, but there was no mistaking it. Miriam.

'Where the hell are you? Where have you been?'
Emma exploded. 'You just up sticks without telling
anyone where you're going, and – I paid your rent the
other day, Annie's really pissed off with you. What's
going on?'

Miriam, who had been trying to interrupt her but
was unable to stop Emma's barrage of questions,
laughed. The sound made Emma's blood boil, all the
stresses of the past fortnight welling up in one great
mass.

'What the fuck are you laughing at? It's not funny!
Where the hell are you, Miriam?' she demanded.

'Calm down, Emma. I'm in Scotland, I'm safe, and
I'm staying at a castle up here.'

Miriam sounded utterly relaxed and unconcerned
by anything that had been going on in her absence.
Emma stared at the phone in disbelief. Then, struck
by the idea, she asked, 'Is Dr Cavendish with you?'

101

Miriam laughed again. 'Yes, he's up here. But we didn't come up together. Not really, anyway. I haven't seen that much of him.'

'So what are you doing up there? When are you coming back?'

'That's what I'm calling about, Emma. I want you to come up here too.'

'Go up to Scotland? What for?'

'I was invited up here to join a circus that's being put together by Lord Garner. It's the chance of a lifetime – well paid, and it's really special. Listen, I can't explain on the phone. You'll just have to come up.'

'What about the course? And our flats?' Emma asked, bewildered by this sudden turn of events.

'This won't last for too long, and we'll easily make enough money to cover the rents and a whole lot more. There's something different about this, Em – you have to come up here and experience it.'

There was something contagious about the obvious excitement in Miriam's voice. Emma found it difficult to keep sounding angry as she asked, 'I'm not coming up to get in the way of anything between you and Cavendish, am I? Because if that's what this is all about, some weird way of making him jealous or something, I don't want any of it.'

Miriam laughed again and her delight was so evident that Emma smiled despite herself. 'Don't be silly, of course not. So you'll come up, then?'

Emma, already glowing from the sound of her lover's voice, unexpected after these two long weeks, at first nodded at the phone before realising that her friend couldn't see her. 'Count me in, I'm coming up.'

Five

There were still patches of snow to either side of the track, pooling under the trees where the sun had not yet reached. The crisp air tightened the skin on James's face and he rubbed his hands together to stave off the cold, the feeling almost all gone from his bluish fingers. He hadn't come prepared for the walk, he reflected ruefully as he trudged along the track, trying to avoid another long puddle. His shoes were already covered in mud, and icy water had soaked through his socks.

He'd found the track easily enough on his OS map, which he was lucky to have brought at all; he'd expected to have been able to get a bus to Ardegan, or at least a cab. But Peter had been right – there didn't seem to be any way of getting there other than walking. The nearest he'd been able to get by bus was Porthness, where his enquiries about further transport had been met with sullen stares or by people simply ignoring him. One severe woman with her hair tied tightly back in a grey bun and her lips compressed into a thin line had, by contrast, approached him and asked him where he was going. When he'd replied she'd spat on the ground to one side of him, made the sign of the cross and walked away. James had almost burst out laughing. He'd heard that the people up in this part of the Highlands were not known for their friendliness, but this felt like he'd just walked onto the set of a Hammer film.

A sound behind him broke him out of his reverie and he turned to see an open-topped carriage approach. His eyes widened as it drew closer. There were horses up here, he was sure of it, so why would anyone choose to have their carriage pulled by huskies? The dogs were only twenty metres away from him now, snarling and pulling harder on their leashes, their eyes reddened and their canine stares fixed upon him. Startled, he drew back, stumbling against the raised edge of the track.

The driver of the carriage gave a guttural cry and pulled back on a set of reins, tugging at the harnesses of the animals even as they strained towards James, their bodies quivering, their teeth exposed. A line of spittle hung from the jaws of one of the animals closest to James, then fell to the ground.

'I'm glad you've got those dogs under control,' James said to the driver, his voice sounding unnaturally loud in the quiet of the woods. Even the dogs had fallen strangely silent now. The driver stared back at him impassively. James couldn't see much of his face, save for his eyes, as he wore a large cap and had a scarf wrapped around his jaw. The rest of his body was similarly well covered, in a greatcoat, and his hands were sheathed in thick gloves. But even through the man's clothes James could see that he was stocky, remarkably broad.

'Dogs?' The voice came from the passenger, evidently a woman, and had a peculiar tinkling quality that made James think of ice and caves. He stepped to the side to see her properly, the body of the driver having blocked her from his line of sight. One of the huskies lunged at him, only to be pulled back at the last instant, snarling, by the driver.

The woman laughed delightedly and clapped her hands together. She was dressed from head to toe in furs, the ensemble completed with a round fur hat and fur-lined gloves. James stared at her face, unable to make out her expression behind her dark glasses, until her crimson lips parted in a smile, her brilliant white teeth glinting in the sun, and she let out another peal of laughter.

James smiled nervously.

'Are you going far?' she asked, a gently mocking smile still on her lips.

'To – to Ardegan,' James stammered, feeling nervous and foolish and not knowing why.

'Oh?' Reaching a gloved hand to her face, the woman lowered her sunglasses and scrutinised him. James had never seen eyes quite so green. 'We're going that way. Would you like to ride with us?' She moved to one side and patted the space she'd left beside her.

James didn't need any further encouragement and stepped up to sit beside her. But he shivered as he sat down: it seemed colder here, somehow – probably just the chill of his sweat now that he'd stopped walking, he thought.

The woman turned to the front and barked a command at the driver. The dogs began to pull the carriage and it was soon moving quickly again, faster than James had expected, the wheels running smoothly, barely making a sound as they moved along the uneven track. The woman turned to James again.

'And why should you wish to visit Ardegan?' James had been trying to place her voice and now he thought he had it: her English was perfect, save for a slight over-formality, with the merest trace of a Middle European accent.

'I'm visiting friends,' James lied.

'Indeed? At the castle?' she asked sharply, looking him up and down. James was suddenly acutely aware of the blandness of his clothes. The T-shirt, jeans and denim jacket that made him blend into the background in the city seemed grotesquely out of place here.

'No, just in the village. Are *you* staying at the castle?'

The woman smiled. But there was no warmth in her expression and James nearly flinched as she bared her teeth, irrationally afraid that she might lunge forward and bite him.

The carriage gave a jolt and before he could help himself James had lurched to the side, his hands clutching at the air lest he fall, finally grabbing the furs covering the woman's legs. His hands sank into their rich softness, tugging them to one side and exposing the woman's legs. In the instant before the carriage steadied again and the woman had pulled the furs back into place, hissing, James had taken in a sight that was instantly etched into his mind.

She was wearing neither skirt nor trousers beneath the furs, but a pair of stockings that gleamed in the sun with the brilliance of a thousand diamonds. His gaze had involuntarily travelled up her legs to the tops of her stockings, lingering on the near-bluish whiteness of alabaster skin above and the shadows beyond. But what had made his heart stop was the carvings on the suspender clips. They were minute, finely fashioned, but their shape was unmistakable: each was a sculpted miniature of a grinning human skull.

'I'm sorry,' James apologised, half wanting to ask her about what he'd seen. She had turned to the front now and remained silent. But as they neared a bend in the track she shouted an order to the driver again and the carriage slowed to a halt.

'It would not do for me to take you to Ardegan like that.' She indicated his clothes, conveying a curt dismissal with a nod of her head. 'There is a path there. You will find the village at the end, ten minutes away.'

James climbed down. Then he turned back to thank the woman, perhaps to apologise again, aware that she was displeased. But the carriage started moving again as soon as he had stepped off and neither the woman nor the driver turned when he called out a final 'Thank you!'

The air seemed to grow warmer as James emerged from the woods, the chill less evident in the air, which soon filled with the dizzy buzz of bees and the sweet smell of woodsmoke. He could hear the revelry not long after the woman had dropped him off, the noise of pipes, drums and joyous whoops coming to him in waves. The unfamiliar sounds made him feel nostalgic, although he couldn't have said why, or what for. But something in him was moved.

The maypole was the first thing he saw, towering above even the squat church steeple. Even so, it was garlanded with flowers at the top and ribbons spiralling down from it twisted now this way, now that, as he watched. As the sounds grew stronger so too did the smells, a heady odour of cider and roasting meat making his mouth water. Then he saw the first few villagers, dancing around the pole.

Something else caught James's eye, something he took for a tree at first, a tree at the edge of the green where the festival seemed to be taking place. But he noticed it swaying where there was no wind and then he saw that it had legs, clothed in green and brown but legs all the same. There must be a man inside, he realised, wrapped in leafy branches thick around him and green – a ball of foliage around his entire upper body, covering his head. The image came to him of an old woodcut of a person dressed almost identically to the one he'd just seen, along with the name 'Jack-in-the-green'. As he wondered if the person could see through the branches, and why anyone would want to dress this way, the legs kicked together and the figure turned towards him, seeming to incline in his direction.

James's heart stopped and he leapt to the side of the track, pressing himself against the hedge, suddenly filled with an unaccountable dread. The man's clothes, glimpsed through the foliage, had not been normal; they looked as though they'd been made especially for the occasion from some coarse natural fabric, except that they showed signs of wear. His shoes, too, each seemed to be made from a single piece of leather, curled over and stitched together, giving him a medieval look.

James looked down at his own clothes again. He'd only had a glimpse of the people on the green but none of them had been wearing clothes like his. He knew – he was certain – that dressed as he was he would not be welcome.

He found a gap in the hedge and pressed through, blinking at the dust and midges swarming around him. There was a field here; one end abutted the village green and as long as he avoided the gate leading onto it he'd be able to watch what was going on through gaps in the thick hedgerow.

A few cattle looked at James expressionlessly. Most of them were lying down and flicking lazily at the flies with their tails. One – a bull, he realised with a start

– wore a ring of hawthorn blossom around its horns, which had been painted a garish yellow. He wanted to take a closer look but gave the animal a wide berth, keeping to the side of the hedgerow until he could peer through at the green. There was something turning on a spit, and people dancing, but it wasn't until he was closer that he realised what was wrong with them, something vaguely disquieting that he hadn't fully realised from a distance.

The women wore long flowing white robes. Their hair was garlanded with tresses of flowers, and James's heart ached to see the beauty of some of them: long-legged, full-breasted and naked under their robes, the pink tips of their nipples and the dark thatches between their legs clearly visible through the gauzy fabric, their bare feet glistening in the remains of the morning dew.

The reports Peter had given him had told stories of lewd dances and men going about as animals. But James hadn't expected to see it so literally: the men were wearing full animal masks that entirely covered their heads. Some were articulated: he turned at a clacking noise to watch a man with a horse's head snap the mask's jaws, the wide staring eyes of bottle glass momentarily blinding him with reflected solar glare. Others were feral, the bull masks having an awful majesty and the wolves painted a hungry green. Some of the men wore hides as well, even tails, while others were dressed in a rough clothing similar to that of the Jack-in-the-green.

A procession was taking place. A young woman, dressed like the female dancers that James had seen but with a more elaborate garland on her head, was being carried on a heavy chair bedecked with ribbons by four men dressed as wolves, their long snouts fixed in the air, who now pushed the chair high up and spun it round, once, twice, three times. The girl's hair swung around her head, petals from her garland floating to the ground. She looked flushed, her eyes glassy, her lips swollen, and James wondered why, until the chair was lowered to the ground, and the wolfmen's arms took her under the shoulders to pull her up and off.

She squirmed against them and stood up with an anxious expression of concentration on her face, biting her lip. She tottered unsteadily and kissed the men, holding their ears in each hand. Then James saw it, something gnarled and wooden, glistening with moisture in the sunlight, a worn shaft sticking straight up from the chair, and he caught his breath. The woman who'd been sitting on it now fondled the crotch of one of the wolf boys; there was a swelling there, a straining the others had too, bulges they seemed only too happy to let her caress, until another girl, waiting her turn, called excitedly to them. The first girl danced away, the large garland was passed to the new girl, and the wolfmen helped her to sit on the chair, pulling up the back of her robes and giving James a flash of the naked swatch of hair beneath. Once she was seated and moving her thighs against the chair a flush of colour rose in her cheeks and the wolfmen picked up the chair's legs to hoist her in turn into the air.

The girl writhed against the shaft and called out in a wavering cry of joy, her hair whipping round, until she too was brought down, only to tease herself by grinding her hips against the chair and clutching at her breasts with both hands, massaging them and pulling at the nipples till they stuck out hard beneath her thin robes. Then the procession moved on, out of James's immediate line of vision, and he looked round some more, his heart pounding, his breath shallow. This was beyond anything Peter had imagined; it looked as though the whole community was involved. Headlines, feature spreads, even book proposals flashed through James's mind. He shifted position, too excited to stay still. This was his big break, he had no doubt.

The dances had become ruder now, and James could see why: there were a number of cider stalls dotted about and everyone seemed to be drinking from pewter tankards that flashed in the sun or from rough-hewn wooden cups. Some of the boys were slightly the worse for wear, stumbling around, but this didn't stop the girls they danced with from making grabs for their crotches, or from bending over to shake their bottoms in the air. Some girls even lifted their robes to flash their furry mounds, occasionally giving a glimpse of the pink wetness inside, then laughing and dancing away as the drunken wolf boys lunged towards them.

A few of the girls went further and freed the wolf boys' erections. Then they danced around the lads, occasionally gripping their cocks and giving them sharp tugs as James's eyes popped wider in disbelief. One girl even crouched down in a squat and James could see her head bobbing up and down on a boy's cock. None of the others appeared to mind this – some even stopped to watch and cheer her on, waving foamy tankards at her or pouring cider down the wolf boy's throat.

As James watched he heard the ringing of bells and looked at the church. But there was no bell there, and this close he could see that the steeple was in disrepair, the stonework crumbling. He looked at the roof, which was riddled with gaps; it sagged towards the middle, where naked beams were visible. Some birds had been nesting there and monochrome streaks spattered the ruined walls. The stained glass was gone, only the skeleton of its leadwork remaining, and even some of this was bent and twisted out of shape. What had happened here?

But the bells still rang, and James turned back to the festival to see where the sound was coming from. Burly men, the first he'd seen without masks, grinning from ear to ear and ringing hand bells, flanked a grotesque figure wearing motley – some crudely stitched jester's outfit of black, yellow and red – who skipped about and cracked a long whip. Unlike the bell-ringers, his face was disguised, in a roughly varnished Punch mask painted a sick white with rouged cheeks and lips. The ends of the hooked nose and pointed chin were also daubed red, and a high-peaked hat of yellow and red curved up to a point above the grotesque face.

The crowd scattered before his sharp, quick forays with the whip. But most of them were laughing as they fled, some of the girls even flashing the Punch by whisking their robes up, soliciting cracks of the whip on the bare globes of their bottoms.

The Punch figure whipped one of the girls who bent over and stuck her bottom out for him, her robes hiked up around her waist, until he ran over to catch another who jumped just out of reach. The first girl joined the others, who were running now in the direction that the Punch had come from, rubbing her bottom with both hands. Suddenly there was a thud against the gate.

A wolf boy was slumped there, sitting on the green. James leapt back, terrified that he'd been spotted. But the boy was motionless and James stalked towards him, slowly at first, then more boldly as he heard deep, even snores coming from him. The boy had drunk too much. James saw the tankard, still clutched in one hand. Half its contents had spilled down the boy's leg.

A hush had fallen over the green and James looked up from the drunk boy to see only a few other figures lying sprawled on the grass. The faint sounds of bells and horns showed him which way the rest had gone.

Slowly and carefully, James eased the gate open and the boy sprawled full-length on the ground. James grasped the boy by his shoulders and began to drag him behind the hedge, inching his way along, his ears pricked for the slightest change in the boy's breathing. The youngster's snoring hitched once, when James first picked him up, then returned to its previous leisurely pace, even as he was being dragged. Eventually he was lying out of sight of the green.

The boy was about the same size as James and the young reporter undressed hurriedly, stripping his clothes off and leaving them bunched up in the hedge a little way distant. The cattle munched away at their grass as they watched him impassively. Then James eased the boy's shoes off carefully, and heard him mumble contentedly as he wriggled his toes in the grass. Next came the trousers, and James saw that the boy was naked beneath them. After a moment's hesitation he stripped his own underwear off and pulled the boy's trousers on, feeling the unfamiliar coarseness of the fabric on his bare legs and crotch. He paused, looking at the bundle of clothes, then took the wallet from his trousers and slid it into his new pockets. It wouldn't do to tempt fate.

The boy's jerkin came next. But James was afraid that he'd wake up and, after silently apologising to him and hoping that it wouldn't add to the lad's headache too much later, he rapped the heel of his shoe against the back of the boy's head. The youngster's legs kicked and his snoring promptly stopped.

James, terrified that he'd hurt the boy, checked his pulse: the lad's heartbeat was slow but regular. James stripped the boy's jerkin off and put it on himself, then took a deep breath and pulled the wolf mask off, having to rock it from side to side to ease it away from the young fellow's face.

James spent a few seconds staring at the boy, who couldn't have been more than eighteen. His freckled face and unformed features looked peaceful, and his long straight hair was damp and close to his scalp from wearing the mask. Then James put the mask on himself, smelling the boy's acrid sweat and the cloyingly sweet smell of stale cider as he peered through the eyeholes. It was well made: he worked his jaw and felt the lower half of the mask move, and his lips were close enough to the mouth hole for him to work out how the wolf boys had been eating and drinking. He could see well, too, although his breathing sounded laboured within the mask and he could hardly hear anything apart from the heavy sound.

After one final look at the boy, James opened the gate again and stepped out onto the green. He picked his way through the gnawed bones, crushed petals and discarded wooden beakers, and walked past the dangling ribbons of the maypole as they fluttered in the wind. When he came level with the church he saw the heavy door hanging off its hinges, dust and rubble scattered on the nearby ground.

He'd seen the last of the crowd heading towards the woods on the far side of the village. He stepped anxiously into the street leading down to the trees, glancing from side to side to see if any of the houses were occupied. But apart from the garlands of flowers and ribbons over many of the doorways, and wizened corn dollies in some of the windows, there was no sign of life in any of the houses. Some doors had even been left open, and swung to and fro in the breeze.

As James reached the last of the houses a curtain at one of the windows twitched. He paused, peering in and wondering why this person had not followed the others. But then the curtain was drawn back over the window. The door was closed but he could see over it a lighter patch on the brickwork where something shaped like a cross had been until recently.

Beyond the houses the street stopped and a sun-dappled path led on into the woods. James could hear piping and cheering again over the soughing of the wind in the leaves, although the bells seemed to have stopped now. He followed the trail. The shoes he'd taken had thin, soft soles and he could feel every twig, every pebble and lump on the earth beneath him as though he were barefoot. He paced through the woods, which grew thicker around him the deeper he went, the sounds of the others becoming louder and louder now.

After hopping across a stream he could see a bright patch ahead, a clearing in the woods; the others were gathered there. The dancing had stopped but the piping and cheering hadn't, and as he drew closer he realised that the people were gathered around in various groups.

James joined the nearest one, standing at the back until he thought he'd blended in. Nobody was speaking, although a few were still drinking, cider spilling down the sides of their masks. To his right the Punch figure was dancing in a grotesque lumbering fashion with a man wearing a bear mask, lashing the bear man with his whip every time he seemed to tire.

James watched, fascinated, until the Punch seemed to turn towards him and the whip fell to its side. Scared, James edged forward to join the others, craning his head and jostling with the other men to get a better view.

A naked woman was lying spreadeagled on the ground, supported only by a wooden X-frame to which her wrists, ankles and waist were being attached with thick ropes by a couple of the bell-ringers. She was young, perhaps in her late teens, and straw-blonde, with a pretty snub nose, a dusting of freckles on her cheeks, high, pert breasts tipped with long pink nipples that were stiff in the breeze, and a tawny swatch of hair between which the neat lips of her sex pouted between her legs. James started forward, anxious that she was being made to do something against her will. Then he saw the expression on her face, a heavy-lidded look of contentment. She was panting, rocking her head from side to side and pushing her hips down then up on the frame. James swallowed heavily and tried to fight his mounting arousal. He had to stay sharp and aware of everything around him here: it wouldn't do to get distracted.

There were other women in the crowd, watching; one wiped a tear from her cheek, her lips quivering. Another woman put her arm around her and held her close, saying, 'Don't fret, my love. They'll need others for next time and maybe it'll be our turn then.'

One of the men standing beside her guffawed and reached a huge hand down to clasp and squeeze her bottom. 'Never you mind, love. What need do you have to go into the woods when you have us to take care of?' The women laughed, the one who'd been crying seeming to forget her despair, and they turned back to watch the girl.

The two bell-ringers conferred and James caught one of them saying, 'Check to see if she's ready.' Then, to his astonishment, the other crouched down

116

beside her, reached his hand between her legs and, as she let out a long, deep moan, eased first one then two fingers into her, sliding them in and out a few times experimentally before dragging them up along the full length of her crease and holding them up for the other man to inspect. Even from where James was standing he could see them glistening in the sun. A murmur went up from the crowd.

The other man nodded and a woman stepped forward from the crowd, holding a bunch of wild flowers. The man who'd inspected the girl took them and bent down again to peel the girl's sex open with one hand. Then he dragged the stems of the flowers up and down her crease. The girl giggled, the laugh catching in her throat and turning into a sigh of unmistakable arousal, and the man eased the stems into her sex, pushing them in slowly until only the flowers' heads protruded, bunched at the centre of her hair, the whites, yellows, blues and reds clear and bright against the swollen pink skin of her sex lips and the tufty blonde hair. The display made an extraordinarily vivid contrast with the milky whiteness of her skin. Her eyes were closed now, her lips full, and a light flush had crept onto her cheeks.

A cheer rose from the crowd and James joined in the clapping. Then two of the wolf boys stepped forward, and joined the two bell-ringers in taking a corner each of the X-frame and lifting the girl into the air. James followed the crowd as they fell into line behind the carriers, forming an impromptu procession. Cheers came from the other groups now; they'd been doing the same thing and three more girls were hoisted into the air, making a long chain.

The piping and drumming started again, fitting into a rhythm although James couldn't see anyone conducting or leading the band; a few of the men had pipes in their pockets or, hanging from their shoulders on leather thongs, small drums that they beat now with their hands. He could see the full range of heads now: the wolves outnumbered the others by far and seemed to represent the younger, more able men. There was only one bear, being belaboured again by the Punch's whip and dancing as the procession moved away from the clearing and further into the woods along a well-trodden path. A few bull heads with terrifyingly sharp horns were worn by the burliest men; the horse heads, with their glassily staring eyes and nightmare clattering jaws, were worn by thinner men; and hare heads, each one with huge erect ears, a startled expression and long whiskers sprouting on either side, belonged to the younger boys.

None of the girls seemed to wear any masks and it was only now that James spotted one man in a stag mask with huge antlers framing the head and a long shaggy mane that reached halfway down the man's back. The stag didn't speak to anyone or play an instrument; his clothes were different too, made of a similar material but more free-flowing and dyed a purplish colour. He didn't play with the girls, either. Dimly aware that this person was important, different from the others, James suddenly realised that he was the same build as the coachman he'd met earlier. Alarmed by the thought that he might be recognised, James tried to move away from the stag man in the procession. Then, embarrassed, he attempted to move away in turn from one of the girls, who smiled sweetly at him and leaned forward to stroke his crotch.

He was erect, turned on by what he'd seen, and he stared as the girl turned and pushed her buttocks against him, squirming from side to side, the cheeks of her rear rubbing against his hard cock over and over again. Then she turned around and pushed her front against him, grabbing at his crotch once more. James could feel her breasts against the thin jerkin and his cock twitched at the sight of her stiff nipples brushing against him. He felt a powerful urge to respond but held himself in check, scared that he'd give himself away. The girl leaned towards him, still holding his cock, and whispered into his ear, 'I'm yours if you want me. Take me after we've laid the offering down.' But he pushed her away silently, wanting to offer some kind of apology but sure that it would only make things worse.

The girl backed away, a confused expression on her face, as James pushed himself further along the procession. When he was a safe distance away he turned back to see her approach another woman. After she had said a few words to her, both of them looked at him curiously, expressions of distaste and suspicion on their faces. Alarmed, he stumbled back, only to find that the procession he was in had stopped.

Of course! He'd seen it on the map before coming here but everything he'd seen since had put it to the back of his mind. He looked around. The mound was long, as long as any he'd seen before, maybe forty feet, and surrounded by oak trees, old, gnarled and towering above them. At its end was a horseshoe-shaped entrance with a couple of stone slabs marking a hole, a dark recess in the mound.

The remaining processions marched around the mound and arranged themselves at three other points around the long barrow. From the position of the sun James saw that his group was at the north end of the mound, with the others waiting at the remaining cardinal points. The men carrying the girls laid them on the ground and a silence fell, broken soon by a high, weird note, long and drawn-out. Startled, James looked round to see where it came from and saw the stag man with a long horn to his lips, holding the instrument in the air, his cheeks rounded and red with effort.

To James's horror, a distant howl answered the stag man's signal and the hairs prickled on the back of the reporter's neck. The stag man dropped the horn to his side, turned and began to walk back down the path, the others trooping behind him. James fell to the back of the procession, partly to keep away from the woman whose advances he'd spurned, and who was talking to other people now, some of whom were turning and looking his way suspiciously, but also because he wanted to slip away and hide in the woods to see what happened to the girls when everyone had left.

James began to drag his feet, looking at the trees beside the path, remaining in the shadows, and before long he was out of sight of the others. He waited for a few minutes in case any of them came back. But the piping and drumming, which had begun again as soon as they'd left the long barrow, were growing distant now; the others would be almost back at the green. He turned around, his heart in his mouth, and ducked into the woods, reluctant to remain on the path but trying to follow it as closely as he could at a distance, stepping gingerly over twigs, treading as lightly as he could. Soon he could see it again, the mound looming in front of him washed in white sunlight, with one of the girls in front of it.

James found a hollow by one of the oaks, took off his mask and crouched down, nervous now but excited too, his pulse racing, as he waited to see what would happen. He'd barely stopped panting from the effort of moving through the woods when he heard a howl coming from his right, much closer now. The girl ahead of him squirmed in anticipation. Then he saw the figure, running with a long, loping stride through the field to the east of the mound. James pressed himself closer to the ground as the figure approached, slowing its pace and allowing James to take a good look at it through the trees.

It was a youngish man, maybe thirty or thirty-five years old, well proportioned and athletic-looking but with a feral cast to his face. His black hair was thick and shaggy and ran over his chest, down his arms and even over his shoulders, wiry and bristling. He didn't look local; his eyebrows seemed to join together, giving him one bushy line over his deep-set eyes, and his skin looked brown, although that could have been from exposure to the sun and the wind. He was naked, the hair on his chest petering out to a thin line as it descended across his stomach before expanding again to flank his crotch, framing the long cock that dangled between his legs. His feet were caked with clayey brown soil from the field that he'd just crossed. James wasn't sure exactly what he'd expected to emerge when the stag man had blown on his horn but it certainly hadn't been a naked man.

The man had reached the line of oaks separating the field from the long barrow now and he pressed through, stepping with an exaggerated care over the branches underfoot. Then he stopped, rearing his head up and sniffing at the air. He seemed to look directly at James. Petrified, James closed his eyes and held his breath, willing his body not to move, acutely conscious of the pine needles pressing into his body, of every root and rock underneath him, of the chatter of birds in the branches above. His fear made every sense acute and he even heard the resumed pacing as

121

the naked man moved on, pressing further into the woods and emerging on the other side, by the mound.

James opened his eyes and breathed out slowly and quietly. The figure was standing beside the girl nearest to him, his head cocked to one side as he looked quizzically at her. Then he loped round to the right, presumably having spotted the next girl along, and James craned his head to see him standing by her in the same position, his head angled to one side. Then he vanished, only to reappear several minutes later on the other side. The girl in front of James was moaning now and pulling against her bonds.

When the man returned to the front of the mound, to the girl lying ahead of James, he had an unmistakable erection, his long cock standing almost vertical from his thick swatch of pubic hair. There was something strange about the way he walked, something that James couldn't quite put a finger on, and the reporter was racking his brain to work out what it was when the man leaned down over the girl, knelt between her thighs and wrenched the flowers from between her legs with his mouth. Then he dropped them to one side before clasping her thighs with both hands and throwing his head back to unleash a blood-curdling howl.

James felt the hairs on his neck stand up and he tried to shrink still further into his hollow as the figure threw himself down on top of the girl, gripped her shoulders and plunged himself into her. His hips began to pump furiously and the girl let out a long keening wail, peaking each time he thrust inside her. James stared in amazement, already wondering how he'd describe the scenario and whether he dared approach the naked man later to try and secure an interview. Then it began.

First the man's buttocks tightened as he craned his head up again to let out another long howl. James, his heart in his mouth at the sound, assumed that he'd just come, but then his hips started pumping again. He looked darker now, as though his body hair had suddenly got longer, and his strokes were more frenzied, hammering into the woman underneath him. His back seemed to hunch over and his shoulders swelled as though he were inflating himself bodybuilder-style. But this was more impressive than anything James had seen before and the reporter's jaw dropped as the man's hair thickened visibly. Thick ropes of muscle suddenly appeared on his back, bunching tautly, then lengthening and quivering. The arms seemed longer now too, stretched out beyond any human length, and the calves of his legs had similarly elongated, the feet larger and flatter, digging into the soil as the man's bottom, entirely covered by thick shiny hair now, continued to pump away.

James swallowed, unable to believe what he was seeing, only able to gape still more as he saw the man's face change, his ears lengthening in fits and starts until they were pointed, pinned back against his head. The nose protruded further and further, becoming more like a snout as the teeth lengthened and thick saliva dropped onto the girl's face. And that was when James panicked.

He still had the presence of mind to rise from his hollow slowly, the beast in front of him apparently too busy in its task to notice him. But when he was up he turned quickly, the wolf mask forgotten as it rolled into the hollow behind him. Then James ran blindly through the woods, not caring how much noise he made, how many branches he broke, running into some that left long red weals on his skin. He was nearly in tears when he came out of the woods and found himself on the path again.

He looked to his right: a dark tunnel led through the trees to the oak grove and the long barrow, and . . . and on the left, the sun shone through the leaves more and more intensely until the exit from the woods became a white-out from where James stood. But he knew it led to the green. Whatever was going on there – the music seemed to have stopped now – it had to be better than what he'd just seen.

As James neared the green he tried to resist the powerful temptation to turn and look over his shoulder. It couldn't have been real, that much he was sure of. Perhaps there had been some hallucinogenic drug at work: something in the fabric of the wolf mask, maybe – he'd heard that such a thing might be possible. Or perhaps watching the boys in the masks, combined with staying out in the sun, had made him see things out there, some bestial transformation when all there had really been was a naked man and a naked woman.

James emerged, blinking, into the sunlight. The revelries had died down but a few people were still milling about at the end of the street by the green. Acutely aware that he didn't have the wolf mask on now, to his dismay James saw that the men there were still masked. He almost turned back but pressed on: anything, he repeated to himself, was better than what he'd come from. He'd cross the green, go into the field again, collect his own clothes and leave. At the very least he needed time to take stock of the situation, and with luck all the villagers would be too cider-addled to notice him.

He made it to the end of the street and had just taken his first few steps on the green, keeping his eyes down, when a call in front of him made him lift his head. A woman stood twenty metres away, staring at him. Then she cried out again.

'Impostor!'

James slowed his steps. Behind the woman a few others were gathering, all staring at him curiously. Then, to his horror, he saw the boy whose clothes he'd taken. He was wearing James's clothes. James was struck with a curious sense of disembodiment, as though he was witnessing himself for the first time. The boy saw him too and both of them stopped dead for a second, until James saw the boy's arm raise up. James turned and started to walk back the way he'd come.

'There's my clothes!' He heard the boy's voice behind him, calling out loudly. 'That's the man who took my clothes!'

James looked over his shoulder. A larger crowd had gathered now. The women were advancing on him, their faces no longer merely suspicious but contorted in rage, and the men, their masks looking more sinister now that they were all turned impassively towards him, were moving too. James broke into a trot, then started to run, picking up his pace as a roar went up from the crowd.

Six

As the coach pulled into the main stop at Porthness, Emma saw that Miriam was there, waiting for her. A huge grin broke out on her friend's face when she saw Emma and she started to wave frantically, almost jumping up and down in her excitement.

Emma had spent each part of the trip so far – the train to the airport, the plane to Aberdeen, the coach to Porthness – working out what she was going to say to Miriam when she saw her at last, how best to repay her for the pain she'd caused her, the worry. But as soon as she saw Miriam she grinned despite herself, excited to see her friend again, all her worries forgotten in the simple fact of being together once more.

Miriam nearly knocked Emma over when she climbed off the coach, hugging her hard and leaning back so that she almost picked Emma up off the ground.

'Whoa, there,' said Emma, laughing. Then she studied her friend more closely. 'You look really well,' she admitted.

'Must be all the clean air.' Miriam grinned. 'Come on, we'll dump your things, go out for a drink and catch up.' She turned and looked at the bags the driver had unloaded from the coach. 'That one's yours, isn't it? I can smell you on it.' She smiled broadly at Emma's look of confusion. 'Come on, I'll take it for you.'

And with that she'd hefted the strap of Emma's bag over her shoulder and was marching determinedly down the road. Emma had to walk fast to catch up with her.

'It's OK, I don't mind taking the bag,' Emma offered. 'Where are we going, anyway? Where's this castle you were telling me about?'

Miriam turned to her and pouted in mock sorrow. 'Buses don't go that far, I'm afraid. Actually, you can't really even get a cab there either. It's sort of car-free.'

Emma wasn't about to be fobbed off with this. 'Hold on!' she exclaimed, putting a hand on Miriam's shoulder. Then she ran her fingers over the taut muscle. She was sure that Miriam hadn't been so muscular before. 'How are we going to get there, then?'

Miriam grinned. 'We'll walk. Do you good, get all those London poisons out of your system. We don't have to go along the road – there are some beautiful woodland paths. Bluebells are out now, too; it looks glorious there. And don't worry,' she continued, putting up a hand to quell Emma's incredulous complaint. 'I'll carry the bag. I'm fitter than I was, you see.'

It was true; she'd picked up the bag effortlessly. Emma stared at her in wonder. 'So why don't we go there now?'

Miriam looked at the sun and frowned.

'Because I'd rather not get there in the dark, because you must be tired after your long journey, and because there are one or two things I need to do before taking you there.'

Emma stopped. 'One or two things?' she echoed. 'What do you mean?' But there was no answer from Miriam and she had to run to catch up with her again.

'Ah! Here we are!' Miriam smiled at Emma. She'd stopped outside a grotty-looking hotel that had a weather-beaten sign advertising colour TV and free tea and coffee in every room. Emma's heart sank.

'You're joking, right?' she pleaded. But Miriam had already opened the door and was making her way towards the reception desk where a matronly woman of about sixty stared at them frostily from behind a thick pair of glasses, her dead-fish eyes watching them suspiciously.

'Hello!' Miriam boomed, slapping a hand down on the counter. The receptionist moved back a fraction, then composed herself.

'Can I help you?' she asked. Emma would have been hard pressed to imagine a less helpful tone.

Miriam didn't even seem to have noticed and carried blithely on. 'We'd like to book a room, please, just for one night.'

'A room, is it?' The woman stared at Miriam, who beamed back at her, then at Emma, whose attempt at a smile died on her lips. 'To share?' She drew herself up at this, as though it were the most outrageous suggestion she'd ever heard.

'Mm-hmm.' Miriam continued to smile at her, while Emma wished she were back home, back on the coach, back anywhere but here. She'd never known her friend to be so bold, except when she was stripping. It was normally Emma who took the initiative when they were with new people, but their roles seemed to have been reversed.

The woman, finally buckling under the weight of Miriam's happy stare, turned and plucked a key from the wall, then held it out to Miriam as though it were a pair of dirty knickers. 'Number nine has two single beds. I hope that'll be acceptable,' she said.

Miriam made to grab the key from her, but the woman pulled it away at the last second. 'That'll be forty-nine pounds, payable now. And if you wouldn't mind signing the visitors' book.' As Miriam scrabbled for her purse, the woman turned her stony glare on Emma. 'Both of you,' she said pointedly.

When they'd checked in and gone into the room, a functional but characterless cubicle, Emma lay down on the bed and let out a long sigh. 'What a fucking dragon!'

Miriam paced around, opening drawers, peering into the bathroom and lowering the blinds.

'Sit down, you're making me dizzy,' Emma complained.

Miriam turned to her, a gleam in her eye. 'I've got a better idea,' she said, sitting suddenly on the side of Emma's bed and making it bounce. 'Let's go out and get pissed.'

As James ran down the village street, unsure where he was heading, he saw more doors opening. People stepped out to see what all the commotion was about and one of the bell-ringers reached out to catch his jerkin. But he was too fast, dodging round the man and sprinting towards the end of the street.

Another door opened, the last house on the right where he'd paused before. A man in a threadbare dog collar and black gown emerged, blinking in the light, and tried to grab James's arm.

'Get in here, quick!' he hissed, motioning to the dark corridor behind him.

James paused, looking back at the crowd of angry villagers, close now, and forward at the path through the woods. Then he ducked past the man and into the house. The door closed behind him and he turned to stare at the man, who regarded him with a bemused expression.

'They won't come in?' he asked, failing to keep a note of panic out of his voice.

The other man shook his head and smiled a tired smile. 'Most of them shun this place, and those who do not still have a certain respect. For I, you see, am – or perhaps I should say *was* – the vicar of this parish.' His voice was slow and heavy with melancholy.

He walked past James and beckoned him further into the house with a flourish of his arm. James was almost too relieved to take in the dingy surroundings as he walked into the living room – the walls piled high with books, a half-collapsed sofa along one side of the room – but a few things caught his eye. There were no crosses on the wall and only two icons, both of which were hanging at an angle on their hooks and one of which had its glass broken. He turned to the man.

'So you're the vicar? What the hell's going on in this village?'

The man sighed and sat down on the sofa, motioning James to take a chair opposite him. 'Please,' he urged, and James sat down. 'The villagers here have fallen prey to a very ancient temptation. They have little time for the one true Lord now. Yet I cannot condemn them entirely, as the temptation is strong. Still, the church has encountered such behaviour before, and the church has prevailed.' He looked up, closing his eyes and seeming to draw on reserves of memory. 'Such practices used to be common. If memory serves, it was Caesarius of Arles in the fifth century, shocked to find . . .' The priest broke off and rose from his seat.

'Let me find the reference,' he mumbled as he began to rummage through the piles of books. James leaned forward, and was about to tell him not to worry about it when the vicar held one of the books out triumphantly. 'Aha!' he crowed, then flicked through the pages, found what he was looking for and began to read. ' "The heathen – and what is worse, some who have been baptised – put on counterfeit forms and monstrous faces . . . some are clothed in the hides of cattle; others put on the heads of beasts, rejoicing and exulting that they have so transformed themselves into the shapes of animals that they no longer appear to be men." '

He closed the book and sat down again. 'Of course, what has happened here is far worse.' The cleric looked anxiously up at the door and James followed his gaze. There was nothing there, just the dark corridor.

'I saw something – in the woods,' James started, unsure of what he should say. But the vicar stopped him anyway.

'You were in the woods?' he asked, his expression keen now as he leaned forward, searching James's face. 'Just now? What did you see?'

'I saw –' James's voice faltered, and he continued in a lower tone. 'I'm not sure exactly *what* I saw. Four women had been tied to stakes, naked, and taken out to the woods.' The priest nodded, his eyes bright. 'I waited in the woods after the crowd had left, to see what would happen; one of the women spoke about some kind of offering?' The vicar nodded again. 'A man ran from the field to the east of the woods. He was naked, and I saw him throw himself on the girl and have sex with her.'

'Was that all he did?' The vicar had leaned back into the sofa again.

'No.' James took a deep breath. 'He seemed to turn into some kind of animal. Do you know anything about it? I don't understand what I saw. I'm –' James

131

paused, on the verge of telling the vicar why he was there, then thought better of it. 'Can you help me? I want to get into the castle.'

At this the cleric started and he began to mumble to himself, repeating, 'The castle', as he glanced distractedly at the door. James once more followed his gaze but again found nothing. Finally the priest spoke, his voice low and sombre. 'To be accepted by the villagers, at least – and I imagine that it might allow you into the castle – you must be marked. The villagers have a mark –' he looked up at James '– usually here, on their shoulder. Like three claw marks.'

'Yes, I saw them. But where –' James started to ask, only to be interrupted by the priest speaking again, his voice more strident now.

'I told you that I *was* the vicar here. I no longer feel that I am qualified to describe myself in this way. I have failed my God!' His voice rose, then fell to a murmur as he went on. 'For I too have succumbed to the temptation that has befallen this foul place. The spirit has been strong, but the flesh is weak. And if I, chosen to spread the Lord's word in this place and among these people, have been too weak to resist temptation, what can I expect of the others?' The vicar looked up now and James was startled to see the tears glistening in the corners of his eyes, raised wetly to him in supplication.

There was a noise at the entrance to the room and both men turned. A naked girl stood in the doorway, regarding them both calmly with vivid green eyes. She looked young, in her late teens perhaps, and her raven-black hair was long and straight, tumbling over her shoulders. With a start, James saw that her eyebrows met, a thin line of hair above the flashing green of her eyes. He stared at her for a few moments,

132

drinking in the sight of her full breasts tipped with splashes of pink and the naked flesh, stripped bare of any hair, between her thighs, before turning back to the vicar.

'Who is she? Why isn't she wearing any clothes?'

The vicar smiled, a long sad smile. 'This is May. You can come in, May,' he addressed the girl. She moved into the centre of the room and returned James's stare. 'Of course, I call her May but she won't tell me her real name. She hasn't spoken at all, in fact, except to growl. A real wild child.' He smiled again as James looked back at her, more wide-eyed than before. 'I found her like that, curled up on the step outside the back door, one night. All this –' he waved a hand vaguely around '– had begun by then, but I didn't know the shape that it would eventually take.

'I thought she might be a runaway; perhaps she was escaping a bad family situation, or trying to get away from a life of drugs. Naturally I wondered why she was naked but the main thing seemed to be just to get her indoors. The nights here can be cold, you understand.'

The priest looked up at James, who nodded mutely before returning his gaze to the girl.

'I tried to make her wear clothes but she tore them off each time I put them on her. It didn't matter what it was, she refused to wear it. I started to worry then, about what would happen if members of my congregation knew I had a naked girl staying in the place.' The cleric smiled thinly. 'Of course it seems ludicrous now to worry about such a thing, considering all that's happened, but at the time it was important.'

'Surely you could have got someone else to look after her? Called the authorities, that kind of thing?' James blurted out. The girl continued to watch him but she seemed more excited now and was making a low growling noise in the back of her throat.

'Ah.' The vicar smiled sadly again and shook his head. 'The authorities, you understand, won't come here now. Most people shun the village; but some embrace what has happened here and come to join them. And May offers a certain . . . solace for an old, lonely man in this place.' The vicar had a glint in his eye now too and the atmosphere in the room seemed charged, electrified somehow.

'What do you mean?' James asked, his voice barely louder than a whisper.

'Does she not look like what you saw in the woods?'

'Yes.'

'I'm sure she can transform herself fully, but I have found a way to prevent her.'

'And still you want to have this – this creature in the house? Isn't she dangerous?'

The priest rocked his head back and laughed, a long slow croaky laugh. 'Oh, she has appetites but they can be controlled.' Looking at May, he motioned towards James with his head. The girl suddenly lunged forward, to land on her hands and knees in front of James before her hands flashed up to scrabble in his crotch, trying to pull his zip open.

'What the fuck?' cried James, leaping up, hands over his groin.

The girl was snarling now, flexing her hands against the floor, arching her back and trembling. The vicar stood and reached behind the chair, pulling out a long-handled leather quirt, the thongs tied into knots at intervals along the lengths. 'Stand back!' he said to James, his eyes wide and bright as he watched the girl.

The cleric brought the quirt down on the girl's bottom with a fury that astonished James, who fell

134

back into his chair. The girl's eyes widened, her mouth circling in an 'O' of shock. Then she gasped and turned, scurrying around on all fours until the vicar caught her by the nape of the neck and knelt down in front of her. Her bottom was facing James now so that he could see the angry red welts raised by the quirt on the pale flesh of her buttocks.

As the priest held her head down with one hand, he brought the quirt down with the other, dragging the knotted thongs over both cheeks with each vicious stroke. The thwack of the impact filled the room and rang in James's ears. Then the girl's snarling had subsided and she was sobbing softly, her buttocks quivering as she tensed with each stroke.

'She's had enough, hasn't she? Leave the poor thing alone!' cried James, staring aghast at the unexpected punishment. But the vicar ignored him, his beating having fallen into a steady rhythm, almost caressing the girl now. Her bottom seemed impossibly swollen, dark red all over and with purple streaks showing where the knots had bruised her.

Then the vicar stopped and turned to look at James. He was red in the face, perspiring slightly, and he wiped the drops of sweat from his forehead with a sleeve. 'She's ready now,' he announced.

James didn't understand. 'I –' he started, shaking his head.

The cleric, to his astonishment, pulled the girl's buttocks apart, making her naked sex lips part wetly, flashing the moist pinkness inside. James caught his breath and then started up from his chair as the vicar reversed the quirt and eased the knotted leather handle into the girl, pushing it in inch by inch as she quivered beneath his touch until it was all the way in. The thongs hung down over the bare lips, giving her sex the appearance of some wilted jungle bloom.

James stood up, his face burning now, and made for the door. But the vicar's voice stopped him.

'Wait! You cannot leave now. It is not safe. You will stay and witness my degradation.'

James slumped back into the chair, unable to take his eyes from the girl's bottom as the vicar began to fuck her with the handle of the quirt, holding her down by her neck again as he plunged the thick leather shaft inside her. It glistened when it came out and a drop of moisture fell onto the carpet.

'This –' the vicar's voice was laboured as he ground the hilt of the quirt around the mouth of the girl's sex '– is why I've stayed. I try to punish her. You can see how I've tried to punish her! But it only makes her more excited.' The girl was moaning now, pushing back on the coarse handle inside her, the vicar fucking her even harder, ramming it in now and twisting it with each stroke. There was a visible tenting under the man's robes.

'But don't judge me!' the cleric called out, his voice wavering with the effort. 'Don't judge me unless you've suffered the same temptations yourself.' He sank back onto his haunches, looking exhausted, and again wiped the perspiration from his brow. Then he stood up and walked to the door before turning back to look at James.

'If I leave you in here with her, I wonder, will you condemn me then?' Then the priest left the room, closing the door behind him. James turned back to the girl who still crouched on the floor in front of him, moving her hips slowly in the air, her head on the ground, her back arched up to present her buttocks. The thongs of the quirt still dangled down over the pouch between her legs.

As James watched, unmistakably aroused despite himself, the girl reached between her legs with one hand and closed her fingers tight around the quirt handle. He thought that she was going to pull it out, that the display had been for the benefit of the vicar alone. And she did pull on it, making him momentarily ashamed of his arousal as he watched her sex lips bulge out around the handle, intensely aware of the slick juices on it; but then she thrust it back in and started to fuck herself with it.

James leaned forward. She'd turned her head, and was looking at him with wide expectant eyes, even as her hand worked the handle further into her cunt.

'You don't have to do that,' James said, hoping that she'd understand and stop. 'He's gone now. Maybe –' his voice faltered '– I can help.' He didn't know what he could do but he was sure that anything would be better for her than this madhouse.

But May had started to moan now, fucking herself with short hard stabs and rubbing her breasts against the coarse carpet, writhing in front of him, a slut on heat. James sank back, despairing. There was no doubt about it: she was enjoying herself. And the bulge in his pants showed that he too was not immune to the situation.

She'd noticed it as well and was looking from his eyes down, pointedly, to his crotch. Then, perhaps assuming that he didn't like her playing with the quirt, she left it alone and began to rub at the pink flesh hanging down underneath, peeling the lips apart, her fingers flicking over the pearl hidden in the folds. James was acutely aware of a wet slapping sound as her fingers burrowed in her sex. His balls began to ache.

Part of him longed to touch May, to sink his hardness into her warm tight welcoming hole. But he was still shaken by what he'd seen earlier, scared as much as he was turned on. As though she were able to sense that his resolve had begun to falter, she reached round above the quirt to where the brown star of her anus was staring at him and smeared its rim with the juices of her arousal.

James stared, one hand unconsciously dropping into his lap to touch the length of his shaft. Fixing him with her stare, pursing her full lips and letting out a breathless sigh, May eased a finger into her bottom-hole, rotating it until it was buried up to the first knuckle. James felt his cock twitch. The girl again dropped her fingers to her sex to gather up more juice, the thongs of the quirt quivering as they hung down between her legs. Then she returned a finger to her anus, rubbing around it again until the skin was glistening and pushing not one but two fingers in, the strain showing on her face, the ring of her anus bulging inwards until she relaxed, then outwards as she pulled her digits out.

The invitation was unmistakable. May wanted James to bury his cock to the hilt in her forbidden hole. Flashes of what he'd seen at the long barrow came unbidden into his mind and he quickly scanned her body, checking for unnatural elongations, spurts of hair, anything that would warn him that it might happen again here. But there was nothing and he stood up, his erection tenting his trousers. May looked up at him expectantly, twisting two fingers inside herself, working her bottom-hole, relaxing it ready for penetration.

An uncertain smile crossed James's lips as he looked back at her. Then he succumbed, dropping his trousers and pulling his pants halfway down his thighs before falling to his knees behind her. She gave a little cry of excitement and began to try to push her fingers apart inside herself, stretching.

Then he was there, poised, his cock huge and angry red, the tip ready to burst. He knew that if he'd stayed there watching May toy with herself any longer he would have come there and then. He reached forward and touched her for the first time, feeling an electric charge in his fingers as he tugged on her hand, the anal ring everting as her fingers pulled out, then closing slowly, the dark pink of her rectal passage seeming to be sucked inside and closed off by the puckered whorl of her tight ring. Mesmerised, James put his thumb to his mouth and lubricated it with his saliva. Then he pressed it to her anus, feeling the girl clench her muscles involuntarily then relax, and he was able to push it into the moist squishiness inside her, feeling the hot walls pulsing around his thumb.

After working his thumb around a few times, feeling how elastic May was, James pulled it out and scooped up some of the juices from her cunt. The thongs of the quirt brushed his wrist and he watched her shiver as he grazed her clit, then rubbed her grease around the tip of his cock, adding to the pre-come that was already making it glisten in the dim light.

He pressed it to the tight ring and eased himself forward, feeling at first only the resistance, the unwillingness to stretch and allow something so invasive to penetrate her. Then May was pushing back, evidently willing herself to relax, and the tip slid in, slowly, millimetre by millimetre, but it was going, and James pushed harder, the sensations of hot tightness surrounding his cock and filling his head. He was dimly aware of the girl catching her breath as the head slid completely in, then the rest followed more easily, digging deeply into the depths of her bowels until he was in up to the hilt. His balls rested on the thongs of the quirt, the leather strips stroking the sensitive taut skin and making him twitch.

As he pulled out, watching the anal ring tugging at him, trying to suck his cock back in, May reached behind herself again and touched her cunt, the fingers lightly tracing the length of her crease. Feeling her relax, James pushed himself in again, a little harder now, then started to fuck her tight bottom with short shallow strokes, watching as the hand between her legs speeded up to match his rhythm, burrowing faster now, the fingers working busily inside herself.

May's ring was more relaxed now, greasy with rectal mucus, and James slammed himself harder into it, the impact of his balls against the thongs of the quirt driving the handle into her cunt with each stroke. He thrust deeper and longer now, pulling himself almost all the way out, feeling her ring begin to tighten around his head, then pushing back in.

May was panting, her fingers fanned out and rubbing over her sex as though she were polishing it, then slapping at it, sharp little slaps that made her ring tighten each time. Then her gasps ran together and she was starting to squeal, low-pitched at first then higher, and James felt her start to spasm around his cock, a long trembling grip through her anal sleeve. It seemed to tug on him, to milk him so that he felt his own peak hit, and he buried himself up to the hilt inside her, his balls acutely sensitive on the thongs, an exultant cry springing from his lips as he emptied himself inside her.

When it was over, James pulled himself out. As he watched her anal ring close slowly on air and a dribble of his sperm push out to run down the wrinkled swollen skin of her naked sex and wrap itself around the handle of the quirt, he heard the low throaty chuckle of the vicar, standing in the doorway.

Verity looked at the sky. The sun was low now, the clouds golden in the west. She smiled at the other villagers she passed as she walked across the green. Some greeted her with a nod and a wink or with comments about seeing her on the chair earlier and she grinned back at them. But she refused to be drawn into conversation. It would be night soon and she was far from sure when her next chance would come.

Behind her smile she seethed with frustration and hurt. She'd put on the best show she could today; one of the boys holding the chair had told her she was their favourite person to sit in it. She'd even given one of the town elders, old Tom Harris, a suck – though not in public, as his wife might have seen and grown jealous. Mrs Harris was a fearsome dragon, not someone whom Verity wanted to cross.

They were meant to be past that sort of thing now – jealousy came from possessiveness, old ideas they'd tried to put behind them – but she could still see it in the eyes of some of them, especially the older ones: the old men, hungry for the sight and touch of a young body like hers, and their wives, their skin wrinkled and sagging, looking daggers at the younger girls if they approached their men.

And she'd sucked Tom Harris off, for nothing. Verity had gone up to him after sitting in the chair, knowing he'd watched her, knowing he'd liked looking at her for years, and showed him she was willing. He didn't need much encouragement, leading her into the woods a little way, into a dell of bluebells, then telling her to kneel and suck on his cock. He'd got it out, soft and wrinkled, and had made her show

141

herself to him, to tease him till he got hard, showing him where the fat cock of the chair had been inside her, displaying her sex still open and wet from it. She'd told him what she wanted, what she expected, but he'd just laughed and tugged at her hair until she'd taken him in her mouth. He'd come on her face, too, not even giving her any warning before he spurted it all out; she'd thought he'd just wanted to rub his cock on her cheeks again. But some of it had gone in her eye and some in her hair, and he'd even used her hair to wipe his cock dry and clean so that she'd had to run to the stream to clean herself, staring at her broken reflection and willing it to happen today.

And what had it all been for? They'd chosen the Bewley sisters, Katie Watkins and Gemma Horton to go instead. Verity had stared at old Tom Harris then, when they'd said who they'd chosen; she'd expected to be called up, and had made herself especially ready, only for *that* to happen. Tom Harris wouldn't even look at her, but the way he looked at the other girls made her think that maybe they'd done something with him too.

Verity was at the edge of the green now and she took one last anxious look around before darting down the path to the long barrow. Girls weren't meant to go down there, especially unaccompanied, after there'd been an offering: nobody was quite sure what might happen, but there were rumours, dark rumours. Verity had heard some of them and the thought made her sex twinge with anticipation.

She hurried through the woods, still barefoot from earlier, taking care not to step on anything sharp but keeping her eyes out for flowers too, darting off the path to gather the bluebells she saw. It was chillier now, out of the sun, and she hugged herself, pressing her arms against the hard nipples poking through her thin dress, rubbing at the goose pimples on her upper arm. She slowed when she got closer to the barrow itself, one side in shadow while the other was bathed in a golden light, for fear there might still be something there.

But after she'd listened for a while, her ears pricked for the slightest sound, Verity tiptoed out and circled the mound. The frames that the girls had been put on were still there and would be collected tomorrow, and her pulse raced as she saw the bunches of flowers lying scattered next to them. She wouldn't use those; she would collect her own.

Verity stepped out into the meadow, relaxing as the sun warmed her, and ran her fingers through the top of the long grass. There were dandelions, buttercups, speedwell, even a few poppies, as well as flowers she could not name, and she gathered what she could into a bunch. Then she returned to the mound.

It was obvious where she should go: the only place that was still in the sun, the western end. Trembling a little, excited and scared now in equal measure, she put the flowers down and then pulled her dress over her head, to leave it in a heap by the cross. Then she lay down, buckling her feet into the lower straps and positioning herself as best she could in imitation of the girls she'd seen there earlier. But not before she'd eased the stalks of the flowers into herself, pushing them up until only the petals protruded, an exotic bloom peeping out from between her legs. She hoped it would be enough: she wasn't sure if they'd come at all without being called by the horn. But she'd done all she could now.

Verity closed her eyes and tried to relax. Her heartbeat throbbed in her ears, and the sole of her left foot itched terribly. But she ignored it, concentrating instead on how her friends would look when she told them what she'd done. She suppressed a giggle as she pictured Jeannie Rose's face, her mouth open in astonishment, then curled her toes in delight at the thought.

Suddenly she heard a twig crack. She froze, every atom of her being straining to hear more. There was nothing for a few agonising seconds. Then she heard it. Heavy, deep breathing. There were footsteps too, and they were getting closer now, and closer still . . . She squeezed her eyes shut, fighting a terrible temptation to scream, to sit up and tear off the bonds around her feet and run as fast as she could back to the village.

Then her sunlight was blocked and Verity knew that it was in front of her. She heard it squat, then the flowers inside her were being twisted and were suddenly pulled out. She gasped at the sensation, then swallowed. She wasn't even sure if she'd be able to scream now. Her whole body was starting to shake. Something else touched her down there: a finger, and she groaned as it rubbed up and down her crease, smearing her juices along the length of her sex. As it leaned closer towards her she couldn't stop herself from moving her arms, reaching round to embrace it. She expected to touch bare skin or fur, only to find the coarse fabric of a jerkin under her fingers.

She opened her eyes and widened them in disbelief. A wolf mask loomed close to her face, cidery breath now wafting over her, and some boy had put his finger inside her. 'Get the fuck off!' Verity screamed, pushing hard against him.

The boy fell back, laughing. 'You should have seen yourself, Verity Collier. The look on your face –' He burst out laughing again, holding his sides theatrically.

Verity's eyes narrowed. 'Is that you, Patrick Taperell? If it is, I'm going to brain you so hard, you'll never –' She leaned forward to scrabble at the buckles round her ankles, only for the boy to grab her wrists and push her back.

'Uh-uh – no, you don't,' he said, shaking his head.

'Let me go!' cried Verity, pushing against him again. But her struggles only made him grip her all the harder.

'What, let a juicy girl like you go, when I've found her all tied up like this?' he murmured in her ear.

'It *is* you, Patrick, isn't it?' She was sure of it; she'd been to school with the boy and they'd sparred and flirted there, but nothing had ever come of it. Verity rather wished something had. 'Go on, take off your mask at least.'

The boy released one of Verity's wrists, cautiously, holding his hand in front of him as though he expected her to punch him in the face. Then, in one swift motion, he whisked off his mask. Patrick Taperell's face, the hair damp with sweat and pressed down on his forehead from the mask, grinned down at her.

'*Now* will you let me go, Patrick Taperell?' Verity asked, smiling a little at him and wiggling her hips. This wasn't what she'd come here for, but it'd do.

'I will not,' he said, returning his hand to her wrist. 'There's talk going round the village that you sucked old Tom Harris.'

Verity flushed a deep crimson. 'I did not!' she protested.

'Then why're you blushing, then?' Patrick laughed. Then, quickly and before she could stop him, he'd fastened one of the bands around her wrist.

'Hey! What are you doing?' she cried, dismayed.

145

Patrick chuckled. 'It'll be better like this. The wolfman won't come otherwise.' He pulled a face of mock horror and Verity smiled despite herself, only for him to fasten her other wrist to the cross. 'There. You'll be going nowhere now. Maybe I should just leave you for the elders to find in the morning.' The thought made him laugh. 'That'd make a fine sight – little cold you trembling in the morning chill, your hair all wet with dew. Up there – and here, too.' He clasped a hand over her sex and she gasped. 'Wet enough here already.'

He grinned at her then, and began to move down her body. 'Patrick?' she asked uncertainly. 'You wouldn't leave me all alone here, would you?' But her final question tailed off into a long groan as his head nestled between her thighs, his hands peeling the lips of her sex wide apart and his tongue licking her, mixing his spit with her grease, making her even wetter than before.

Verity pulled against the wrist buckles, enjoying the delicious sensation of being unable to move, unable to resist as Patrick's tongue wormed its way around her slippery folds, rubbing gently at her clit then pushing deeply inside her, sucking at her juices. She gasped in pleasure, her feet curling down.

'Oh, Patrick,' she whispered.

Then the tongue darted down further, licking around the base of her sex and tickling the sensitive band of flesh before her anus. And then he'd taken a tentative stab there, where she'd never been licked before, and a bolder one, pushing the tip of his tongue inside, the tightly clenched muscle relaxing to let him in.

'Oh Patrick, you filthy fucker,' Verity purred, wanting to put a hand on his head, to play with his hair as he licked her, pulling deliciously shivery

146

sensations out of her swollen quim. He moved back up to suck and nibble at her sex lips, darting his tongue in small stabs at her clit. Then he clamped his mouth over the hood and sucked hard at it, Verity squealing at the sensation. He paused then, pushing a thumb inside her, slowly, deliberately twisting it around, coating it with her juices, then running it down until it pressed against her anal bud.

Verity tried to stop him, whispering, 'No, Patrick, it's wrong.' But her protests were half-hearted, her anal whorl slick enough by now with her grease and his saliva for his thumb to slip in easily, and she felt her muscles tighten around the unfamiliar invasion.

Patrick had returned his attention to her clit now and was alternating sucks on it with hard rubs of his tongue against it, flicking it from side to side, all the while fucking her bumhole with his thumb, pushing it in and out, twisting it about, until the sensations blended into one, one delicious feeling of being used, being played with like a toy. Verity closed her eyes as the waves of pleasure began to mount, slowly at first, then more strongly, and then stronger still, the rhythm of Patrick's sucking and thumb-fucking driving her to the edge. Then she was there, screaming in ecstasy, not caring any more if anyone heard them, as Patrick sucked the tip of her sex into his mouth and pressed his teeth against her clit.

Her hips bucked against him, her limbs straining against their bonds, and Verity felt her arsehole clench around his thumb in ripples, keeping her at the peak, until finally she began to come down. Patrick was kissing her sex now, her clit too sensitive to be touched, and was slowly pulling his thumb from her anus.

Embarrassed by how easily she'd come and lost control in front of this boy, but still dizzy with the force of her orgasm, Verity opened her eyes and gazed down at Patrick's face. He grinned knowingly at her, his skin smeared with her juices. Then she looked up, at the thing looming behind him, the lips of its mouth pulled back in a bestial snarl.

Seven

The door opening felt like razors being scraped across Emma's brain. The knocking had appeared in her dream, she dimly remembered, growing louder and louder, and now whoever it was who wanted to come in had grown tired of waiting. Emma opened a bleary eye and met the gaze of the maid, whose eyes widened as she dragged her stare away from Emma's and took in the sight beyond.

'Two girls in one bed!' Emma heard her mutter in a rich Scotch burr. Then she saw her hurriedly make the sign of the cross and leave, closing the door gingerly behind her. It was still loud enough to wake Miriam up.

'Who was that?' she asked lazily, her eyes still closed, her body burrowing deeper under the duvet.

'The maid.' Emma closed her eyes again. It was far too early to get up, however much light was filtering through the curtains. At least she'd had the foresight to leave a glass of water on the side table, and she reached over and drank it gratefully, swallowing the cool liquid in great gulps. Now if she could only sleep for a few more hours, perhaps the dull insistent throbbing in her head might go away.

'The maid?' But Miriam had sat up now. 'Did she see us?' Emma groaned non-committally and pulled the duvet up around her shoulders. But Miriam seemed agitated. 'Emma! Did she see your tattoo?'

Dimly a memory began to emerge in Emma's mind, of a drunken visit to a tattoo parlour in town, open late at the weekend to take advantage of drunks with bravado. She groaned again, louder this time, as the dull ache that filled her brain began to coalesce around her shoulder. She remembered admiring the mark on Miriam, the paw or claw or whatever it was meant to be, Miriam had seemed even vaguer than usual. She'd decided to have one done herself to mark their happy reunion – Miriam had even insisted on paying the tattooist – before they'd returned to the hotel to lick each other until the dead weight of the vodka had finally brought unconsciousness. Oh, the vodka. Emma buried her face in the pillow.

Miriam shook her, lightly at first, then harder. 'Emma, you've got to wake up! Did the maid see your tattoo?'

Emma pushed her away, irritated now, sleep seeming ever more distant with Miriam's insistent demands. 'I don't know,' she mumbled. 'Probably.' She felt the mattress rise beneath her as Miriam got up, and she sprawled wider on the bed. Light flooded into the room as Miriam pulled back the curtains, making Emma wince even through her closed eyelids, and she pulled the duvet over her head. But she could still hear Miriam.

'Oh shit,' her friend said. There were bumping noises as Miriam moved around the room. 'They're coming.'

This was too much. Emma opened her eyes, shading them from the light with a hand. 'Who's coming? And draw the curtains, will you? That light's killing me.'

Miriam ignored her, stumbling off balance as she tried to pull her trousers on. Then, as Emma pulled the duvet over her head again, she sat down on the bed and shook her friend.

'Emma? You've got to get up. We've got to get out of here. Something very bad's going to happen if we don't leave now.'

Emma tried to ignore her, digging herself deeper under the duvet. If she played dead Miriam would ignore her, would stop playing this stupid game and let her go back to sleep. God only knew how Miriam was able to get up anyway; she'd drunk at least as much as Emma. But she was moving around faster now, pulling on her shoes, checking at the window again, then returning to Emma's side.

'Emma? Please?' There was a note of desperation in Miriam's voice and for the first time Emma turned to her, to look into her eyes. Miriam was panicked, there was no doubt about it. But there was no way Emma could get up. Not just yet.

'You go,' she mumbled into the pillow, turning away from her friend. 'I'll stay.'

Miriam paused, hovering over her, then stood up. 'Come to the castle when you're ready. Tell them that I sent you,' she said, her voice colder now. 'I have to go. Don't say I didn't warn you.' And with that she was gone. Emma listened to her footsteps growing fainter down the stairs, then allowed herself to relax again, to sink into the soft mattress, sliding deeper down, down . . .

A hand was shaking her. Miriam had come back. Couldn't the girl take a hint? Emma reached up to shake it off, still half asleep, only to find her arm held in a vicelike grip. She opened her eyes, suddenly wide awake and alarmed. There was a woman leaning over her, someone she'd never seen before, probably in her mid-forties, wearing a long grey dress buttoned up and with a high collar, a thin silver cross dangling from a necklace, her greying hair tied behind her head in a tight bun, pulling the skin of her face so far back that it had an unnatural sheen. There was a maniacal look in her eyes.

'What –?' Emma began as she turned in bed to get a better look at the woman. As she did so, she realised that there was a man in the room too, a bearded man also dressed in grey, standing by the door. She sat up in bed. The woman's grip on her arm didn't slacken for a second. 'Who the hell are you? How did you get in here?' Emma demanded angrily. She was not a little scared.

'So!' the woman crowed, her eyes fixed on Emma's shoulder. 'You're one of them! You slut, you dare to bring your filth away from your cursed village to infect us?'

'What the fuck?' Emma struggled to get up and away from the woman but she was held firmly down. The woman was stronger than she looked. The strength of the insane, Emma thought wildly. That was it, the woman must be mad. Too late, she realised that this was what Miriam had wanted to avoid. But how had she known this was going to happen? The woman turned to the man, who advanced, holding a length of rope and a handful of pieces of sacking.

'No, don't!' Emma struggled as the man clamped a hand over her face, pushing a wadded-up oily cloth against her mouth. Emma shook her head from side to side but the man grabbed her hair to hold her head in place, then pinched her nostrils. As she gasped for air, he crammed the gag into her mouth, then pulled a sacking bag over her head. This done, he grappled with her arms, easily taking hold of her two wrists in one hand, and tied them together with a rope. Then he did the same to her ankles.

Emma felt herself being lifted up as though she were a child and hoisted onto a broad shoulder. She squealed and bucked her legs back, trying to unbalance herself, but a warning hand slapped against her buttocks. She realised with a mixture of shame and anxiety that she was only wearing a long sleeveless T-shirt with no underwear, and the irrational fear entered her head of the other hotel guests being able to see her nakedness, before she thought again of the far worse things that were happening to her.

It would be good to be seen, she realised. Someone must see me; someone will help. Then, as she was carried down the stairs and out through a door, she thought that she must remember which way she was being taken; to be able to escape, it was important to know first where you were. Emma clung to the thought as she heard a car door open. Then she felt herself being slung bodily inside to lie along what she assumed was the back seat. A rough blanket was flung over her. She squealed again as the car door was closed, more panicked now – why had nobody stopped them? – and kicked her heels against the door. Then the front doors were opened and the car started.

Emma tried to keep track of where they were going, counting time between the turns, but after the fifth or sixth turn she realised that it was hopeless and she wondered instead why she had been taken. The woman's language had been strange, more extreme than she would have expected from someone simply offended by the idea of two women sleeping together, although she knew that some of the communities here were more conservative than anywhere in the rest of the country. And the cross ... maybe these people were religious fanatics?

Emma heard the crunch of gravel as the car slowed to a stop. The back doors opened and she was pulled out and slung over a shoulder again, her skin tightening against the cold air. A door was opened and she was carried down several corridors before finally being sat in a chair, her wrists secured to the back.

'Put the blanket over her legs, Brother Joshua. I don't want to see her – indecency.' Emma heard the woman's voice, quivering as it paused before the last word. Then the sacking was lifted and the gag removed.

Emma winced at the sudden light, squeezing her eyes shut briefly. Then, before she could stop herself, she began to babble. 'Please let me go, I won't tell anyone you took me, just let me walk away and we'll pretend none of this ever happened.'

The woman, sitting behind a desk opposite Emma, smiled thinly. Emma looked around. The room felt like a prison cell, painted a drab institutional pale green, with flakes of paint peeling off to show the dull colours the room had been painted in before. There were no windows; the only light came from a bare light bulb hanging from the ceiling. There was a radiator in one corner, painted the same colour as the rest of the room, but it didn't seem to be on: the room was freezing. Emma changed tack.

'Whatever you think I've done, I haven't. I don't know why you've taken me. There must be some mistake.'

The woman cleared her throat. 'Have you finished?'

Emma stared at her incredulously.

'I expect you'd like to know who we are and why you're here. That, I am at liberty to tell you. We are the Order of Sanctity, dedicated to Saint Desdemona, and you are here because you are a member of that demonic cult ravaging the very fabric of our land.'

Emma paused before replying, unsure that she'd heard the woman correctly. 'I'm a member of a demonic cult?' she finally exploded. 'What the fuck gives you that idea?'

The woman's thin lips tightened. 'If you use language like that in my presence again you will be gagged. As for how we know you belong to the cult – you have the mark.' She nodded towards Emma's shoulder.

'What? This?' Emma turned her head to look at the tattoo. 'But I only had this done last night. You can see it's fresh – it hasn't even healed over properly! Look!'

The woman turned to the man standing by the door, the same man who Emma presumed had carried her from the hotel, and gave him a quizzical look. He nodded. The woman turned back to Emma.

'You may be only newly a member of the cult, but you belong nonetheless.'

'But I only had it done because my friend had one!' Emma protested. 'I don't know what it stands for!'

The woman stiffened. 'There are other ways of determining whether or not you belong with them. All I need to do is tell you the story of Saint Desdemona and see how you respond.' She smiled thinly. Emma simply stared back at her.

'About a hundred years ago, a convent stood on this spot. It had been here for about three hundred years and all had gone well until the convent was visited by Father Tarnhelm, a precursor to that wretched Garner of yours.' She glared at Emma, who could only shrug and shake her head.

'Tarnhelm introduced the custom of having each of the nuns handed a slip of paper every morning. On

155

one of these slips would be marked an X. The person who received the X would be obliged to play the part of temptress to the others, trying to lead them into sin and seeing which ones followed. I suspect that on some days all the slips were blank but everyone assumed someone else was the temptress and acted as though it were the case.

'At first it might have seemed a good plan. The nuns would set each other theological riddles or traps, subtle temptations such as to suggest that "To obey the letter of the rules is only for imbeciles who cannot understand their spirit." But the cycle of temptation soon deteriorated until the nuns would make lewd suggestions to each other, and then not only suggestions but overtures. Some became well versed in the art of seduction and Tarnhelm must have delighted in hearing the details of the nuns' falls from grace at confession. Indeed, I believe he only initiated the routine to see which nuns would fall into the life of a whore first. Then he would take the opportunity to exploit their weakness to the full himself.

'Some of the nuns would even pretend to be the temptress when it was not their turn, until nearly all the innocents were locked into a cycle of temptation, sacrilegious lust and penitence that was exploited to the hilt by Tarnhelm, who twisted their regret further into guilt by making them recount in the confessional every detail of what they'd done. Then they would have to show him themselves and act out their filthy actions with the Father Confessor first as voyeur, then, later, as participant.'

A wildness had taken hold of the woman's eyes now as she stared with a glazed expression at the wall.

'Once the disease had taken hold it spread like an epidemic. At first they used pictures of men that they shared while touching themselves. Or they pushed rosary beads inside themselves and made up lewd rhymes to chant as they pulled them slowly out.'

Emma stared at the woman, her mouth opening in disbelief. But the older female ignored her, punctuating her tale now by banging her hand on the table.

'One of them stole into the chapel at night and broke the stained glass, then used a shard of glass to whittle down a length of wood that she'd taken from a fallen bough in the grounds. She'd never seen a man's –' here the woman paused and a strangled expression crossed her face before she continued '– parts, and had only the drawings the other nuns had shown her to go on, all grotesquely oversized weapons with monstrous heads. When it was in a shape approximating what she thought it should be she sanded down the surface using stones she'd found while gardening. Then she oiled the wood using grease she'd stolen from the kitchen, her lust and curiosity leading her from one sin to another.

'When it was finally ready she used the remainder of the grease she'd taken to oil herself, although in truth she need not have worried: her fear and excitement lent her a natural lubricant. She hid in a private cell, one designated for prayer and silent meditation, and tried to ease it inside herself. But she was too tight at first and cried out in pain. One of the other nuns, Sister Esmeralda, who'd become the most enthusiastic temptress, overheard her as she passed the room and after listening outside for a brief period she entered, to see the other nun engaged in an act of fellatio on the phallus while pushing two fingers inside herself in an attempt to widen her entrance. Her eyes were closed.'

The woman's own eyes had narrowed now and she

seemed rapt in the telling of her tale, her body trembling slightly.

'She was so lost in her own lewd imaginings that she failed to hear Sister Esmeralda enter the room and was shocked to be caught in this position. But Esmeralda was a more experienced wanton and congratulated the other nun on her initiative. Esmeralda had been using candles on herself before, in secret, but now that she'd found another nun with the same idea – and a bolder version – she decided to take her filth one step further. Before this the nuns had not touched one another, nor had they discussed the urges that nearly all of them felt, save with Father Tarnhelm.

'Sister Esmeralda changed that by taking the phallus from the other nun and demonstrating its use. The candles she had used meant that she was stretched and broken already, but even for her it was difficult. Yet still she persevered and had soon pushed the head inside herself, letting out little coos of pleasure that first astounded and then delighted the other nun.

'Yet Esmeralda's greatest pleasure was in corrupting others. Soon after she'd demonstrated that the phallus could be used she helped the other nun prepare herself for its use by becoming her lover in the basest way possible, licking her and using her own fingers inside her. After that the nuns stopped at nothing. The monstrous phallus was passed around from nun to nun, each one instructing the next in its use, demonstrating it first on themselves, then on the others.

'Esmeralda, in whom some remaining shred of decency manifested itself in an utterly perverse desire to marry her sluttish behaviour to punishment, also began another trend. The wooden phallus had largely replaced the candles used hitherto and had now developed into a veritable fetish object, a focus of idol worship, its body marked with striations where the nuns had dug into it, seeking new sensations and seeking also to mark the phallus, already honeyed with the juices of almost every one of them, as their own. Esmeralda began to use candles again, but lit ones this time, kneeling on all fours and reciting prayers or singing hymns as the molten wax ran down the stalk to sting her swollen excited flesh. She showed others too, and soon they made a competition of it, to see who could let the candle burn down the furthest before crying out for it to be extinguished. Some of the nuns, keen to excel in the game, even took to plucking out their hairs near where the candle would go, further demonstrating, they imagined, the mortification of the flesh.

'And finally one of their number, perhaps Esmeralda again, greased her bottom-hole and pushed the candle inside, the ease with which it was done suggesting that the hole concerned was not entirely virgin. The candle was lit and the nun's rear held high in the air, her bottom twitching as the hot wax began to pool around the stretched ring before dripping down into the crease below. The nun was able to keep the candle lit for longer than before and this became the new mark by which they judged themselves, a sick parody of the rituals of abjection and mortification that they should have prized themselves on.

'And yet not all of the nuns succumbed. One, Sister Desdemona, accepted the role of temptress but would do nothing with it. She would never be drawn into the sordid games of the other nuns, even as the convent descended into anarchy, even as the Mother Superior – no less – allowed herself to be flagellated by Tarnhelm in a sexual way. All the nuns save for Sister

Desdemona had given up any pretence of goodness, of purity, of sanctity by now. The temptations were little more than licence to behave in ever more obscene fashion, until some even spoke of consorting with the Horned One, of putting on the heads of beasts and returning to the old ways.

'Sister Desdemona did not criticise the others or attempt to seek help outside the convent. She merely continued in her own way, praying even as the others whispered obscenities into her ear, seeing to the daily needs of the convent while the nuns played breathless games in the rose garden. Tarnhelm was furious, of course, and the Mother Superior was frustrated: some of the nuns had begun to believe – heresy above all heresies! – that the road to the Lord was through indulging in the worst sexual excesses. But with Desdemona still there, remaining pure, a jewel in a mire of filth, their belief could not be final: she acted as a beacon to the others, showing them how far they had lost their way.

'Tarnhelm and the Mother Superior did everything in their power to break her. Routinely using the scourge, they punished her for imagined infractions, and once they allowed the other nuns to wrap her breasts in rose stems, the thorns pricking her delicate flesh. But she continued to pray, more fervently now, although she made no attempt to leave. Tarnhelm finally hit upon a scheme that he must have been sure would work. Gathering all the nuns together, he announced that Sister Desdemona would be punished for having soiled her bed during the night – a complete fabrication, of course. But Sister Desdemona did not complain and submitted to her punishment. Yet it was no ordinary scourging Tarnhelm had in mind. He had the Sister bound to a chair with no seat and forced her to drink glass after glass of water, pouring it down her throat even though she begged them to stop. He then placed an image of Christ below the chair, ensuring that she was obliged to urinate on the figure of the Saviour.'

The woman paused and nodded to the man, who moved towards Emma and unexpectedly slid his finger into her crotch, under the blanket, forcing it against her sex, still greasy from the night before. He pulled it out with a smug smile and held it up where it glistened in the light. The woman's features tightened and she stood up.

'Since you find the tale of our beloved Sister Desdemona's martyrdom so arousing you are obviously at least an incorrigible slut, and most likely also a member of that accursed cult.'

'But that wasn't –' Emma started. But the woman cut her off peremptorily.

'We have ways of curing sluts of their disease. Bring her to the training room,' she ordered the man.

After escorting Emma down a corridor to another room, which contained some kind of exercise bike, the man pushed her down into a chair by the wall and started to pull up her T-shirt. She didn't know what was going on – was he just after a quick look, or was he going to touch her down there again? – and started to kick and scream. But the man simply wrapped a strip of rubber with a red ball attached to it around her head, forcing the ball into Emma's mouth so that she couldn't make any sound apart from a high-pitched keening.

Then he stripped the T-shirt all the way off her. She glared at him, pressing her thighs together, trying to cover herself but acutely aware of his stare on the neat little trim where she'd had her pubic area waxed only a few days before.

Almost as soon as he'd stripped Emma bare, the woman came in. The man turned to her.

'I'm afraid I've had to gag the slut. She was screaming like a baby.'

The woman smiled and nodded. 'That's quite all right. I've come to expect that sort of behaviour from this sort. But we'll train it out of her, won't we?' she asked, addressing Emma who shook her head from side to side and gave a muffled squeal.

'You can take the gag off her now, Brother Joshua,' the woman continued. 'I'm sure she'll be getting a good idea by now of what's in store for her if she misbehaves.' Brother Joshua unclipped the rubber strip from behind her head and she spat out the red ball.

'I expect you're wondering exactly what we have in store for you,' the woman resumed, turning back to Emma. 'This bicycle has been specially designed for just such wantons as yourself. We have tested it, of course, but you'll still be one of our first subjects and it will be intriguing to see how you respond.'

The woman moved over to the bicycle and touched the seat, which was covered by what looked like rubber nubs of varying lengths and had a web of straps hanging down from it. 'As you can see, this is a modified exercise bicycle. You sit here –' she indicated the seat '– where you will be held in a harness, and you put your hands here –' she motioned to the handlebars '– where you'll be cuffed in, of course.

'As you pedal, this seat will vibrate. The vibrations are designed to arouse you sexually and you will have electrodes attached to you down there –' the woman looked pointedly at Emma's crotch '– which will run to the computer –' Emma followed her gaze to a bank of blinking lights on the wall '– and determine the level of your arousal.

'Should you allow yourself to become aroused, the electrodes will give you a short sharp shock. This will also happen if you stop pedalling or slow down below a certain level, which I am sure you will discover for yourself soon enough. Is that quite understood?'

'Yes,' Emma whispered.

'Good. Brother Joshua?' The woman motioned to the man. He took Emma under the armpits, lifted her up and dragged her, struggling, to the bike, where he easily parted her legs despite her efforts to keep them closed, sat her down on the seat and buckled her into the harness. Its straps bisected her bottom cheeks on one side and framed her pussy on the other before joining a loop around her waist.

Brother Joshua then took two clips attached to long wires running from the computer and bent down, his face level with Emma's crotch.

'Lean back,' the woman called out. When Emma didn't move, the man pushed her, and the woman, who'd moved behind her, held her by the shoulders as her sex was slowly exposed. She was still damp from the night before, as they'd already discovered, and the fear and anticipation of what was going to happen to her only heightened a sense of arousal she was ashamed to admit to herself. Emma's cheeks coloured as Brother Joshua dipped a finger inside her. There was nothing sexual about the move but the way in which he did it, just checking her like some scientific experiment, made her juice a little more. She felt her nipples firm up and stick out.

Then Brother Joshua attached the first clip to the mouth of her sex. Emma swallowed, expecting it to hurt, but the springs loading the clips couldn't have been too strong as the grip merely felt uncomfortable – as did the second one, which he attached to the hood of her clitoris. Then the woman released her

163

and she sank back down onto the seat, feeling her weight mash the clips – painfully, this time – into her sensitive flesh.

The man cuffed Emma's wrists to the handlebars, placed her feet on the pedals, which were, she was glad to note, of soft rubber, and looked quizzically at the woman. When she nodded, he threw a switch that was set in the wall, and the bike began to hum and vibrate slightly.

'I'd start now, if I were you,' offered the woman, smiling thinly. 'Otherwise you'll get a nasty shock.'

But Emma just sat there, still too numbed by everything that had just happened to move, looking from the woman to the man as though expecting them to release her, to admit that it had all been a joke, that she was free to leave now. Then the shock hit her, jolts of electricity coursing through her pussy and up into her chest, making her whole body shake, a horrible feeling that left her skin ringing. Panicked, she began to pedal – and felt the seat move beneath her.

From the corner of her eye she saw the woman move to the door. 'How long are you going to leave me here?' Emma called out, unable to keep the mounting panic out of her voice.

The woman chuckled. 'Well, ideally you should have no sexual response to the stimulation. But, given your behaviour so far, I'm not sure if you'll be able to manage that during your first session on the bike. Brother Joshua will stay here and I'll leave it up to him to work out when you've had enough.'

She left, and Emma turned to see the man staring at her.

Despite herself, she could feel her body responding to the moving seat, the long vibrating nubs having already worked her sex lips apart and begun to press

164

into the soft pink folds beneath. Emma tried to think of something – anything – to take her mind away from the thrum of the seat, the vibrations that were shaking her to the core and making her melt inside: the farm where she'd grown up, the school she'd been to, the dull lessons she'd had to attend. She tried to remember the faces of schoolfriends, but the faces of lovers she'd had came unbidden into her mind instead: the memories of furtive fumblings, of small cries of release out by the bike sheds. She felt herself sink further onto the seat, feeling the rubber press against her clit, hard now, unable to stop herself from giving in to the feeling ... until another jolt of electricity bit through her sex and she let out a sob of despair.

'Please.' Emma turned to the man. 'Please stop it.' She felt another wave of arousal flood through her and tried to lift herself off the seat, dreading the inevitable shock. Brother Joshua looked impassively back at her.

'I'll do anything for you,' Emma begged. The vibrations of the seat made it hard to think clearly but she could see that the man was aroused – the bulge in his pants was unmistakable. 'You could turn off the machine and I'll help you with that,' she offered, looking pointedly at his crotch. Her voice was breathless now; she'd begun to pant, unable to stop herself.

Brother Joshua flushed, looking embarrassed. 'I'll not allow myself to be tempted by you, slut.'

With a groan, Emma slumped back down onto the seat, feeling it move her in just the right way, the nubs kneading her tender flesh, caressing it like thousands of tiny hard tongues. She felt herself flood onto the seat again, only for the electric jolt to course through her, stiffening her legs and leaving her aching afterwards, a sob catching in her throat.

But this time Emma was too far gone for it to dent her arousal. The charge had even made her more swollen down there, she was sure, more sensitive than ever before. She started to grind herself against the seat, pushing down as hard as she could, pedalling faster, feeling the seat vibrate quicker, feeling the energy build up inside her, unstoppable now. The fire started in her womb, then sent out tendrils that filled her body from her fingertips to her toes before exploding in her brain. Another jolt hit her at just the same time, filling her cunt with molten fire, and she arched her back and screamed, the come gloriously high, bucking her in the seat. But it was painful too, as though her sex had been scalded.

As Emma came she stopped pedalling and another jolt hit her soon afterwards, purely painful now. Her pussy had become oversensitive and she started to pedal again, sobbing as she felt the seat rubbing against her. 'It's too much,' she cried. 'Please stop it.'

Blearily, through her tears she saw a smile twitch on Brother Joshua's lips and he moved over to the computer. He flicked a switch and the bike juddered to a halt, the machinery still whirring then slowing with a gradually descending whine.

'Four minutes, thirty-two seconds,' he called out. 'Faster than our first test subject.' He smiled, evidently emboldened by her weakness. 'But then, we *knew* you were a slut.' He moved towards Emma, then reached down with gloved hands between her legs. 'Hmm,' he said thoughtfully as he probed, Emma squealing as he pinched her oversensitive clit. 'Fully erect clitoris, about seven millimetres. Perhaps this'll teach you not to respond so easily.'

166

As Emma started to shake her head, scarcely able to believe what was happening to her, Brother Joshua moved back over to the machine. The bike seat began to vibrate again.

'But they might hurt her!' Miriam exclaimed.

The mistress didn't seem concerned and took her by the arm to walk her towards the rose garden in front of the castle.

'Can't you do anything?' Miriam asked, exasperated.

The mistress turned to her and smiled. 'I have faith that your friend will find her way here. She will be unharmed.'

Bewildered by the other woman's certainty, Miriam allowed herself to be pulled along. Insects buzzed lazily around the trellises in the rose garden – the tight buds of the flowers were already visible. It was warm today, but although the mistress still wore her furs she didn't seem to be put out by the heat. Miriam couldn't imagine sweat on that alabaster skin for a second.

The mistress continued to pull her through the avenues of rose bushes towards a wall at the end. Miriam had not been to this part of the garden before and saw for the first time that there was a small door of plain unvarnished sun-bleached wood set in the wall. The mistress seemed to be walking towards it and Miriam, suddenly scared, began to pull back.

'Where are we going?' she asked. 'I should be practising for the circus. There are preparations for the feast tonight,' she said wildly, looking behind her. The burly coachman stood at the other end of the rose garden, watching them.

The mistress's grip on Miriam's arm tightened.

'This is the only preparation that need concern you,' she hissed. 'After this you will be one of us for ever.'

'No!' Miriam, panicked by the note of grimness in the mistress's voice, tried to pull away but the other woman only held her more tightly. As she struggled another pair of hands took her shoulders and held her firmly. She turned to see the coachman staring impassively at her.

The mistress let out a long breath. 'Think of everything that has happened to you, Miriam. Are you not happier now than you were? Do you not feel stronger, bolder than before?'

Miriam didn't feel strong at all now but she managed to mutter, 'Yes.'

The mistress laughed and transferred her grip to Miriam's elbow. 'I understand why you are scared. Any great change fills the uninitiated with fear. But fear must be resisted. Change must be embraced, each leap into the unknown made without fear of the consequences.'

Miriam stared at her, confused.

The mistress pulled a long, elaborately decorated key from the pocket of her furs and inserted it into the lock of the door in the wall.

'What is this place?' Miriam asked breathlessly.

'This? This is the walled garden,' announced the mistress. She swung the door open silently and ducked to step through. Miriam followed, the coachman pushing her through the door.

Beyond the walled garden's entrance a long, tall and neatly trimmed yew hedge filled Miriam's field of vision. Directly in front of them a gap in it showed only another hedge beyond. The mistress turned to Miriam and put a hand up to stroke the marks on her neck, a wistful look on her face. 'You have been bitten once already. Now we shall finish your initiation.'

She turned left between the hedges, then darted immediately right, the coachman pushing Miriam directly behind her. Miriam tried to keep the layout of the maze in her head but she was quickly made dizzy by the endless twists and turns and eventually allowed herself to be passively led through the hedges. What the mistress had told her filled her with fear – she couldn't help feeling it. But there was another kind of anticipation, as well as pride. Not all of the people at the castle had been marked as she had: many of the girls in the circus group, including Alice, were there simply, as far as Miriam could make out, because they supported Garner's ideas. She didn't know why she'd been singled out, selected especially for this treatment, but she knew enough to take it as a compliment. And given how much better she'd felt since the first change, the thought of the changes that might follow now thrilled her.

As though he realised that Miriam no longer needed to be forced, the coachman relaxed his grip on her. Now she followed the mistress unaided, the twists and turns of the maze, the hedges that blocked off anything else from her field of vision, having a hypnotic effect on her. When they finally emerged into the centre she was disorientated and confused to find herself in open space again.

The centre of the maze was circular, with an upright human-height wooden X secured in the ground. Leather straps hung from wrist-and-ankle securing rings.

The mistress turned to Miriam. 'Strip,' she ordered.

As though in a dream Miriam peeled her clothes off, unflustered by the gaze of the coachman on her naked skin. The sun was directly overhead now and Miriam's toes curled into the short grass at her feet. She enjoyed the sensation.

The mistress beckoned towards the cross with her head. 'Climb up.'

Miriam obeyed and the coachman slipped her ankles and wrists into the worn leather straps, then tightened them so that she was held firmly in place. Miriam flexed her muscles experimentally. There was no give in her bonds.

The mistress then unbuttoned her fur coat and let it slip from her shoulders as the coachman moved behind her to take it from her. Miriam was astonished to see her without the coat, partly because she'd come to associate it with her but also because of what she wore underneath. Her stockings ended at the tops of her thighs, death's-head clips attaching them to her suspender belt. The motif was repeated on the ribs of the corset she wore over a white negligee: the empty eyes of the grinning skulls seemed to bore into Miriam's brain. She wore a necklace of carved severed heads too, the faces green, the necks a bloody red, with tongues variously swollen and distorted in grotesque postures of death. But most remarkable was the large tattoo covering her shaved pubis: an angular death's head gently curving to the swell of her belly.

The coachman came forward again and handed the mistress a small jar into which she dipped her fingers before pressing them to Miriam's sex. Miriam stiffened at the unexpected icy cold of her fingers and the casual authority with which she applied the salve.

She then turned her back on Miriam and began to chant in a low hypnotic tone, the coachman echoing her words.

Spirits from the deep
Who never sleep;
Spirits from the grave

170

Without a soul to save;
Spirits of the trees
That grow upon the leas;
Spirits of the air,
Foul and black, not fair;
Water spirits hateful,
To ships and bathers fateful;
Spirits of the earthbound dead
That glide with noiseless tread;
Spirits of heat and fire,
Destructive in your ire;
Spirits of cold and ice,
Patrons of crime and vice –
Oh spirits, be kind to me!
Wolves, vampires, satyrs, ghosts!
Elect of all devilish hosts!
I pray you send hither,
Send hither, send hither,
That great grey shape that makes men shiver!
Shiver, shiver, shiver!
Come, come, come!

By the time the mistress had finished, the salve had begun to do something to Miriam. It was making her sex swell, it seemed to her, prickling her slightly, although the sensation was not unpleasant.

The mistress turned back to Miriam and took a long look at her, her head cocked to one side. As if aware of the unspoken question in Miriam's eyes she said, 'I will return to release you myself when it is done. That is, of course, if he does not do it himself.' Then she turned away, and she and the coachman vanished into the hedges.

As the mistress departed Miriam's fear began to return. Was she going to see something like the creature that had attacked Dr Cavendish? It had been a fearful sight, a loathsome thing in appearance, even if Miriam was grateful for everything it had given her. But as the memory of it returned to her she started to struggle against her bonds.

Then she heard it. The squeak of a door. At first she thought it must be the mistress and the coachman leaving the maze, but then she remembered that that door had opened smoothly, noiselessly. This was a different door.

Miriam's heart was beating fast now and her mouth had gone dry. She turned her head from left to right, trying to catch a glimpse of the entrance to the centre of the maze. But the cross was positioned so that it was impossible for her to see. She could hear, though, and she held her breath at the first sounds she heard: a pitter-patter of feet – or something harder than feet – moving quickly around the hedges. There was a new smell in the air now too, mingling with the yew and the mild scents of the rose garden: a smell of something feral and goatish, coming closer.

The running sound grew louder, pausing then moving back the way it had come. And there was something else on top of it, a chittering sound of annoyance when the running stopped.

The smell, which had seemed rank at first to Miriam, now took on other qualities and she breathed in great draughts of it, letting it fill her lungs. She'd never smelled anything quite like it, a heady scent that seemed to pass straight from her nostrils to her groin, making her sex swell and moisten in response. Her sex lips were still tingling from the effects of the salve and her nipples were lengthening, acutely sensitive in the gentle sunlight.

The sounds and smell were closer still now and Miriam groaned in anticipation, grinding her hips in a slow circle against the cross, her pussy aching with need. She felt the first trickle of her arousal begin to run down her leg, her fear forgotten now, willing the thing to come closer, to take her, use her . . .

There was a grunt of surprise behind her, then the sound of a few slow, cautious steps, Miriam's acute hearing picking up everything there was to hear, and she closed her eyes to help her concentrate. When the hand touched her she cried out in surprise at the strength of the sensation as well as from shock, her skin trembling. She opened her eyes to look down at it, half expecting to see a furred claw. But it was a hand, hairier than most, the nails more hornlike and longer than usual, but still a hand. It moved up from her belly to caress the underside of her breast. Then it pinched her nipple and Miriam moaned, craning her head around to try and see. The smell was overpowering now.

Then the hand had released its grip and after a hop to her side the creature stood in front of her. Miriam's eyes widened and she opened her mouth to speak, to scream, but no sound came out. The being put a finger to its lips and smiled, then moved round fully.

Miriam's stare drank in the sight. It was smaller than most men, maybe five feet tall, with short curly hair and a straggly beard hanging down from its chin. Two short horns, yellowed and with a slight twist, sprouted just beyond its hairline and it regarded Miriam with a bored, slightly tired expression in its oval goat eyes.

Its chest, torso and arms looked human, save for the stark lines of long erect black hairs that ran down each forearm. But from the waist down it was closer to a beast, its legs thickly furred, the hair matted and dull, the joints impossibly bending back the wrong way so that it seemed to have an inverted knee, the legs ending in off-white hooves. As it moved from side to side, studying Miriam, she recognised the sound its hooves made, the one she'd strained to listen to earlier.

But her attention was most drawn to the thing between its legs: a long cock with a furred shaft and an elongated head. It seemed to pulse as she watched it, growing until it reared up, grotesquely large, nearly touching the thing's belly, with a pair of furred balls cupped neatly below.

The creature moved towards her now and reached for the bonds that secured her wrists, staring at her and chittering anxiously. Miriam tried to smile at it but she couldn't read its eyes nor its alien expression. She knew that she should have been scared and part of her was. But she was also exquisitely aroused: the combination of the salve she'd been given and the pheromone-loaded scent of this thing, this beautiful creature, was almost too much for her to bear.

As the being released her second wrist grip Miriam put her free hand on its shoulder, feeling it flinch at first from her touch. Then it grew calmer, its chittering becoming less agitated, and she caressed the tight curls on its head before tugging at its short horns as it unfastened the leather straps from her ankles. It took her by the hand, in a perverse and unexpectedly chivalrous gesture, and motioned to the grass.

Miriam lay down, feeling the blades of grass flatten out under her, and spread her legs, displaying herself for the thing. It stared at her greasy sex, touching its cock, then lay down on top of her.

Miriam took hold of the cock, reaching between the creature's legs to guide the penis towards herself. The head was long and wedge-shaped, like the head of a snake, and she brushed it up and down over the entrance to her sex, shivering each time it pushed over her clitoris. But the thing was chittering impatiently now, running its hands over her belly and breasts, leaving long red marks where it clawed at her skin. She smiled uncertainly up at it, spread her legs as wide as she could and began to ease the head of its cock inside her.

This close, the thing's scent made her near-delirious with lust and she badly wanted to feel its cock inside her. It was so big, perhaps too big, and she tried to close her hand around its furred shaft to gauge its width and see if it would fit. But she couldn't reach all the way around it and in the process accidentally grazed the creature's balls with her knuckles, which seemed to drive it into a frenzy. It gripped her breasts hard and pushed with its cock: half of the head slid in and then stopped, the flanged curve before the shaft began proving too large.

Chittering in rage and frustration, the thing pulled and slapped at Miriam's breasts, pinching the nipples and tugging hard on them, and she squealed as she felt her milk spurt out onto its face. It stared down at her, milk dripping into its beard, its eyes wide with surprise. Then it squeezed her breasts again to see the bluish-white milk jet out. Miriam moaned at the intensely pleasurable sensation – and then it was as though something inside her had given way and she relaxed to let the end of the creature's cock in, her eyes popping wide open at the strain, the sensation of fullness, of being stretched to the limit. Then the shaft followed, sliding in easily after the oversized head but still filling her sex.

It started to fuck her with short, sharp stabs that made her catch her breath each time, plucking at her nipples all the while and dipping its head to lick at her breasts, squeezing the milk into its mouth.

Miriam ran her hands over its back and down to its buttocks, gripping the fur on each cheek and pulling it hard, drawing the thing deeper into herself, wanting still more of it inside her. The being's cock filled her with sensation – and then the thing began to tremble, its shaft seeming to swell even larger within her. As she moaned in ecstasy at the sensation of its seed, thick and ice-cold, spurting inside her, its jaws gaped and it bared its yellowed teeth before sinking them into her shoulder.

Eight

When James awoke the sun had not yet risen. He felt exhausted, drained, but the thought of everything that had happened yesterday made him overexcited as well. He knew he had to leave the village before its occupants woke up. The vicar had locked the girl away after James had used her three times, surprising himself with his energy, and he'd curled up to sleep on a dingy sofa in the living room, not even bothering to ask the vicar if it was OK or if there was anywhere more comfortable.

His clothes had been found; there was no point in trying to retrieve them. But at least he'd had the foresight to keep his wallet with him and as he opened the door and peered out into the already lightening gloom he knew what he was going to do in Porthness, as soon as he could. There was nobody in the streets. Probably all nursing cider hangovers, James thought. The shapes of the houses were beginning to solidify in the clear light of dawn. There was a chill dampness in the air but the sky was clear, the rare strand of cloud tinted a violent pink by the rising sun. James realised as he walked cautiously towards the green that he had never heard so many birds singing.

The ground was still strewn with petals and garlands, their colours becoming ever more vibrant in the growing light, and the ribbons from the maypole on the village green swayed to and fro in the gentle breeze. The glint of something shining on the ground caught James's eye and he reached down to take a look. A number of coins had become embedded in the earth, churned up a little from where the dancers had circled the maypole, and James scratched at one, trying to pick it out of the soil, until it came loose in his hand. He'd been expecting a two-pound coin – it was the right size and weight – but he quickly realised that it wasn't one, was in fact like nothing he'd seen before. For a moment he thought it might be a Roman coin but although the minting looked rough it was also fresh. One side of the coin bore the image of a wolf's head in profile, crudely done, with a stippling effect around the edge. There was no writing and no numerals. On the flip side was the profile of a man and although it too was roughly done James was sure he'd seen the man before. It only took a few seconds for him to realise that it was Garner. His heart thudding now in his excitement, he scrabbled for the other coins, wiped the mud off them onto his tunic and put them in his pocket. There were no words or numbers on any of the coins: if they had a value it was probably denoted by size and weight and maybe by the metals used, although James couldn't tell what they were. Copper for the smaller coins, possibly, and gold plate for the larger ones; none seemed to be silver.

James stood up again and looked around. There was still nobody in view. The thought of trying to walk back to the next village along the muddy track through the woods seemed less and less attractive. He decided to try the road, cracked and furrowed but at least dry, with wild flowers adding dashes of pink and blue to the blackish grey of the tarmac.

He glimpsed a flash of even brighter colour to his right, in a grove of oak trees on the edge of the village, where only a few more houses were dotted about. After quickly looking behind him to check that there was nobody else in view he darted towards it. The low sun painted the mossy bark of the trees orange and he saw that in the centre of the grove was a low circular stone structure with a hole in the middle. He peered into it and saw, ten feet below, his reflection dancing in the water. There was a wooden bucket to the side, attached to a length of rope, but what had caught his eye from the road was a large colourful picture in a wooden frame, leaning against one of the trees facing the well.

It was huge, well above James's head, and as he drew closer he could see that it was made from flowers, pine cones, pebbles, quartzes and lichens, all pressed into a bed of moist clay. The outside edge was ringed with two garlands, one of white flowers enclosing one of blue. But it was the picture itself that astonished James. Up close all that he could make out were the textures of the materials: the tendrils of the lichens, the petals of the flowers. But further away he could see a bearded man at the left of the picture, with furred legs that bent back the wrong way, like the back legs of a dog, a flute held to his mouth and a giant erection springing between his legs. It looked like he was running, and to his right was a woman, dressed in the long white robes that he'd seen on the girls the day before, except that her garment was half torn, exposing one of her breasts. She seemed to be running too, but was looking back with a coquettish smile as though encouraging the bearded half-man – a satyr, was it? James couldn't be sure – to catch her.

After memorising the details of the picture James left the well and turned back onto the road. After the last houses, fields and meadows rolled away on both sides of the road and here James finally saw people. He ducked down at first, scared of being spotted, then realised that he was fairly well hidden from view by the hedgerow that ran along both sides of the road.

He could see two girls with long dark hair in the meadow to his right, both dressed in white robes, bending down and rubbing their hands in the meadow grass, then covering their faces with the dew. They turned to face the sun, fully risen now, its golden light silhouetting their bodies so that James could see that they were naked underneath their robes.

Struck by the strangeness of what they were doing he paused to watch them as they washed in the long grass. Then, as one of them began to turn, he hurried on, his face averted, his head hung low to hide himself from them.

His attention fixed on the ground, James soon noticed that the road surface was improving. The further away he got from Ardegan, the scarcer the cracks and holes in the road became. He could also have sworn that he was colder now, although he knew the idea was absurd – surely with the rising sun he should be warmer, if anything. Before the road took him round a bend over the rim of a hill and out of sight of the village he turned for one last gaze at the castle looming out of the village on the hilltop. The sun reflected off the windows and forced him to shield his eyes with a hand.

James was ravenous by the time he reached Porthness but nobody seemed to want to serve him breakfast. He was simply ignored in the first café he went into, the owner speaking over his repeated requests and serving the next customer. He'd put it down to rudeness and had left. But after he was forcibly ejected from the second café he knew that he was unwelcome here. It must be the outfit, he reasoned, and considered trying to buy some normal clothes. But he'd already seen that there was a tattoo parlour in the town; as soon as he'd been marked, he planned to head back.

James had never had a tattoo or a piercing in his life and he didn't take the idea of being permanently marked lightly. Still, he couldn't think of any other way that he'd be able to get into the castle or be accepted by the villagers as one of them. As it was, he was worried that they'd recognise him and chase him again – and he didn't like to think about what they might do if they caught him. But he couldn't pass up on this scoop; he didn't even want to phone the paper in case they sent someone else up who might spoil it for him. And before anything he needed some breakfast.

He finally persuaded a few market traders to sell him some food, buying a couple of apples from one and a pastry from another; even through his hunger he was so aware of people staring at him that he found it difficult to eat. Most of them looked disgusted and would turn away as soon as he looked back at them, refusing to make eye contact. A handful smiled enthusiastically and James was aware of some of the grey-clad people he'd seen here before scurrying around in the background but vanishing from view whenever he turned to look at them. If he hadn't known better he would have thought they were following him.

The tattooist, a burly man in his fifties, only his face and hands apparently free from colourful designs, took one look at him and raised his eyebrows. 'I know what you're here for,' he stated even before

James had had a chance to speak. Then he pulled out a sheet of paper bearing the design that James had seen on some of the villagers' shoulders, the three parallel marks that the vicar had described. James nodded.

'Been doing plenty of those lately. Even had a couple of girls in last night; one of them had one already, the other one wanted the same. They'd had a bit to drink, but their minds were made up, and anyway –' he gave James a conspiratorial glance '– I know what they're for.'

'I'm going up to the castle,' James started, not knowing what else to say.

'Oh aye.' The tattooist nodded. 'And you won't get in without one of these. Just sit on the bed there and roll your sleeve up. It won't take long.'

This really was suffering for his art, James thought ruefully as the needle pierced his skin. The tattooist hadn't lied: it took less than half an hour, and only another ten minutes for James to be talked through the aftercare for the tattoo.

'How much do I owe you?' James finally asked as the tattooist began to potter round his studio, the session obviously over. The burly man turned and looked him up and down suspiciously, his forehead wrinkling.

'You mean you don't know?'

This left James at a loss. He reached into the pocket of his tunic and pulled out his wallet to open it. 'Just tell me how much I owe you,' James said uncertainly. 'I've got money.'

The tattooist peered at James's wallet, then looked back into his eyes. He looked angry. 'What the hell do you think you're playing at?'

James, panic rising in his throat, extracted a couple of notes and held them out, part of his mind stupidly telling him that he should get a receipt so that he could claim this back as expenses from the paper. But the gesture only seemed to make the tattooist angrier and he clenched his fists.

Suddenly struck by an idea, James reached into his pocket again and pulled out the coins that he'd found earlier that morning. The tattooist's face lightened and he reached forward to pluck the largest coin, the first that James had found, from his palm. 'I knew you had to be kidding me,' he said, leaning over to slap James on the back, grinning widely. 'Garner's boys don't have any use for that *old* money.'

James nodded dumbly and tried to smile back, aware that a disaster had been narrowly averted.

Outside, the air had chilled noticeably and James hugged himself, breathing out a plume of steam. There wasn't any point in hanging around here any more: a brisk walk back to Ardegan should soon warm him up. The raw skin of his shoulder chafed against his tunic as he began to march down the pavement, making him wince, and he rolled up the tunic's short sleeve, hoping that the cool air would help numb the pain.

As he peered at the marks – serrated black shapes rising from the angry red of his skin – he heard a scuffle behind him and before he could turn round a sack had been roughly put over his head. There was more than one person attacking him, maybe three, and as James struggled against his unseen assailants, shouting for help, his hands were wrenched behind his back and tied with what felt like coarse rope. He heard a car screech to a halt before he was held under each shoulder, his legs kicking wildly, almost picked up, and hurled bodily into the car.

Somebody else climbed into the back with him and held his legs down as the car pulled away. The position he was in, lying on his bound wrists, was painful, and he asked from under his hood to be turned over, his voice sounding muffled even to him. But he heard nothing in response. More bewildered than scared, James eventually gave up trying to talk to his captors and tried instead to work out what was going on.

Had Garner's people found out that he was trying to gain access to the castle as an impostor? Had the tattooist tipped them off, having become suspicious with his fumbling of the money? Maybe this was some local police force who'd taken a dim view of the tunicked inhabitants of Ardegan and were picking them off whenever they ventured too far out of their own domain; he hadn't seen anyone else dressed like him in Porthness. But if they were police, surely they would have used cuffs and a more professional blindfold. Or they would simply have arrested him on some trumped-up charge, rather than going in for all this cloak-and-dagger nonsense.

James was still working through the possibilities when the car ground to a halt on a gravel drive and he was hauled out, feeling the freshness of the air, welcome now. He was taken through a doorway and down a corridor, his shoes squeaking against a lino floor, then through another door that had to be unbolted first. His hood was wrenched off and he was pushed forward, hard, so that he stumbled into a room, blinking in the harsh light, as the door slammed shut behind him.

There was a young woman in the corner, dressed only in a long T-shirt that barely covered the tops of her thighs. She had long tawny blonde hair, and was attractive, even through the fear and exhaustion clearly apparent in her wide eyes. She was sitting bound to a chair and shrank from him as James was pushed in. He tried to smile at her and his own fear and uncertainty must have told in his expression because her look softened. He peered around the room: bare walls, peeling dull green paint, no windows, a radiator running along one wall. The room was a little cold; the radiator hadn't been switched on. There was something else too, something that hovered over the faint smell of lino and disinfectant: a definite smell of sex hung in the air.

'What is this place?' James asked the woman finally.

She shook her head and shrugged her shoulders helplessly. 'I don't know. I was in a hotel when they came and brought me here. I think they're some kind of cult; I met the woman who seems to be in charge and she told me some crazy story about a nun they worship.'

James had seen the mark on her shoulder, visible through the thin material of her T-shirt. 'You've been up at Ardegan castle?'

The woman shook her head again, looking puzzled. 'My friend's started working there; I think she's training to be in a circus. How did you –' she began, then saw him staring at her shoulder. 'Oh, that. They've been very excited about that *here*. Apparently it means something, although God knows what.'

'It's the mark all the villagers get at Ardegan. Or all of them who want to go to the castle, anyway,' James told her. Then he shook his head and grinned again, more easily now. 'I'm not one of them, by the way. My name's James. I'm a journalist and I've been sent up here to cover everything that's going on at Ardegan.' He looked expectantly at the woman, who just stared blankly back at him. 'Haven't you heard about any of it?'

The woman shook her head and smiled weakly back at him. 'I just came up to meet my friend. I got this tat done because I liked hers and we'd had a few drinks. And now this! They put me on some weird machine that –' An expression James couldn't read ran across her face. 'Anyway, we've got to get out of this place. These people are fucking crazy.'

James nodded, thinking that if he told the woman what he'd seen at Ardegan she might well think that he was crazy too. And the further away the memory was the less plausible it seemed, even though he knew what he'd seen. 'What's your name?'

The woman smiled again. 'Emma.'

'Well, Emma, does anyone ever come through here? To bring food, or water, or anything?'

Emma nodded. 'They brought me a bowl of something a few hours ago and fed me. I tried to ask the man what was going on, when they were going to let me go, that sort of thing, but he didn't say anything, didn't look into my eyes, even, just kept on spooning food into my mouth. I would have refused it but I was starving.'

James looked around the room, tugging against his bonds, trying to reach the knot around his wrists and pulling at the rope in an attempt to loosen it, all to no avail. Suddenly struck by an idea, he walked over to Emma and turned around, lifting his wrists towards her face. 'I hope you've got strong teeth.'

They'd been free for what must have been over an hour now, although with nothing to mark the time it was hard to be sure. Every muscle in James's body tensed as he waited by the door, listening for the sound of someone coming down the corridor, the muffled footsteps he could just make out if he concentrated. It was a good thing that Emma was a brave girl, he reflected as he smiled at her encouragingly. She'd watch him to see if he heard anything, then assume the pose they'd agreed on: slumped down a little in the chair, her T-shirt resting on the tops of her thighs, pushing her breasts together with the tops of her arms, looking as inviting as she could. Which to James was very inviting indeed, although the response seemed horribly inappropriate given the situation they were in.

The sight of her posed like that reminded him of May and kicked off such an intensely erotic recollection that he entirely missed the newest set of footsteps and was only alerted when he heard the key turn in the lock. He turned to Emma urgently but she'd heard it too. She slumped still lower in the chair, positioned so that she would be the first thing whoever opened the door saw. James just hoped it would be a man.

The door swung open and James heard a soft intake of breath. Then came two uncertain footsteps as a large man swung into view, his head turned towards Emma, who was smiling now, looking at the man from behind a few blonde curls hanging down over her face. He was carrying a tray with two bowls on it too, and James silently thanked the gods that his hands were full. He stepped noiselessly behind him and swung his fists in a haymaker at the man's head.

The force of the blow knocked the man back against the door with a resounding clang. He crumpled to the ground like a puppet with cut strings, one hand still clutching the tray as the bowls of gruel spilled their contents onto the floor. Emma had stood up excitedly as he fell and James took her hand and peered out into the corridor. Nobody seemed to have heard the commotion, so they both stepped out.

The corridor stretched away on both sides, neither direction leading obviously to an exit, so James took a punt and pulled them to the left, moving as quickly as he could past the seemingly endless rows of doors without making too much noise. As they neared the end of the corridor, which made a 'T' with another, he heard voices and footsteps coming from their right. Panicked, he turned the handle of the nearest door. It was locked. Emma looked aghast. He hurriedly turned the next handle but it seemed to be locked too. In desperation he pushed himself hard against it and it swung open to reveal a lit room, similar to the one they'd been locked in but with large shelves running along the walls. He pulled Emma in quickly behind him and closed the door, praying that they hadn't been seen, holding his breath and listening against the door for anyone coming down the corridor.

There was no sound and he turned, relieved, to Emma, to find her pointing excitedly at a box, one of a row on a shelf. She squeaked excitedly, 'My clothes!'

Before he could respond she'd pulled the box off the shelf and was frantically digging out the clothes and then pulling them on, her knickers first. She gave James a dirty look as he watched, so that he blushed and turned away to allow her to finish dressing, only to turn back too early and see her pull the T-shirt up over her full breasts. He turned round again, his cock thickening in his pants at the sight, before she could see him. He briefly considered checking the other boxes himself for more clothes, but he reasoned that as they'd be going to the castle as soon as possible anyway he wouldn't need to change. Instead he scanned the room for anything else he might be able to use and gave a start as he saw a familiar pattern on a bundle of clothes. James tugged at the material and had his suspicions confirmed when the jester's outfit he'd seen the day before unfurled in his hand, the heavy mask swinging down and almost falling to the ground. James had to lunge forward to stop it. He stared at it for a few seconds, wondering how it had got here. Then he spotted a map that had been spread out and fixed to the opposite wall.

As Emma tied her trainers, he stuffed the jester's outfit back onto the shelf and crossed the room to study the map. James was familiar with some of the area already, from the map he'd seen earlier, but this was on a larger scale and gave him a better idea of the surrounding villages. Ardegan was marked, with an X positioned over the castle and various rings drawn around the village with a marker pen. He found Porthness and looked closely around it, sure that wherever they were it too would be marked. Sure enough, there it was, just three or four miles from Porthness, marked with another X. He memorised the road layouts around the property, then turned back to face Emma who was now grinning broadly.

Miming an elaborate *shh* at her with a finger to his lips, James listened at the door. There was no sound and he opened the door to peer out. The coast was clear and he beckoned to Emma to follow him. When they reached the adjacent corridor he checked again, then felt a wave of relief pass over him. The building had clearly been some kind of institution before, rather than somebody's home: there were green exit signs clearly marked, and before long James and Emma had pushed on an emergency-exit door and were out in the grounds and running towards the nearest clump of bushes.

* * *

It was Paul, on his way to a meeting in the main hall, who discovered that they'd gone. He quickened his step when he saw that the door to the cell was open and found Brother Francis there, lying on the gruel-spattered floor. Paul put his hand to the cereal. It was still soft: they couldn't have been gone too long. Then, horrified, suspecting that Francis might be dead, he touched a hand to the man's head, flinching as the prone figure groaned.

His panic mounting, Paul ran from the room, taking the corridors at full pelt as he raced to the main hall. He passed a few others on their way there, telling them breathlessly to check the rooms, that Emma and James might still be in the building. By the time he'd reached the hall there were so many people milling around that he ignored them, scanning the crowd desperately for the woman he needed to tell. In the end it was she who found him.

'You look alarmed, Brother Paul.' Her voice, gently mocking in a way that Paul had not heard from her before, made him start as it came from behind his shoulder.

He spun round and took her by the shoulders, ignoring her raised eyebrows as he gripped her arms. 'They've gone!'

'Who?' she began, then paused. 'The prisoners?'

'Yes! They've gone! And they've hurt Brother Francis. He's injured, lying in the room.'

The woman's features tightened, although she didn't seem particularly surprised. 'Have the other rooms been checked?'

As if in response to her question the men Paul had met earlier ran into the hall and came up to them, answering her breathlessly themselves. The prisoners were nowhere to be seen but there were clothes scattered on the floor of one of the storage rooms and an exit door was still open.

To Paul's shock the woman smiled. 'Shouldn't we
–' he started, keen to leave and track them, confident
that they couldn't have gone too far. But she
interrupted him with a raised hand.

'You want to see your wife again, to take her away
from the heathens.' She said it flatly, a statement
rather than a question, but still Paul nodded.

'We will go there tonight. You will wear the clothes
we took from them today –' a raiding party had
descended on the Ardegan woods at dawn and had
found the jester's outfit discarded in a clearing, a
great prize '– the guards will let you in, then we will
follow. Tonight your wife will be returned to you and
the evil will be vanquished. Yes?' Paul nodded again,
and the woman turned to walk to the dais.

Paul took his chair with the others, still convinced
that they could catch the prisoners, and exchanged
worried glances with the men who'd searched the
building, one of whom shrugged helplessly.

As the sound of chairs scraping against the varnished
floor died down the woman coughed. Paul noticed a
change in the atmosphere in the room as everyone
leaned forward, tense, to hear what she had to say.

'Our guests have left,' she began, 'spurning our
hospitality.' She smiled thinly and a few members of
the Order chuckled uncertainly. 'But no matter.
Tonight is the night of the feast at the castle and their
departure only hastens the inevitable. Tonight they
will all be in one place, revelling in their pagan
filthiness. To you this may seem blasphemy. To me it
is an opportunity. Will we leave them alone to
celebrate their heathen rites?'

She paused, evidently waiting for a response from
the crowd. One or two voices cried out, 'No!'

'Will anyone else be bold enough to cleanse them
from our midst?'

The reply was bolder now, more voices joining in. 'No!'

The woman smiled grimly again, raising her own voice in turn. 'And how should we cleanse them? What would be a just and fitting end for the disease they have wrought among us? Should we simply ask them to leave?'

A few laughs were drowned out by angry muttering.

'Have they not brought hell to our community?'

The muttering grew louder and Paul joined in, caught up in the spirit of the moment.

'And with what shall we pay them for bringing hell to Earth? Is theirs the hell of ice? Of darkness? Or of fire?'

There was a pause as the full import of what she had said began to sink in. Then one weak, tremulous voice piped up: 'Burn it down!'

Others joined in, the chant mounting until it filled the room, reverberating around the walls as the woman watched them, nodding, her own eyes alive with a fiery intensity.

Nine

The castle door was closed but they could hear music behind the heavy oak portal. Emma turned to James, who shrugged.

'Let's knock,' he suggested. He had just put his hand up to do so when a grille in the door slid open and a face peered out at them.

'Are you expected?' the man asked.

Emma moved in front of the grille. 'Yes! My friend Miriam sent for me.' The man nodded, and scowled at James. 'He's with me; he's a friend,' Emma reassured him.

The man raised his eyebrows and James pulled up his sleeve to show his tattoo. Emma did the same and the door creaked open.

'You're just in time for the big feast,' the man said as he shut the door behind them, grinning now. 'You'll have to change, though,' he told Emma, frowning as he took in her clothes. 'Lord Garner won't have people wearing clothes like that, especially not today. If you wait there a minute I'll see if I can rustle something up. Usually the mistress would look after you but I'm sure she's busy with all the preparations. I know where the clothes are kept, though. Wait here.'

Emma barely had time to thank him before he'd run up a flight of steps in the wall of the courtyard and vanished through an open doorway. James started to relax – at least it seemed friendly here and it hadn't been as difficult to get in as he'd feared. Whether it would have been so easy without Emma was a different matter, though. He was on the verge of telling her how happy he was that they'd met up, even under the circumstances, when a shrieked 'Emma!' from their right stopped him in his tracks.

They turned and James saw a beautiful girl with long dark hair leap into Emma's arms, almost knocking her down. The pair hugged long and hard, then kissed each other on the lips repeatedly while James pretended to take an interest in the stonework of the castle wall.

'You made it!' Miriam finally held Emma out at arm's length, studying her. 'And I'm so glad you're OK. You *are* OK, aren't you?'

'Mm-hmm.' Emma nodded, but tried to look cross with her friend. 'No thanks to you, though. Who the fuck were those people? They seemed to think I was part of some kind of cult, with this stupid tattoo.' She began to roll up her sleeve for emphasis but Miriam stopped her with an urgent 'Shh!', and looked around nervously.

'Listen, they're – they're just local people who don't understand what Lord Garner's been doing here. I shouldn't worry about them – they won't come up here. Did they come up to the hotel room?'

'You know they did, Miriam.'

'So how'd you get away?' Miriam looked puzzled.

Emma turned to James for the first time since Miriam's arrival. 'Miriam, this is James; James, Miriam, the friend I was telling you about.' James put out his hand and was surprised by the strength of Miriam's grip as her lip curled back in a feral grin. 'James was picked up by them too, after having had the same tattoo done. We got away together.'

'Is that right?' asked Miriam, looking James up and down. He felt nervous, and nodded. 'So what's your interest in the castle, James?' The way she stressed his name made him swallow and he was struggling to think of something to say when the man who'd let them in returned with a bundle of clothes in his arms. Gratefully James turned to the man, aware that Miriam's stare was still on him.

'Well, let's find you somewhere to get changed, shall we, Emma?' he proposed with forced jollity.

'There are some rooms down there that you could use,' said Miriam, waving a hand vaguely to their left. 'I've got to go now. I'm performing in the circus and we're having our first outing at the feast. When you're ready you can join the others in the great hall. It's up there.' She pointed to a door recessed from the wall, at the top of a short flight of steps. 'See you later!' And with that she was gone, running to the other side of the courtyard and disappearing behind one of the doors.

'I don't see why I have to wear this,' complained Emma, holding the shirt and tunic out in front of her. 'I've only just got my old clothes back. And isn't this what Miriam was wearing?'

James nodded. 'It looks like everyone wears the same clothes here. Come on, I'll wait outside while you change.' Emma curled her lip in disdain, then headed to the rooms that Miriam had pointed out.

As he waited, James listened to the music coming from behind the door of the great hall: drums, flutes and violins, not much different from the music he'd heard at the village festival. He'd been worried that someone might identify him in the village as they walked towards the castle but he'd hardly seen

195

anyone there at all. The maypole was still up on the green and he'd looked anxiously at the vicar's house, half hoping for a glimpse of May, but there had been nothing. They had probably all come here already, he realised.

Emma returned, scowling as she looked down at herself.

James grinned. 'At least it fits. Come on, let's go inside.'

The first thing that hit them as they entered the hall was a wave of steam, thick with the smells of beer, cider and roasting meat. The hall was packed with long trestle tables covered in flagons and with dishes that held legs of lamb, whole roast chickens, great hanks of roast beef, joints of pork covered in crackling, as well as bowls of cooked vegetables. At a glance James counted four roasts to each table, with a whole ox on a spit at the head of the room by the table that was furthest away from them – where there were a number of empty seats near a huge, ornately carved chair that he assumed must belong to Garner.

There seemed to be no order to the feast: people were helping themselves, swigging down gulps of cider, some of them cramming chicken legs or huge chunks of beef into their mouths, all laughing, with a small band playing to one side of the tables. Nearly the same amount of space that had been given over to the tables was empty and James wondered if it had been set aside for dancing later on. Emma had spotted someone, evidently someone she knew, a burly man in his late forties who grinned widely at her and stood up to greet her.

Alone, James felt nervous again and quickly scanned the crowd to see if he recognised any of the faces from the village. To his surprise he saw the vicar, dressed just like the others – no dog collar now – his eyes glazed over already from drinking, grease from the roasted meat dripping from his chin as he shared a joke with his neighbour. James looked quickly away, only to spot two of the women who had identified him as an impostor in the village only yesterday. He coloured and began to fidget with his hands, wondering where he should go, turning away so that his face was hidden from them. Then a cold hand gripped his arm.

'You have come to the castle after all?' The woman in furs who'd given him a lift in her carriage stared at him. James could only nod, speechless.

'You didn't seem sure before. And now –' She surveyed his clothes, nodding appreciatively. Then, before he could stop her, she rolled up his sleeve and looked at his tattoo. 'You are marked. It is good. Tell me – why have you come here?' She fixed James with her piercing stare.

'I – I –' James stuttered, unable to lie to her.

She smiled. 'Let me rephrase the question. What do you do? What skills have brought you here?'

'I'm a writer,' James replied.

'Ah. Good. Lord Garner will be most pleased. Already we have one such here –' she indicated the man deep in conversation with Emma '– but perhaps your style is less specialised.' She turned to face him again. 'You are a journalist, are you not?'

James felt his gorge rise. He seemed to sink into her eyes, to lose all sense of self-control, as her ice-cold hand dug into his arm. 'Yes,' he whispered.

'And you come here to expose us, for your newspapers?' Her voice was heavy with sarcasm and James was surprised when she put her head back and laughed, a clear peal of mirth.

There seemed little point in denying it now. 'How do you know? I mean, how did you find out?'

The woman smiled at him again. 'There are more sources of information available to those who truly know than any journalist would use.'

James paused, expecting that at any moment he would be ejected bodily from the room. He'd already seen the coachman from the day before and the coachman had seen him – was watching him closely, in fact. But nobody made a move towards him; the revelries continued. Absurdly, he felt a pang of hunger.

'You – you don't mind my being here?' he asked.

'*Mind?* You funny little man! We positively *welcome* you here. Our May Day celebrations will involve something very special, something that has not been attempted before. Lord Garner and I are keen that the festivities should be documented.' She turned and swept her arm in an arc, encompassing the hall. 'After all this, you can tell your newspapers what you like. It will be too late for anyone to stop us then.'

'This "something special" – do you mean the people who turn into wolves? I've seen them, you know. Out in the woods, yesterday.'

The woman turned back to him. 'You have? And still you came here? You are brave – or stupid. But no, the special event will be different. You will see: Lord Garner will want you there, I am sure. Come.'

She took James by the hand and led him towards the top table. Panicked, he looked around for Emma, only to see her still talking to the man she'd spotted earlier. When they reached the table the woman indicated a chair, and sat down in the next seat along. 'Eat,' she prompted. James stared at the dishes of steaming food in front of him, then turned to look quizzically at her.

'Use your hands, you fool!' she said, tearing hunks of meat from a roast leg of lamb, attacking the meat with a savagery that stunned James, then laughing after she'd swallowed several mouthfuls. 'Eat,' she said again. James followed her example.

The meat tasted delicious and as he tore more chunks from the lamb, picking up a bone to gnaw at the flesh, the woman poured from a flagon of cider into a horn cup. James was thirsty and took a deep draught, smiling gratefully. She smiled in turn and laid a hand on his shoulder encouragingly.

The music stopped and there was a lull in the noise of the room. James paused, more meat in his fingers, as the double doors at the far end of the hall opened. One of the band members put a long horn to his lips and blew a short sequence of three notes. Everyone turned to face the doors.

There was a creaking sound. Then four girls strode into the room, tall and naked, with leather harnesses around their waists attached to a carriage behind them, little more than a lavishly cushioned chair mounted on wheels. Each girl wore a wolf mask, identical to those that James had seen the day before, and something glinted in their nipples, a metal bar through each pink tip, attached to thin chains that were in turn linked to reins held by the man in the carriage.

They pulled the carriage into the centre of the open space, then moved towards the head table. The revellers were silent now: the only sounds were the creaking of the wheels of the carriage and the laboured breathing of the girls. As the carriage swung round James could see that the girls had been given tails, fixed somehow to emerge from their bottoms. A couple of them were given a flourish as they neared the table.

So this was Garner. It was a hell of an entrance, James had to admit, staring at him. He was a big man, well over six feet tall, and broad too, dwarfing the others around him, who appeared like children now. James could see as the girls came closer that sweat was running down their sides. Garner was bearded, a thick auburn shock of curls that almost obscured his mouth from view, and his hair was cropped short, making his forceful brow appear even more fearsome. He wore on the upper half of his body a sleeveless green jerkin that was crossed by a gold-embroidered sword belt; a huge gold chain hung round his neck, from which hung the wolf amulet James recognised from the newspaper photos, and a golden torque of Celtic design circled the prodigious muscles of his upper arm.

As they reached the table Garner stepped out of his carriage and sat heavily in his chair. The wolf girls remained where they were, standing perfectly still. Then Garner waved a hand in the air, the band started up again, and the conversation resumed, more raucously now, as if each of the guests were vying with each other to show their appreciation by eating the most meat, drinking the longest draughts or swearing the loudest insults.

Garner turned to the woman and smiled. Then he saw James. The corners of his lips curled down in a frown. James's intestines coiled coldly and he felt a powerful urge to push his chair back and run. But the woman, sensing his unease, put a hand on his shoulder.

'This is James, my lord. He has come to tell the world what we have done here.'

Garner squinted at James, who stared back, trying to smile. There was something wild in Garner's eyes, something that gave rise to an uncontrollable panic in James, and he tried involuntarily to stand again. But the woman's hand on his shoulder held him down.

Then Garner's attention had turned away from him again. James gratefully took a swig of cider, only to cough part of it out when Garner clapped his hands together and boomed out, 'Let the show begin!'

There was cheering and applause, which died down into scattered clapping as all heads turned to face the double doors again.

Miriam peered out into the hall, then turned back to Alice, who was trembling with excitement, the mesh of coins covering her chest and her sex chinking together lightly. 'He's here,' she announced. Alice stepped forward to peer out too, then looked at the row of girls, six of them including Miriam waiting to go out. She clapped her hands, nodded to Miriam, then stepped out into the hall. Miriam led the girls as they skipped out behind her.

'Ladies and gentlemen,' Alice announced, 'the first show we have for you tonight is an obedience test for the dogs you see behind me.' Despite knowing what was going to happen, Miriam coloured when Alice swung an arm around to indicate their naked bodies, their hair bunched up in absurd knots, small furry muffs around their ankles and wrists, as though they were poodles being put on show, and bands around their arms marking each of them with a number.

'Sit!' Alice suddenly ordered Miriam, and she squatted. 'Spread your legs.' Miriam did as she was told, exposing herself to the audience, her gaze roving over them to catch the stare of Cavendish (who looked excited), Emma (who looked shocked, her mouth an O of astonishment) and Garner (who smiled benignly as the mistress whispered something in his ear). The crowd looked excited too, a few of the men shouting bawdy comments, but they quietened down when Alice addressed them again.

'See how obedient she is, ladies and gentlemen! Roll over!' Alice instructed Miriam, and she rolled onto her back, her legs and arms up like a dog playing dead, aware that the lips of her sex, squeezed together, would be peeping out at the audience. Alice tickled her belly and tugged on her nipples, then turned to the audience again. 'If any of you ladies or gentlemen would like to test the condition of the dogs, please nominate one and they will come to you.'

'I will!' a woman's voice cried out, unexpectedly. Miriam rolled onto all fours again to look at the speaker and found Emma grinning at her. Miriam arched her back, fully expecting to be called for, but Emma made a show of looking over all the others before finally calling out 'Five!'

Miriam's stomach lurched in disappointment and she turned her head to see number five, another newcomer called Barbara, spring up and strut towards Emma's table. A stinging lash caught Miriam on the bottom and she jumped up, putting a hand to her rear.

'Turning when not ordered to is disobedient, number one,' Alice said crossly, holding her crop erect as though about to hit Miriam again. Miriam, her bottom cheeks burning where Alice had marked her, turned to face the front again.

As Miriam watched, Emma inspected Barbara, peeling her lips back to comment 'Good teeth!' Then, telling her to bend over, she inspected Barbara's anus and called out loudly to the audience, an expression of annoyance on her face, 'This one's been used!'

Miriam couldn't help giggling, even through her jealousy. But for this she received a second stroke, harder than the first. She sucked in her breath hard, trying to resist the temptation to put her hand back and feel the mark.

'Number one's not being very obedient, is she? I wonder if she can make up for her lapses by demonstrating obedience with a member of the audience?' Alice called out.

A man sitting at the nearest table, whose body was twisted round to watch the show, shouted out, 'I'll have her!' through a mouthful of chicken. He was waving a bone around in one hand and a horn of cider in the other, spilling the amber liquid over its rim in his excitement. Alice grinned, raised an eyebrow at Miriam and sent her on her way with a light tap of the crop.

As Miriam approached the man, who had turned fully around now to face her, she realised that he was overweight. Huge, in fact: his body was a corpulent blob. He was sweating, too, and licking his lips as he watched her, grease running down the unshaven rolls of his chin. As Miriam stood in front of him, wondering what indignities he'd put her through, her sex already greasy at the thought of being made to perform for him, she could hear other people, emboldened by Emma and the fat man's example, calling the girls up.

'Sit!' the fat man ordered. But his piggy eyes narrowed in disappointment as Miriam squatted to the ground. 'Not like that. Like you did before!'

Colouring again, Miriam spread her legs and felt the lips of her sex peel wetly apart. The fat man peered down between her legs and grinned broadly.

'Looks wet down there. You sure you haven't been disobedient with anyone else?' He chortled, the rolls of his stomach shaking. 'Touch it,' he ordered.

Obediently, Miriam put a finger to the slippery

folds, then shivered as she ran her fingertips down the length of her slick crease.

'That's right,' the man muttered, leaning back and groaning as he struggled to undo the buttons of his trousers. He was erect, Miriam could see, his cock springing up once he'd freed it. He looked around uncertainly. Then, happy that the other girls were being made to do much the same if not worse, he pointed to his cock and leered at Miriam.

'Suck it,' he ordered. Miriam gave him a dirty look before advancing, still in a squat, until her head was level with his crotch. He wrapped his fingers through her hair and pulled on it, hard, forcing her mouth down onto his erection. She put her hands out to steady herself and he tutted.

'You can play with my balls with one hand. I want to see you rubbing yourself with the other.'

Her mouth full of cock, her tongue running over the head, which grew even larger as she sucked on it, Miriam obeyed, cupping his balls in one hand and stroking her quim with the other.

The man groaned and relaxed, content now, the hand on her head pulling her on and off his cock in a steady rhythm as he fucked her mouth. Miriam could feel her pussy beginning to ache with need, her clit a hard nub between her fingers now, and she was wishing that he'd just bend her over and fuck her, stuff his hard cock in her greasy hole. She felt her sex twitch at the thought. She shivered as she felt the desire mount in her, strumming her clit faster, slapping on it, the hand holding the man's balls starting to flex as she felt her muscles going into spasm. She knew that she was going to change, that she shouldn't, she'd promised not to, but she didn't care any longer. Then she felt the white heat of the crop bite into her buttocks, twice, three times, far harder than before.

As the change urges subsided, Miriam looked around to see Alice holding the crop up threateningly, giving her a warning look. Then she returned her attention to the man's cock, sucking hard on its end now and squeezing his balls, her own needs quashed by the fear of punishment, the training that she'd received.

'That's right, slap the dirty cocksucking bitch,' the man leered breathlessly. Miriam could feel his ball sac starting to tighten and she squeezed it again, hard. Then she dug her long red nails into the sac, bobbing her head up and down on the tip of his cock at a furious pace now, until she felt it pulse. She sucked hard on the end as he emptied himself into her, his balls twitching, the hand in her hair tugging at her spasmodically. She swallowed the great gouts of come, relishing their flavour and sucking every last drop from him, greedy for more, then looked around guiltily as she felt her arousal mount again, as the man's softening cock slid from her mouth.

'Won't get many bookings with a circus like that,' James pointed out to the woman in furs. He felt more relaxed now with a bellyful of food and cider.

The woman smiled. 'In fact you're wrong. We've already had bookings for several cities and we hope to plan an itinerary all the way down to London.'

'Doing *that*?' James asked incredulously. He'd watched Emma's friend Miriam suck an obese man until he came, and two of the other girls were being fucked, one sitting on a man and the other laid down on a table, dishes and plates having been unceremoniously swept aside to make room for her. 'You'd be shut down before you'd even started.'

The woman laughed. 'Of course, the show they'll tour with won't be *quite* the same as this. It'll start with more standard acts – but yes, it'll definitely be *adult* entertainment rather than, ah, fun for all the family. I've never been very much in favour of *families*: have you?' She placed a hand on James's thigh and squeezed his leg. 'As for the puritan element who'd seek to prevent displays such as this, the ritual we are about to perform will crush them and usher in a new era of freedom, of licentiousness, of every man and woman able to use their birthright to the full: pleasure without guilt.

'Until then, those for whom desire burns deepest must be trained or simple arousal might change them into something – different. Look.' She drew James's attention to the tattooed girl who was lashing Miriam with her crop as Miriam lay on her back, holding Miriam's legs with one hand as she left a series of red welts on the already patterned buttocks. The tip of the crop occasionally landed on Miriam's swollen sex and the dog girl's fingers frantically scrabbled at her slit, her head thrashing from side to side. The people sitting nearby had begun to move away anxiously and there was a look of mounting panic on the tattooed girl's face.

'Miriam is newly transformed, and has not yet learned how to control her animal urges,' the woman stated flatly.

'You mean . . .' Startled, James watched Miriam again, checking to see if any of her limbs had begun to elongate or if fur had begun to sprout on her skin. 'You mean she's one of those wolf people?'

The woman nodded. 'We are training a few, like Miriam, to spread our way of life. The circus will allow them to travel throughout the land, gaining new recruits and changing others.'

'You're insane,' James said.

The woman laughed. 'After what we're about to do, what was impossible yesterday will become second nature to all. You'll see. Lord Garner likes you; he wants you to watch.'

As though he'd been listening, Garner leaned over to interrupt her and made a peremptory gesture with his hand. She nodded. 'Come,' she said to James. 'It is time.'

James glanced again at the circus display. The dog girls, including Miriam, had been led off, and another girl, dressed as the tattooed girl had been in a bikini of linked coins – Garner's currency, he was sure – had taken the stage, holding out a variety of ropes and buckles and inviting members of the audience to tie her up. As Garner climbed into his carriage and tugged on the nipple leashes of the wolf girls, people had already begun to advance towards her.

It was dark and dank in the cavern, and the steps they descended were slimy. Each of them held an oil lantern that they'd picked up at the entrance, the light sending looming shadows scattering over the depths. Garner was walking down now, having left his porters at the entrance.

'What is this place?' James asked the woman, his eyes adjusting slowly to the gloom.

'The cavern is far older than the castle,' she replied. 'A chapel was built here three hundred years ago, the church recognising the value of a sacred site, but it has since fallen into disuse.' She smiled thinly. 'There are other things down here, too – far older things.' The three of them had reached a platform now and she swung her light up to illuminate the wall. It took a couple of seconds for James to see that it was covered with paintings. Awed, he stared at the figures, recognisably lupine, even with the few lines used, but erect, standing on their hind legs. He turned back to the woman.

207

'But that's – are these new? They certainly *look* old.'

'They are prehistoric.'

'But I haven't heard anything about these! Surely they're the only ones in Britain?'

The woman snorted. 'Obviously we do not want tourists or –' her arm jerked dismissively '– *scientists* coming here to study the cave. That *we* know is enough, for the moment.'

They continued to the bottom of the steps and turned a corner into another, smaller cavern. This seemed almost perfectly circular in shape, with a slablike flat rock in its centre and several stalagmites protruding from the ground next to it. James held his lantern up and peered at them. They looked worn.

Garner looked quizzically at the woman, who told him, 'They're behind us.'

Wondering who she meant, James looked back the way they'd come and pricked up his ears. Footsteps echoed in the empty space, clearly audible over the noise of dripping water, and another sound – hooves, James could have sworn – and a chittering noise, something like the jabbering of a monkey.

As he watched, another lantern swung into view, closely followed by the coachman, the light shining up on his face giving it a sinister cast. There was someone behind him, too. James stared as the figure stepped into the light, unable to believe his eyes. The creature had tightly curled hair on its head, out of which protruded two short horns. It was naked, its cock dangling between its legs, which were covered in thick hair, bent back like an animal's hind legs, and ended in hooves. James stared in astonishment, convinced at first that it had to be a man in a costume. But there was something in the way it moved, the fear evident in the way its head twitched from side to side, its unreadably alien goat eyes, that made him realise it was real.

Garner stepped up to it and put a hand on its shoulder, which seemed to soothe its trembling. 'Ah, my friend, it is good to see you again, but sad too. You would not be long for this world; I hope you can understand that there is one way in which you can still serve us.'

James moved over to the woman's side to whisper in her ear, 'What the hell is that?' as the coachman, at a nod from Garner, untied the creature's bound wrists.

She turned to him and looked genuinely surprised. 'A satyr. Don't you recognise it? I thought every schoolboy would know what it was. We would not have been able to accomplish any of this without it. But the poor thing's ill. Look.' She held the lamp up and James could see that its horns were flaking and the fur on its legs was matted and patchy. 'It's unstable here but it should still make a worthwhile sacrifice.'

'Unstable? What do you mean?'

'I mean that it is not from this world; we always knew it wouldn't last for ever. And we got it the last time we came down here.'

'How?' James demanded.

'By magic, my dear boy. We conjured it up. It wasn't easy, and a sacrifice was necessary then too. But this should be stronger.'

'What are you trying to do now?'

'You really have no idea, do you?' the woman asked, staring up at him. 'We're going to raise Pan.'

209

Ten

'We can't have you taking part in the next act,
Miriam,' Alice told her. Miriam was on the verge of
tears but none of her pleas or promises seemed to
move the tattooed girl. Behind her the other girls had
let their hair down and removed the ruffs from their
wrists and ankles, although they kept the number
bands on their arms.

'Please, I promise I'll control myself,' she begged
again. 'You know I can do it.'

Alice shook off the hand that Miriam had put on
her shoulder and frowned apologetically at her. 'I'm
really sorry, Miriam, but we can't have you changing
out there. Some of those people are scared now and,
to be honest, I am too. I haven't seen you change
completely and I'm not sure that I want to. You
looked pretty damn close to it a few minutes ago and
I'm not about to take the chance again.'

'Please?'

'Miriam, this whole act is about girls coming. You
know that if I let you go ahead, you'll change. You'll
just have to watch.' And with that Alice had stepped
out into the hall again, the escapologist girl carrying
her ropes and chains off with her to frenzied applause
and whistles. Miriam looked round at the other girls,
each waiting with their bicycles.

As Alice announced them, they pushed the bikes on, a few of them smiling apologetically at Miriam. She peered out at the audience and saw the men's eyes light up at the sight of the bike seats. Emma was staring at them as well, but for some reason she looked sick.

'Ladies and gentlemen, again I invite you to participate in the act –' a cheer went up '– although only to place bets –' followed by theatrical groans. 'As you can see, these bicycles are designed to pleasure the girls riding them.' Alice caressed the long curved phallus protruding from one of the seats, and stroked the raised nodules at its base. 'The girls will ride until one of them has come. Your task is to guess which one is going to come first.'

There was scattered laughter in the audience. A few of the men had already started calling out numbers or offering to help. The first girl climbed on top of her bike, holding the lips of her sex apart and biting her tongue in concentration as she sat on the seat, slowly easing the long dildo inside herself. Then she began to pedal. A cheer went up and there were shouts of encouragement to the other girls who sat heavily on their seats in turn, two of them squirming around once they'd got settled.

A movement near one of the doors caught Miriam's attention and she looked over to see someone in full jester costume, a lopsided Punch mask on their head, come into the room. She frowned: none of the other guests were in costume, and she wasn't sure what this one was doing dressed up. He seemed to move uncertainly too, looking from side to side and then watching the display of girls cycling around. A mottled flush was visible on a couple of their chests now and one or two of them were showing a noticeable shivering of the thighs as their eyes started to glaze over while they made their sixth circuit.

The jester stood stock-still, staring at them. Then he called out, his voice clear even over the hubbub of the audience, some of whom were taking bets, others laying them as piles of Garner's coins mounted up on the tables. 'Barbara?'

The girl with the number five armband, who was a strong favourite to come first if the betting was anything to go by, paused and let her feet touch the ground, wobbling unsteadily as she shifted against the bike seat. She squinted towards the door. 'Paul?'

The jester had taken off his mask now to reveal the grey head of a man in his early sixties. 'Barbara!' he called out again, louder now. Alice looked confused and had begun to move towards the girl, her crop raised, when all hell broke loose.

From the doorway through which the jester had entered came a man clad in the grey clothes that they had all come to fear and loathe, the mark of the religious maniacs. Then more of them emerged, a trickle turning into a stream, until a horde of them was flooding through the doors, more coming through every second.

Most of the audience simply stared in amazement at this but a few continued to watch the girls, two of whom, oblivious to events going on around them, had carried on cycling round the room. As one of them began finally to come, screaming out, her body bucking against the bike seat, her head thrown back in ecstasy, Miriam was gripped from behind by one of the men in grey. She elbowed him in the ribs, then snapped her fist up in his face as he doubled over. She thrilled to the sickening crunch of his breaking nose. But there were others behind him – ahead of him, too – and as more of them gripped her shoulders, one even leaping onto her back to restrain her, she looked around despairingly. Where was Garner now?

'You have got to be fucking kidding,' said James.

The woman shook her head. 'We've spent the last few months studying spell fragments in ancient grimoires. The basic ritual will be similar to the one that we used to conjure the satyr. A sacrifice – and an orgasm. Death and sex.' She stared at James, who started to shake his head.

'You don't want me to –' he began. But she cut him off with a laugh.

'No, no, nothing like that. I will provide the orgasm – by myself.' She motioned at the stalagmites by the slab where the satyr was now lying, its body trembling. James's eyes widened. 'Everything is in place now: the sacrifice, the amulet, the date. All you need to do is watch and take note. You will be the mouthpiece of this event, marking a new stage in the history of man!' James stared at the woman incredulously. She was insane; they were all insane.

She shrugged off her coat and let it slide to the floor. James recognised the clasps at the tops of her suspenders, the miniature human skulls that glinted now in the lamplight. But he hadn't expected the motif to be repeated on the rest of her clothes: grinning skulls adorned the ribs of her corset and the straps of her top, a slender shift through which he could clearly see her erect nipples. She wore a necklace of heads, too, but these were flesh rather than the bone of skulls and looked like the shrunken heads of decapitated men, painted garish colours at odds with the silvery white and black of the rest of the woman's outfit, their tongues lolling out at grotesque angles. But the thing that drew James's attention most was that she'd shaved between her legs, leaving her quim absolutely bare save for a tattoo, in thick black outline, of a death's head, bulging out over her mound.

She stepped over to the stalagmites and caressed one with her finger, then bent down and mouthed the end, leaving it gleaming with spit. Then she licked her fingers and put them between her legs, shuddering as she rubbed herself.

As Garner looked on approvingly and James gaped in disbelief, she climbed onto the stalagmite she'd selected, and rubbed the tip of it along the length of her crease a few times, her fingers lightly fluttering over the top of her sex. Then she gasped as she began to sit down on it, her eyes screwed shut in concentration. James stared as her sex bulged out, the smooth tube of rock penetrating her inch by inch, her hand skimming at her clit in fits and starts as she slid slowly lower and lower onto the rock until she was squatting on it, unable to go any further. She breathed in short gasps as she flicked her fingers at her nub.

Finally she opened her eyes and gazed around herself as if unaware of where she was. When her stare lit on Garner there was a glimmer of recognition and she nodded.

Garner began to chant, Latin words that meant nothing to James, and he started to mark out various symbols on the body of the satyr as it lay prone on the slab, using the wolf amulet he'd removed from around his neck and held now in both hands.

The woman was bouncing up and down on the rock pole now, leaving it slick with her grease, one hand strumming at her clit, a blur in the lamplight, as the other toyed with her breasts, caressing each in turn, then pinching and pulling on her nipples. As her breath came harder and faster, Garner's chanting increased in volume until she started to wail, a long high-pitched sound that echoed off the cavern walls, and to slap at her sex, hitting it hard and sitting as low as she could, squashing herself down onto the column of rock, her whole body bucking, her free hand mashing her breast.

As she came, Garner raised the amulet high above his head, the metal claw glinting in the light. Then he shouted something and plunged it into the chest of the satyr, which let out an unearthly howl, its body twitching.

There was a blinding flash of white light and the ground seemed to shake beneath James's feet. Panicked, he began to move towards the steps. The coachman regarded him impassively. As though from a long way away, a sound came, growing louder by the second. As soon as it was recognisable as a roar, its volume had grown intolerably high, its pitch shaking James to his very core. He clamped his hands over his ears and turned to the steps. But he looked back before he left and saw the woman, still impaled on the stone column and trying weakly to pull herself off it, looking confused and scared. Garner was shouting something at her, something inaudible over the deafening roar, and fear was in his eyes too. James ran up the steps, his lamp swinging crazily as he prayed he wouldn't slip, his ears numb from the bellow. A wild sense of relief struck him as he reached the top, the entrance, where he knew he'd be one step closer to escaping the insanity. He didn't dare look back again.

She nodded her encouragement as the first torches were put to the piles of firewood assembled around the castle walls. Members of the Order were still dragging branches and boughs from the woods to fuel the pyres, their lights flashing around in the undergrowth, and some had started to venture inside the castle. The doors had opened to Paul and he had quickly been followed by others before the guard had had a chance to respond.

She smiled as she surveyed the sight again, then turned to one of the paths leading through the woods. She knew that they would fight without her; as the leader of the Order, she had a more important role to fill. The crackling of the burning pyres and the shouts as the first villagers ran out of the castle, alarmed, quietened as she walked further into the woods. The paths here were well trodden, the gap between the trees above her broad enough for the moon to light her way, but still she stumbled over roots and slipped on stones, feverish in her haste to descend through the woods, to reach her destination.

She'd known about the mound, of course. She'd played there as a child, not understanding what the place was, seeing it simply as a feature of the landscape. But as she and her friends had grown up she'd seen it visited by strangers, people coming from far away, men and women with long hair, in vans, people her parents had shunned not only as outsiders but as those who did not abide by God's rule, who lived loosely together in sin. The elders of the church too did not approve and efforts had been made to dissuade the visitors, barricading the entrance to the mound or daubing graffiti on the side of their near-derelict vehicles.

Yet still they had come, celebrating their heathen rites at marked times of the year. She had even stumbled across a couple one May Day. She'd been a young teenager then, out walking and unable to resist a stab of curiosity about what might be going on at the mound, justifying her visit by the righteousness of telling the church elders who among the locals had dared to go there.

She had missed the revels, it seemed, seeing only a ring of trampled wild flowers left by the entrance and a wooden bowl of water, heathen offerings to a heathen god. She had been on the verge of leaving again when she'd heard it, a panting coming from the side of the mound. Her heart in her mouth, she had climbed onto the top – the back, as she'd thought as a child, when the mound had seemed to her a sleeping dragon, ready to awaken at any time and rear from the ground, scattering moss and rubble over the fields – to peer down at the source of the sound.

She hadn't known what to make of what she'd seen. She'd long since grown distant from her school-friends who joked about boys, the bolder among them kissing them and professing pathetically juvenile loves: she already knew that Christ was her one sole love. But her parents, who she'd imagined would be delighted to see her following the true path, had told her that they wouldn't mind if she knew a boy or two, that perhaps she should spend more time with people her own age, less time with the church elders. If anything, the message had confused her and she'd turned away from them to the elders whose message was so pure, so clear, so easy to understand.

And so it seemed to her that the man on the mound was attacking the woman, that the struggle between them was a violent one, that the woman's eyes were screwed shut, her mouth gulping air, because she was in pain. The sweating, unshaven man was driving himself against her, clawing at her chest, leaving angry red marks where he grabbed and pulled at her – hurting her. Before she could help it she'd called out 'Stop!' to them, still standing on the top and looking down.

The man had looked up first, pausing in his assault. But he'd simply grinned at her, and the woman too, a ring of flowers garlanding her sweat-darkened hair, had opened her eyes and smiled. So she'd run away from there, bewildered, her mind in turmoil over how a woman could be hurt but still smile, could simultaneously feel pain and joy.

She shook her head at the memory, her lips pursed into a thin smile. The path was widening out now, the trees becoming thinner, and as she peered through the gloom she could see the silvery light marking the black maw of the mound. She put a hand instinctively to her side to check that the silver dagger she'd brought was still there, and she peered around on the ground as she advanced, hoping that what she'd heard was true.

In the end it was only by chance that she stumbled across it, literally tripping herself up and catching the curved haft between her feet, falling onto her knees before it, winded. Resisting the temptation to kick the object, to try and crush it underfoot, she reached back, still on her knees, and felt the smooth bone, cold to the touch. Then she picked up the horn. It was heavier than she'd expected, both ends ringed with some kind of dull metal – brass or bronze – and as she turned it in the light she could see that the metal rings were embossed with some kind of heathen design. Disgusted, she almost threw it to the ground again. But she remembered what she had come here for and walked closer to the mound, shivering now, partly from the cold but also from her apprehension, muttering prayers under her breath to protect her from whatever she might summon.

The path stopped and she found herself under the moon, the bright, clear light bathing the mound in silver. She looked up, the sky seeming to spin slightly.

Then, before she had time for her fear to mount, she put the tip of the horn to her lips and blew.

A long mournful tone sounded, so resonant that she dropped the horn as if she'd been scalded. But she knew that she had to go through with it, that if nothing happened now it might be simply because one blast was not enough. She picked it up again, returning it to her lips and blowing another note, then another still.

There'd been a rustling of branches in the woods as she'd blown the first note – birds, she reasoned, their slumber disturbed, or night predators responding to the call. But after the third note there was nothing, just the wind and the faintest sound of commotion up at the castle. She could see it from here too, an obscure orange glow at the top of the woods. At least the fire was taking hold. She'd wait here for five more minutes, then she'd return, she thought, fingering the dagger nervously.

A flash of searing white light made her freeze with fear. It was instantaneous and silent, illuminating every branch of every tree around her, etching each blade of grass in crystal clarity, so that when she blinked afterwards she saw the scene imprinted in bold lines on her eyelids. She looked up, expecting to see darker clouds scudding across the sky, to hear the answering rumble and crack of thunder, but the heavens stayed clear. Confused, she looked around, then realised she was still gripping the dagger, the cold angles of its handle imprinted into her flesh. She let it go and released her hand to her side, feeling curiously self-conscious.

She wasn't at all sure how she'd respond if the creature should arrive. Some of the Order claimed to know of more than one and her stomach lurched at the thought of a number of them arriving, her dagger no defence at all against their hideous bestial lusts. She was panting, she realised. The shock of the flash had left her heart racing and she tried to calm down, to reassure herself that with God on her side nothing could harm her; that the orange glow from the woods meant that they were winning, that they were burning the accursed plague out from the village.

She took a few deep breaths, then looked up at the moon again. She must have been here for five minutes, she thought. It was impossible to tell. She listened again, straining to hear something different, but still there was nothing. It must have been lightning, she reassured herself. She'd heard of it coming without thunder before: rare, but not unknown. Half disappointed, half relieved, she turned, dropped the horn near the mouth of the mound and began to walk slowly back to the path.

It was darker here but she felt more secure, moving back towards the others, the warmth of the flames. She fingered the dagger again. Perhaps there would be some opportunity to use it up at the castle. Perhaps the creature was there, and she should hurry back to help the others, to defend them against attack. Nodding to herself, muttering her thanks to the Lord for the strength that he had given her, she picked up her pace, her stare fixed to the path as she took longer strides, focused with a grim determination.

She didn't even hear them until they were at her feet. Even then they were noiseless, one running in front of her, others pushing from the back, their eyes and mouths glinting in the moonlight. She let out a strangled cry, too shocked to respond any other way, and put out a hand to steady herself, only to find it closing on rough fur. She drew her fingers back as though she'd been electrocuted but the reaction toppled her off balance and she shrieked, louder now, as she fell to the ground, cushioned as she tumbled by the wolves' bodies circling around her.

Their jaws were opening over her, their teeth nipping at her top, and she screamed again, trying to pull the dagger out, imagining the jaws clamping on her flesh, eating her to the bone. But their teeth did not touch her skin as they tore and pulled at the fabric of her clothes, their heads shaking violently from side to side as they stripped her. Wide-eyed with shock and terror, she began to plead with them. The dagger was dragged away with her clothes and she raised her arms and sobbed as they pulled the last shreds of dignity from her, one even bumping against the mound between her legs as it delicately nipped her underwear in its jaws. Then, with one wrench, it tore the garment free.

At last they moved away, as silently as before, to sit in a ring around her, leaving a space at her feet. She sat up, utterly bewildered, cold in the night air, trying with one hand to cover herself up and then reaching to either side to gather what rags she could, too much in shock to cry or scream any more. Then she heard it, or rather felt it: the booming voice, deep inside her, seeming to come from the very pit of her being.

You called me.

She looked around, panicked, still clutching the shredded clothes to her breast.

You called me.

It was louder now, the sound seeming to fill every atom of her being, painfully invasive. As she looked back down the path towards the mound she began to make it out, the silhouette growing larger every second, her stare travelling down from the horned head, the moonlight glinting on the horns and curls, to the oval eyes, the abundantly haired chest and the

221

furred legs – like the hind legs of a wolf, she realised, bending back like those of a beast. But the legs were nothing compared to the sight of what reared obscenely between them as it moved towards her. The voice grew louder and louder, filling her body so that she could think no longer, obliterating her mind as she lay back, her legs falling involuntarily to either side.

Miriam was still struggling, her wrists tied behind her back and her ankles bound together, when she realised the man behind her was trying to undo her knots.

'It's OK, it's OK,' he was repeating as he undid the tight bonds the others had left. She turned her head to see James, the man Emma had arrived with. He looked ashen.

Miriam was still stunned from the flash of light that had whited out the hall earlier. It had obviously shaken the invaders too, because after they'd tied her up they'd quickly made off. Most of the people who'd come to the feast had fled now as well, some having fought with their attackers and followed them out into the courtyard while others, bewildered, had made for the doors at the first sight of trouble. The hall was empty now, save for a few guests who were too drunk to move.

'What happened?' she asked James, rubbing her wrists as he released her ankles.

He shook his head, not meeting her gaze. 'I'm not sure. But we have to get out of here. Where's Emma?' He helped Miriam to her feet.

Miriam shrugged helplessly and was aware of James studying her nakedness as though seeing it for the first time.

'We'll have to get you some clothes, too. We can't

222

have you running around like that.' He smiled, then looked alarmed again, sniffing at the air.

Miriam looked over her shoulder and saw a few wisps of smoke emerge from an open doorway. 'Smoke,' she said.

James turned and saw it too. 'Those crazy bastards have set the castle on fire! Come on.'

Miriam, feeling stronger now, said, 'I'll meet you in the courtyard. I know where I can find some clothes.'

James nodded grimly and ran to the stragglers propped up against the wall of the hall, slapping them and telling them to get up. Miriam dashed down a corridor, her mind a whirl of confusion now. Surely it couldn't be over? The smoke was thicker here and she coughed a little as she let herself into the laundry. Then she saw the piles of neatly pressed clothes, rejected a couple that were obviously either too large or too small, and dressed hurriedly as soon as she'd found a set that fitted.

Outside, she found James and Emma standing by the entrance. People were running around the court-yard, castle people mostly, with a few of the Order scattered about. Some of the former were calling for water and were trying to organise a fight against the fire. But whenever any of them appeared with a bucket, running towards the open doors of the courtyard wall through the thick smoke billowing out, red flames now visible at its base, members of the Order pushed them back, spilling their buckets. 'Let it burn,' Miriam heard them cry. 'Let it burn to the ground.'

And it would, she realised. There was no stopping it now.

James and Emma pulled at her as she stared into the flames. 'Come on, Miriam,' Emma urged her. 'We've got to go. Now!'

Beyond the castle walls the scene was even more chaotic. Castle people were fighting the Order in small groups, a steady stream of both factions running out into the woods. But James's group didn't stop to join in, instead running out and down towards the village. The burning castle, flames licking out of every window now, lit their way. As they descended the steps through the woods that led to the village, Miriam was almost tripped up by something large pushing past her thigh. Then she saw a stream of them: Garner's wolves were fleeing, firelight dancing on their sleek backs.

It was too hot to stay in the castle now, too difficult to breathe, and in the commotion Paul had lost Barbara.

He wandered around outside, taking no notice of the skirmishes going on between the Order and the villagers, just looking hopelessly around for his wife, or for the leader of the Order: anyone who could make him feel better. He felt ludicrous in his jester's outfit. Now that it had served its purpose it felt like a mockery of his true emotions.

And then he spotted her, the leader, stumbling towards the castle, and he ran to her, trying to explain, convinced that she would know what to say, would have the right words to make him feel good again. 'Barbara –' he began, then paused, looking at her more closely. Her hair was stuck up in a wild halo around her head, her eyes were manically large, and she was barely dressed, simply holding torn rags to her chest and crotch. It looked as though she had been raped by the villagers and Paul stepped towards her, his arms out, asking, 'What happened to you?'

But as she saw him her glazed eyes took on a focus and she lunged towards him, knocking him over, dropping the scraps of cloth that covered her and scrabbling at his crotch. Winded by her attack and too stunned at first to do anything about it, Paul simply lay on the ground, his head spinning, as her busy fingers delved into his trousers and wrapped themselves around his cock, still half stiff from what he'd seen in the castle. She moaned with demented excitement when she found it like that and moved her head down to engulf it with her mouth, sucking it to full hardness as he stared at her, unable to comprehend what he was seeing.

Then he tried, gently at first then more forcefully, to push her away. Other members of the Order had seen her too, her naked body writhing and her head in his crotch. He looked around pleadingly as they stared at him, horrified.

'Get off me!' Paul cried, and pushed hard on her shoulders. But she just moaned again, then grabbed his wrists and pinned them to the ground. He'd never have expected her to be so strong: her grip was like iron. He willed his cock to soften but it betrayed him, rearing up and filling her mouth, so sensitive that it was his turn to groan when she released it and licked his balls, smearing his spit-shiny cock all over her cheeks, then bobbing her head over the tip again.

Then she pulled her body further up so that her crazed eyes stared into his, her hands still pinning down his wrists, and she positioned her sex over his cock. As he looked around one last time, his panic slowly giving way to his arousal, he saw the members of the Order who'd stayed to watch crossing themselves and muttering prayers as she sank, slowly, deliberately and greasily, onto his cock.

James had insisted on getting clear of the village. But by the time they'd reached Porthness he could tell that they were all too exhausted to go on any further. To make matters worse it had started to rain, a gentle drizzle soon developing into a downpour, and they were all soaked and shivering.

'Let's try and get a room here. I have some money,' James suggested, patting his pocket. The girls, utterly bedraggled, nodded.

An inn nearby cast an inviting golden glow into the night, and as they drew near James saw a sign for rooms. Willing to pay whatever it cost, just as long as they could rest, he opened the door to the bar and ushered the girls in.

A hush fell over the bar as the drinkers turned to stare at them. The girls headed for the open fire in the corner of the room while James made for the bar.

'Do you have any rooms for the night?' he asked the barman who was slowly and deliberately drying a pint glass.

'We might have,' he replied, looking James up and down. 'You've come from Ardegan, then?'

James looked down at his clothes and tried to grin at the barman. 'Sort of, yeah. But we've left now.'

'Oh aye?' said the bartender. 'We've only the one room. Would that be a problem for you?'

James shook his head gratefully. 'Oh no, that'll be fine.'

'I thought as much,' the bartender replied.

As James paid him, the bartender inclined his head to a woman who'd been watching their exchange, then turned back to him. 'You'll have to wait a while for the room to be made up. But you can wait down here if you like, no problem. Would you like a drink?'

James brightened up. 'I'll just go and ask the girls what they'd like.' But as he turned he saw Emma looking up at him, her face pale. He looked quizzically at her and she led him towards the fire where a ring of men had surrounded Miriam. He tried to get past, but there was no space to squeeze between them and they didn't look about to budge.

'Pagans,' one of them was saying. 'I've heard all about you lot, up in the village. Free love, is it?'

Miriam looked nervous and wild, staring around her.

'We'll give her some free love if she wants – isn't that right, boys?' another asked. As they laughed, the first speaker reached forward and made a grab for Miriam's breasts.

'Hey, don't do that!' James started forward, only for one of the men to turn and force him to sit down, pushing hard on both his shoulders.

'Just you keep out of this and there'll be no harm done,' the man warned him. 'Any funny business and we'll do you next,' he continued, looking pointedly at Emma. 'This one's up for it, no mistake.' He turned to face Miriam again.

Emma clung to James's arm. 'We've got to do something,' she urged. But James was watching Miriam, who'd begun to sway to the rock'n'roll music blaring from the jukebox. Guffawing, one of the men stepped away momentarily from the tight circle to put more money in.

Another one reached out to grab at Miriam's chest again and this time she didn't resist. He took a good feel, mashing her breasts with his hands, then spun her round, groped at the cheeks of her bottom and pushed her towards one of the other men.

'Looks like you were right all along,' he leered. 'Proper sluts, them pagan girls.'

The man into whose arms Miriam had been pushed fondled her breasts in turn, tugging at her nipples. Then he started to pull her tunic off, but she stopped

227

him by putting her hands on his wrists and whispering to him.

'You what?' he asked incredulously. Then he turned to the others. 'We've got a goer here, boys! She says she's going to strip for us!'

A cheer went up, drowning out Emma's warning cry of 'Miriam!', although that didn't stop one of the men turning to gaze menacingly at her again.

'You let your friend here do as she likes, missy, and we'll all get along fine,' he said, waving a stubby finger in her face.

Other men had moved over from the bar now and Emma told James, 'I'm going to get help.' Her face looked stricken. James followed her, only to find that their way out was blocked by a thickset man who stood at the door, grinning.

Emma turned to James, who looked beseechingly at the bartender. The bartender simply smiled back at him.

Sickened, he turned back to the ring of men. A crowd now about three deep surrounded Miriam and James stepped up by the fireplace so that he could see what was going on. He needed to watch so that he could intervene if things got out of hand, he told himself. But when he looked round to check that Emma was OK she gave him a dirty look.

Miriam was leaning forwards, squeezing her cleavage together so that the deep valley was clearly visible under her shirt. James swallowed. Didn't she realise what she was doing?

The men were cheering, some reaching forward to grab at her while others tried to keep them back. Swaying her hips to the rock'n'roll, Miriam turned her back to them and undid her shirt, slowly, one button at a time, until it fell open around the tunic. Then she turned back to face the men, her arms crossed over her chest.

228

Some of them were nursing erections now, their hands adjusting the bulges at the fronts of their trousers as Miriam let first one arm then the other fall, exposing her full creamy-white breasts tipped with hard pink nipples.

As James watched she cupped a breast in her hand, lifted it to her face, then touched the nipple with her tongue. A great roar went up from the crowd, but she'd turned away again now and had taken the hem of her tunic in both hands, sticking her bottom out as she began to peel it up.

The roar swelled again and grew louder still as the men realised that Miriam was wearing no underwear. The tension in the air grew thick as she paused before exposing the thick pink lips of her sex, with a tell-tale line of slick wetness visible along the middle. Then the brown star of her anus was in view, on show to everyone. She pulled the tunic up and over her shoulders and turned to face the audience again, the men howling in disbelief as they stared at her. Then she slowly sank down into a squat, spreading her legs as she went until her swollen sex was visible to the men nearest to her, wet and ready. A couple of them were wanking themselves openly now, their fists pumping at their cocks through their trousers. Miriam leaned forward to unzip the man standing in front of her and release his cock, which sprang out, looking ready to burst.

When Miriam lowered her head onto it, it was as though a dam had burst. All the men surged forwards, scrabbling at their flies, one of them pushing Miriam onto her knees as he fought another off, trying to position himself behind her. Then she was being fucked, with two cocks stuffed in her mouth, others slapping against her face, waiting for a lick, a circle of men around her at each end, their cocks out and being wanked over her as she gobbled at each in turn. The man who'd started fucking her pulled out abruptly and spurted his seed all over her crease, the thick white fluid running down her skin; then another replaced him, plunging his cock inside her, slapping at her cheeks, fucking her hard and fast.

The men in front of her were pulling on her hair, trying to force their cocks into her face. But she pulled her head back, her back arching, and groaned, a low, dismal sound. As her face was stuffed full of cock again her whole body started to twitch, the muscles on her shoulders bunching up and flexing – and lines of hair suddenly sprouted on her back.

The man fucking her paused, his cock still buried deep inside her, and his eyes widened. 'What the fuck?' he muttered incredulously.

James looked around to see Emma staring aghast at the men. He jumped off the step and ran towards her, then took her hand and led her towards the door. 'We've got to get out of here.'

'But what about – I can't leave Miriam behind!' James gripped her wrist tightly and shook his head. The man who'd been guarding the door had moved towards the others now to see what the commotion was all about. Some of the men were moving away in alarm even as others were still thrusting their cocks at the thing in front of them.

As they opened the door James heard a terrible tearing sound. Then came a long blood-curdling howl, followed by a scream that was just as chilling. They ran out into the night, heedless of the rain now, soon followed by the first of the panicked drinkers.

Epilogue

The granite flashed pink crystals in the sun. From the rocky outcrop Verity could see the village, satellite dishes mushrooming from the richer houses. Cheers and shouts came in waves and she squinted into the sun to watch the figures on the green, little more than dots from here. They were playing football, the thwack of leather boot against leather ball echoing over the woods. She tried to picture the green as it had been before but it was difficult to hold the image in her mind: as readily as most of the locals had embraced Garner's ideas they'd turned away from them after the fire. The village had returned to a bland normality that seemed to blot out any memory of what had happened. The maypole was one of the first things to come down, chopped up for firewood, and a few days after that the first cars had appeared, bouncing over the potholes that were now starting to be filled in.

The police had ventured back to the village after the fire too, although they hadn't charged anyone with arson, and a couple of local newsmen had come to survey the ruins. Lightning, they said, and most of the villagers agreed: they'd seen the blinding white flash. And that was that: nobody seemed to want to make anything more of it. There had been a reporter there earlier, while it had still been happening, but as far as Verity knew nobody believed his stories back in London, apart from a couple of crazy American New Agers staying at the inn, tolerated for their easy money and blind enthusiasm for overpriced Scotch.

Verity sighed and stretched her arms, closing her eyes and feeling the warmth of the sun on her face. It was almost time now. She turned and walked back along the path to the ruins, picking her way among the smoke-blackened stones. Parts of the structure were still standing, but only just: one of the children who came here to play would probably bring the whole lot down on themselves sooner or later. Hardly anyone else came up here now – at least, she hadn't seen anyone. She kept her gaze on the grey ash at her feet, out of curiosity as much as for safety's sake, half hoping for a glimpse of bright burnished metal, or even bone, although the police said that no bodies had been found. But there was nothing, and she kicked a charred stone through the dust, marvelling at the cloud that settled slowly in its wake.

Something had been lost of the magic of the woods. Verity could dimly remember how it had been, alive with birds and small mammals, the spirit of the trees bursting from every leaf. Now it seemed like a drab copy of its former self, the games that had enlivened its dells and clearings replaced by dog walkers and even the occasional mountain biker, hurtling thoughtlessly through the glades that she'd rested in before, her heart bursting with joy.

But it wasn't over and the thought comforted Verity as she fingered the puncture wounds on her shoulder. They had started to throb again. She remembered when she'd come here after the fire, feeling the call for the first time. Other girls had felt it too and she'd seen them, spectral figures in white robes, luminous in the light of the moon. But of them all she had been chosen and she quickened her step, half dancing down the track, her anticipation mounting.

She'd kept an eye on the news, of course. If the wolves seemed to have gone from around here, there were reports from farmers of sheep with their guts torn out spreading over the border now. Others too, less certain – sightings of things that were neither beast nor man. She smiled as she remembered the gently scoffing tone of the news items. If they could only see what she had seen.

Verity was close now and could feel the pull drawing her in, stronger and stronger, dampening her fur with the thought of what would happen. If the woods had been partly reclaimed by the others, hardly anyone came this far – the villagers' memories of what had happened here were coloured now with shame and fear. But not for her and those like her, who left the offerings she could see now, the garlands of wild flowers by the mouth of the barrow, the promise of its black maw making her heart race, the corn figures and coins – crudely minted discs of no use now in the village – scattered around the entrance.

As Verity moved closer she looked around, wary of the eyes of the curious. Then she ducked her head into the long barrow. She'd been able to smell it from the woods, a strong smell, goatish, and this close it was almost overpowering. She peered inside and as her eyes adjusted to the darkness of the barrow's depths she saw it: first the eyes, seeming to glow golden in the dark, then the thing rearing between its legs, prepared already, swollen and cradled in one hairy hand. Its teeth glinted as it smiled at her. Licking her lips, Verity smiled back and dropped to her hands and knees to crawl inside, the voice in her head blotting out every sensation save for the mounting heat between her thighs.

They moved by night, not liking to be seen, revelling in the sensation of running through the fields, taking their prey with an easy snap of the jaws, only occasionally lapsing back into their original form. Their former lives were all but forgotten now, nothing left of the shy student and the cold academic even when they walked on their hind legs. It was warm enough now for them to run naked if they chose in this way, although in this form at least they were careful to stay away from farms, choosing to follow the lines of woods, the banks of railway tracks. The sun was stronger now, warming them as they slept in derelict huts or barns, burrowing into the soft hay, and the food was plentiful. The woodlands were alive with deer, the fields with lambs, calves, easy prey for them to gorge themselves on, although she still felt a pang of remorse at leaving their kills only half eaten.

But they had to move. Garner's intent had lodged like a seed in their minds, fed and watered by the presence of the other being, the force they had come from, lying dormant now, still and waiting, biding its time. For their work they had to descend into villages, occasionally even dressing in clothes they found bundled in bags outside junk shops. But they found most of what they needed in the car parks that were still used for illicit affairs, exhibitionists seeking a smaller thrill than the one they would provide. There it was easy to spread their gift, biting the quivering pale flesh of young lovers in the light of the moon and leaving a trail of servants snaking down from the cold Highlands into the very heart of England.

They knew that despite their best efforts they had been seen, in both forms: that due to the ravages of livestock farmers bought guns and prowled their fields, waiting for a glimpse of whatever had attacked their animals. And their bloody assignations elsewhere had almost led to them being caught once or twice, police headlights fixing them on the turn, limbs impossibly elongated and twitching with sprouting fur as they fled from their task.

As they moved further south the roads and buildings became more dense, the hiding places more difficult to find. They had been interrupted in their sleep by derelicts and wild-eyed children clutching bags of glue, all shocked to find them lying naked and filthy on scraps of mattresses in graffitied hovels.

Yet still they were free and they could sense that the others they left in their wake had begun to move, like them, from the safety of the fields and woods to the different pickings to be had in the metropolis. They could sense that what they would begin there would carry out Pan's work, would make sense of a plan as yet unformed, allowing it to reveal itself as the avatar of a new era, an old deity for a new age. As they fought, fucked and fed, gorging themselves on the pleasures of their new life, their hearts quickened at the sense of standing on the swell of a wave, on the cusp of the new reign that they would usher in. They already anticipated the dead pitted motorways, trees and flowers cracking their black tyranny, rusted hulks of cars lying discarded to the side. The grey misery of those they saw trapped in joyless lives, their pale moon faces pressed to the train windows as Miriam and Cavendish moved silently through the woods, were soon to be transformed to ecstatic celebration. Factories were belching their last smoke, to be choked in turn by weeds and vines, while blossoms were replacing rusting bolts, birdsong the restless chatter of machines. Nature's dominion was being stamped again over the works of man.

nexus

The leading publisher of fetish and adult fiction

TELL US WHAT YOU THINK!

Readers' ideas and opinions matter to us. Take a few minutes to fill in the questionnaire below and you'll be entered into a prize draw to win a year's worth of Nexus books (36 titles)

Terms and conditions apply – see end of questionnaire.

1. Sex: Are you male ☐   female ☐   a couple ☐?

2. Age: Under 21 ☐ 21–30 ☐ 31–40 ☐ 41–50 ☐ 51–60 ☐ over 60 ☐

3. Where do you buy your Nexus books from?

☐ A chain book shop. If so, which one(s)?

_____

☐ An independent book shop. If so, which one(s)?

_____

☐ A used book shop/charity shop
☐ Online book store. If so, which one(s)?

_____

4. How did you find out about Nexus books?

☐ Browsing in a book shop
☐ A review in a magazine
☐ Online
☐ Recommendation
☐ Other _____

5. In terms of settings, which do you prefer? (Tick as many as you like)

☐ Down to earth and as realistic as possible
☐ Historical settings. If so, which period do you prefer?

_____

- ☐ Fantasy settings – barbarian worlds
- ☐ Completely escapist/surreal fantasy
- ☐ Institutional or secret academy
- ☐ Futuristic/sci fi
- ☐ Escapist but still believable
- ☐ Any settings you dislike?

_____

- ☐ Where would you like to see an adult novel set?

_____

6. In terms of storylines, would you prefer:

- ☐ Simple stories that concentrate on adult interests?
- ☐ More plot and character-driven stories with less explicit adult activity?
- ☐ We value your ideas, so give us your opinion of this book:

_____

_____

_____

7. In terms of your adult interests, what do you like to read about? (Tick as many as you like)

- ☐ Traditional corporal punishment (CP)
- ☐ Modern corporal punishment
- ☐ Spanking
- ☐ Restraint/bondage
- ☐ Rope bondage
- ☐ Latex/rubber
- ☐ Leather
- ☐ Female domination and male submission
- ☐ Female domination and female submission
- ☐ Male domination and female submission
- ☐ Willing captivity
- ☐ Uniforms
- ☐ Lingerie/underwear/hosiery/footwear (boots and high heels)
- ☐ Sex rituals
- ☐ Vanilla sex
- ☐ Swinging

☐ Cross-dressing/TV
☐ Enforced feminisation
☐ Others – tell us what you don't see enough of in adult fiction:

_____

_____

_____

8. **Would you prefer books with a more specialised approach to your interests, i.e. a novel specifically about uniforms? If so, which subject(s) would you like to read a Nexus novel about?**

_____

_____

_____

9. **Would you like to read true stories in Nexus books? For instance, the true story of a submissive woman, or a male slave? Tell us which true revelations you would most like to read about:**

_____

_____

_____

10. **What do you like best about Nexus books?**

_____

_____

11. **What do you like least about Nexus books?**

_____

_____

12. **Which are your favourite titles?**

_____

_____

13. **Who are your favourite authors?**

_____

_____

14. **Which covers do you prefer? Those featuring:**
    (tick as many as you like)

☐ Fetish outfits
☐ More nudity
☐ Two models
☐ Unusual models or settings
☐ Classic erotic photography
☐ More contemporary images and poses
☐ A blank/non-erotic cover
☐ What would your ideal cover look like?

_____

15. **Describe your ideal Nexus novel in the space provided:**

_____

_____

_____

_____

16. **Which celebrity would feature in one of your Nexus-style fantasies?**
    We'll post the best suggestions on our website – anonymously!

_____

THANKS FOR YOUR TIME

Now simply write the title of this book in the space below and cut out the
questionnaire pages. Post to: Nexus, Marketing Dept., Thames Wharf Studios,
Rainville Rd, London W6 9HA

Book title: _____

TERMS AND CONDITIONS

NEXUS NEW BOOKS

To be published in October 2006

BRUSH STROKES
Penny Birch

Amber Oakley is dominant and beautiful. But just a little too beautiful for her own good. As far from accepting her sexuality as she seeks to portray it, her fellow enthusiasts almost invariably want to get her knickers down, usually for spanking. In *Brush Strokes*, her attempts to resist the attentions of the firm and matronly Hannah Riley quickly come to nothing, and Amber is once more back over the knee, behind-bared as a hairbrush is applied to her well-fleshed cheeks. Rather than give in, she tries to resist, but only manages to get herself into even deeper trouble.

£6.99   ISBN 0 352 34072 X

CORRUPTION
Virginia Crowley

The greater the degree of purity in a person, the darker the taint on their soul if they succumb to temptation. Not even the men and women of the holy orders are safe from corruption as Lady Stephanie Peabody and her host of greedy, voluptuous collaborators engage in the most sinister forms of seductive manipulation. Not even the Prior, the nuns at the convent, or Stephanie's principled stepdaughter, Laura, are safe from the threat of spiritual corruption.

With the aid of a powerful aphrodisiac, Stephanie's coven of cruel, demanding harlots tempt the righteous with the tawdry delights of the flesh – at the expense of their immortal souls.

£6.99   ISBN 0 352 34073 8

THE DOMINO QUEEN
Cyrian Amberlake
**Wherever dark pleasure reigns, there the Domino Queen
keeps her court.**

Whether she's initiating a lonely peasant girl or training a trio of
eager slaves, Josephine deals out tenderness and cruelty with an
even, elegant hand.

Meanwhile Cadence Szathkowicz, the lover Josephine aban-
doned on Dominica, is searching for her. From pulsating Los
Angeles to the strict discipline of Madame Suriko's house in
Chicago, Cadence travels on an odyssey of pleasure and pain.

All she has to guide her is the sign Josephine wears between her
breasts: the tattoo of the domino mask.

£6.99   ISBN 0 352 34074 6

If you would like more information about Nexus titles, please
visit our website at www.nexus-books.co.uk, or send a large
stamped addressed envelope to:
Nexus, Thames Wharf Studios,
Rainville Road, London W6 9HA

nexus

This information is correct at time of printing. For up-to-date
information, please visit our website at www.nexus-books.co.uk

All books are priced at £6.99 unless another price is given.

------ ✂ ------------------------

Please send me the books I have ticked above.

Name   ....

Address   ....

            ....

            ....

            .... Post code ....

Send to: **Virgin Books Cash Sales, Thames Wharf Studios, Rainville Road, London W6 9HA**

US customers: for prices and details of how to order books for delivery by mail, call 888-330-8477.

Please enclose a cheque or postal order, made payable to **Nexus Books Ltd**, to the value of the books you have ordered plus postage and packing costs as follows:

   UK and BFPO – £1.00 for the first book, 50p for each subsequent book.

   Overseas (including Republic of Ireland) – £2.00 for the first book, £1.00 for each subsequent book.

If you would prefer to pay by VISA, ACCESS/MASTERCARD, AMEX, DINERS CLUB or SWITCH, please write your card number and expiry date here:

....

Please allow up to 28 days for delivery.

Signature ....

Our privacy policy

We will not disclose information you supply us to any other parties. We will not disclose any information which identifies you personally to any person without your express consent.

From time to time we may send out information about Nexus books and special offers. Please tick here if you do *not* wish to receive Nexus information.   ☐

------ ✂ ------------------------